Orchid

House

Best Regards,

Kathleen Comstock

Orchid House

Kathleen A. Comstock

Pentland Press, Inc.
England • USA • Scotland

PUBLISHED BY PENTLAND PRESS, INC.
5122 Bur Oak Circle, Raleigh, North Carolina 27612
United States of America
919-782-0281

ISBN 1-57197-201-3
Library of Congress Catalog Card Number 99-75262

Printed in the United States of America

Chapter One

The dream vanished as John Jordan woke with a start. He stared at the dim light filtering through the curtain. What was it that had interrupted his sleep, something dropping, or perhaps a sharp blow? He lay still for another minute. Slowly things began to register. The bed, his bed, the night before at Yvette Peters's solstice party, and now, gradually, the remembrance of the dream. He inhaled, let out his breath, and pulled the corner of the pillow to his cheek, closing his eyes and envisioning Emily's arms that in his dream had been around him.

His instincts, however, turned his thoughts to the window and the soft summer light that had begun to make its way into his room. Had there been a sound? Maybe it was only a fox or coyote, a raccoon on the roof, a bird accidentally smashing into a window. His house was a mile from any road and often the wild animals roamed his property. Was the noise in my dream, he wondered?

What he recalled was the imagined softness of Emily, her touch that ran down his body, like he'd been longing for last night for real. Her arm, already kissed to a bronze glow by the spring sunshine, reaching for the glass he handed her. She wore a long denim skirt with a slit up the back and a silk black blouse that begged to be touched. If I could reach out to you, he'd thought, and the dream had allowed him that.

Why am I embracing a pillow and not her, he asked himself? This made him more alert and he sat up in bed, resenting the emerging daylight and the noise that had disturbed him. The clock on the bedside table glowed green arms, 5:34. Too early to rise for a Sunday.

Anxious for her morning walk, his Norwegian Elkhound, Sami, was already pacing. Once she saw him look her way, she rushed to lick his exposed arm, then swirled in circles, whining and looking at him at every turn as if to say, "C'mon, I'm ready to go!" Her movements didn't stop when John snapped his fingers, his way of requesting her obedience. She persisted with her dance and moved to the window, furiously sniffing the ledge. For a second she stopped, perked her ears then resumed her fervent search.

Rolling on his side he wished the dream back, but could recover only snatches. She'd laughed and he'd lifted her up as they danced. Holding, twirling, touching, and feeling oh so wonderful, but then what? Had they kissed? No, but they'd been nearing one another before he woke.

Emily Turner. The name on his lips as it had been ever since she returned to Winslow, the place where she and John had grown up. He thanked the day he offered to cover for Police Chief Allen, who had to go out of town. Fresh from a seminar on New England antique homes, she had entered the station and asked why the mill had been torn down and was there any committee to preserve some of the older establishments? Her years in California had stunted her appreciation of antiques and she was back to renew her dormant interests.

Dormant. An appropriate word, John had thought on staring at her as she talked. She was even more alluring than when they'd known one another as teens.

He couldn't take his eyes from her when she walked into the party, her slim, athletic body moving towards him, taking him in shyly, as if she were trying to figure if she should squeeze him like a tomato or reach for him as if he were a cuddly toy. Uneven black hair landed helter skelter on her shoulders and over her forehead. Through the shadows of strands, brilliant blue eyes that seemed to look right through him. His entire body had relaxed at the sight of her, a feeling he rarely had. In fact, he hadn't experienced that since he dated Joanne, his former girlfriend who, after a brief two months together, had found the pocketbook and looks of a well-known surgeon infinitely more interesting than John. After the couple moved into some fancy penthouse in Manhattan, he'd received an invitation to an open house party they were having. Thanks but no thanks.

Emily and his former girlfriends were similar, all possessing a brooding yet puerile look, a look he both loathed and was imminently attracted to. Emily's return gave rise to the hope that they might get on track after all these years.

Last night she'd approached him and it looked as though they could have had something, but outside the brush of her hand against his arm, nothing had materialized. The party had been strange in a way he hadn't been able to figure, and that strangeness had played on his interaction with Emily. Or maybe it's a simple case of being a lot more wary now, he told himself. After all, you've returned to Winslow to piece things together in the hopes you can carry on with a more productive life. You're a lot more analytical than you used to be. Your ever-so-insightful counselor, Jean, helped you out there. He tried to push all these thoughts away and force the sweet sensations of the dream back.

As the details of the encounter with Emily last night solidified, however, his mind became the mind that ticked for most of his waking hours; his was a mind that focused on the pros and cons of copping in a small town, a mind that worked on detail and large issues simultaneously in order to maintain an order to this New England enclave of three thousand, a mind that placed a woman next in line to his job. There had been something mysterious about the party, this annual event that only once before in his life he'd been invited to, this display of opulence at which Yvette excelled. In addition, he sensed Emily was worried. At first he thought she was nervous being with him but, as she sipped her water, he'd noted her shaking hand and glances to the patio, as if she were contemplating escape or trying to keep away from someone. After fifteen years copping in New York City, he'd seen enough desperation to recognize it instantly.

He chided himself for not asking her if anything was wrong. He'd been trying too hard to impress her with his nonchalance and knowledge as they discussed local goings-on. He'd been in town already three months, she was the "newcomer" now.

His body ached from the overdose of rich catered food. Come to think of it, how much alcohol had he consumed? He slowly pulled a leg over the side of the bed. Rubbing his muscular and tanned arms he noted increased roughness on the insides of his hands, a result of uprooting tree stumps in the yard over the last few weeks. It wouldn't hurt to buy some lotion. Was he thinking of caressing soft skin? As he shook his head, blonde strands fell into his eyes. How many times did he have to remind himself how women could distract him? Go away, Emily, he whispered.

His head felt as though a hammer was beating on it. The sour taste in his mouth had the distinct reminder of the bourbon he'd downed after coming home. He'd been so straight during the evening, only to sneak a bottle from the party and return to his well-worn chair in the living room with a view of the northeast sky and the moon. Something about reclining there and thinking of her had given rise to increased thirst. Damn, he thought, rubbing his head. Slipped into the dark haven again. The drink had gone down so easily, and now he paid the price. Dulled thought, sluggish movements, a day of waiting until tomorrow when the hangover would pass.

Sami was persistent now, jumping and twirling as she watched John slowly make his way from the bed to his jeans that lay on the floor. She whimpered and stayed close, eyeing John's every move as if one false one would send him back to the bed and she'd not have her way. His head ached, though, and every move seemed to be wrong. He was up way too early, even though he enjoyed early-morning walks, even though it was now summer. It had been after 2 A.M. when he arrived home. No wonder he was sore.

"Screw it," he murmured, slumping back onto the bed. He debated letting Sami out on her own, but decided against it. She'd find the Turner's cat and there'd be hell to pay. On the other hand, he smiled, Emily was also residing there. Emily rather than her crotchety father or nervous mother might be the one to appear outside and call to Sami to lay off. Would she be in her nightclothes? What in fact did she wear to bed? He thought of her naked and noted the tenseness in his groin. She was beautiful, almost forty and beautiful. What he'd do to be with her in bed.

He ignored Sami's whimper and closed his eyes, drifting again to the thoughts of the woman lying not a mile from here, snug in her four-poster bed, breathing this fresh air spiked with dampness, air that was filling with rain.

The drops landed sporadically at first, then faster. A rainy early summer morning, thoughts of a woman, the drugged late-night laziness that invaded his brain. The sounds were probably coyotes, noisy devils.

"Sam," he murmured, "scram."

❋   ❋   ❋

Three hours later the phone rang, jolting him out of an even deeper sleep. Sami let out several snorts and recommenced her sniffing and scurrying to and from the window, now whimpering constantly. John reached over and grabbed the receiver.

"John, get over to the Turner property."

It was Chief Allen. John sat up, feeling his stomach sink. "What's up?"

"Daughter's been found dead on the property," Allen said.

The swirling in John's head kept him from speaking. A dark shiver forced his eyes closed as he held his breath. This is a dream, this is the dream, he thought.

"John?" The chief's voice had a ring of concern.

4

John mumbled. "Are you sure?"

"Positive. Same outfit she had on at the party. The woods between Yvette's and theirs, just in from the orchid house. You'll see my car. Art's there now examining her. Better keep Sami away."

John nodded but could find no words. Sami was whimpering louder now and the phone had begun to drone once the chief hung up. Everything was in slow motion, the thump thump of his heart, the dog and the phone, the ringing in his ears, the room that seemed to shift and expand with each breath. The horrid sensation that filled his every cell. This was a dream.

Another shiver and he shook his head. Get there, you have to get there. It's an ugly mistake. His clothes were on and he ran to the kitchen, grabbing Sami's lead and snapping it to her collar. She raced out the side door and around the back of the house before John could turn her in the other direction. The rain had stopped and the sun was already warming the wet earth. John tugged to pull Sami towards the dog run, but she was determined to make her way to the back of the house.

"Damn you, dog," he yelled. But with all her Elkhound might in force, there was no stopping her. She was at John's bedroom window in seconds, sniffing and snorting, jerking her body as she tried in vain to find something. With a tug, John turned her to him. "C'mon!" With that, Sami lowered her head, dropped her behind, peed, then obediently followed him to the run where he quickly attached her.

For five minutes, John ran as fast as he could. It would go quicker running because to drive a car to that side of the Turner property would mean going out of the way two miles. His body beat to the sound of his feet on the ground, picturing only those blue eyes as they'd stared at him last night, that look of worry or fear. What was it? Why hadn't he reacted more definitively? Why hadn't he dragged her home to make love? That was what he was thinking, wasn't he? Maybe she'd be alive now. He let out a cry that echoed through the trees.

He arrived at the back of the Turner property and began the ascent to the ridge on top of which the house stood. Panting and pulling himself up, he eyed their rambling pre-colonial house to his left, quietly sitting undisturbed and perfect as one of Betty Turner's many flower arrangements.

Sharp voices were coming from the back woods. Orders. An ambulance's lights were flashing. He scraped his arms and face on dangling branches as he made a straight line to the scene. He saw the chief and then his eyes went to the ground.

He stopped short. The medical examiner, Art Johnson, knelt beside her body, blocking some of the view, but John could see her face, her hair splayed around her closed eyes. His heart whispered that she was only sleeping. He inched forward and stood by the chief, her body a few feet from him.

With his arm blocking forward movement, Chief Allen prevented John from getting closer. "Not yet."

Save for a bloodied wrist, there was no sign of injury. A pale arm, paler than it was last night, fingernails dug into the earth and stretched in his direction. He began to shake uncontrollably.

"Nothing obvious," Art noted. "She's been dead several hours." He stood and wiped his forehead. "Legal medical autopsy's in order." He looked to Chief Allen.

"Foul play?" Allen asked.

"Sudden death, no apparent cause. Calls for investigation. She's hardly of an age to just drop dead," Art said. His tired eyes looked on, emotionless. Art had been the examiner for over thirty years, presiding over many deaths.

"The blood?" Allen asked.

"Superficial cut on her finger, like from broken glass. Nothing that would kill. We'll need to investigate."

Then there were words—morgue, hospital, forensics. John continued to stare down at her until she became smaller and smaller, a dot in his mind, a thing that would disappear and the real woman would walk up behind him and reassure him she was still alive. He felt the chief's hand on his shoulder, prodding him. He made a tentative step towards her, eyes on those shut lids wishing them open. Screaming inside for the sound of the soft voice. What had she said last night? "I only drink water now." How his body had reacted, shifting at once to a malleable piece of clay that she could have molded any which way. He had joined her in a glass of water.

He bent down and swallowed back tears that in spite of his efforts fell down his cheek. He touched her arm. Cool, like morning air. He squeezed. The chief warned him not to touch, so he pulled back and stared. The skirt was hiked up to her knees, she was wet all over from the rain. The silk shirt clung to her breasts. She wore no bra. Had she wanted him last night, too? Oh, God, he looked at the ground nearby, what happened to you? Could I have saved you? Those eyes, that look of yours!

It was then he noticed two people on the other side of Emily some ten feet from her body. Betty and Walter Turner, the parents. Arm in arm they held one another, neither comforting nor crying. Nothing. Just like all those years John remembered them. Just like them, just like they'd been to her when she was little. Just like what drove Emily away in the first place. Their nothingness, their not being for her. Standing there allowing the police and rescue squad to handle their very own daughter. No words of thanks, no words of sorrow, not even a scream. Nothing. Just like they'd always been. Standing perfectly straight like the flowers in their gardens, ordered and blending colorfully with the season. Betty in her blue and red print apron and Walter in his crisp jeans and work shirt. Neither shedding a tear.

Walter looked into John's eyes. It was a look John recognized from years back when he'd be chased from their yard in winter for trampling the flower beds with his dog. Walter's empty eyes. An old man looking out on the world emotionless, nothing telling coming from inside. Eyes that had scared John to death when he was little.

Betty clung to him, gripping his sleeve. Her brown curls blew in the slight breeze and she wiped them off her forehead as she stared at her daughter's body. She too gave nothing away but seemed to be holding her feelings by grasping her husband as if he were a pole that would protect her from falling. Her head went up slightly and then down as she tried to focus on the body but invariably turned away, into Walter's shoulder where she took refuge until the next minute passed and she was able to again face the sight.

John recalled an image of them driving around town in their Lincoln, Betty yapping, Walter at the wheel checking out all the places to see if anything was different, anything changed that they could go home and discuss. Emily had once said they thrived on the details of other people's lives, an activity that John now understood kept one from looking within.

Now his heart was heavy like it had been at other death scenes when he worked Manhattan. The familiarity of death descending, the notion that hours before this person had been a part of the human race and now was not. A simple fact so loaded with mystery. Here was this beautiful woman he'd wanted to take to bed last night, someone who years before had black pigtails he'd pulled, someone who—because she was not allowed a dog as a child—sneaked over to his house summer evenings before dinner to play with his mutt. Someone with whom he'd first been friends and then fallen in love, the progression that could have led to a healthy love relationship. Lying dead next to him.

His body seemed to leave him as he lost awareness of his surroundings. A powerful urge to scream hit him. He lowered his head and focused on a small gray stone inches from him. He felt the wetness in his eyes blurring the two people feet from him who watched him like he was art in a museum, blurring the lifeless woman draped in her wet outfit that would soon come off as the coroner disemboweled her and tried to glean a reason for her premature death.

Chief Allen kneeled next to him. "C'mon, John. We'll get her to the morgue. You go home."

He shook his head. "No."

"Walter, go help," Betty said, and Walter stepped to John.

"Son," Walter said, extending an open hand towards John.

From the corner of his eye John saw the large, rough palm but didn't reach for it. He stood and, now closer to Walter, stared at the man. He wanted to scream at the empty look. "Give a damn, for God's sake!" he felt like saying. Instead, he turned towards Art and the chief and headed to the police car as the medical staff passed with a body bag and collapsed gurney.

Two more police cars had arrived and the fire engine. Yellow tape had already been placed within feet of her body. The photographer unloaded equipment from the police Jeep driven by Chuck Mangis, the assistant officer who'd covered for everyone last night.

John noticed sitting on a large rock a young man wearing neon-colored spandex clothing. Sunglasses dangled from a black cord necklace around his neck. Noting John's gaze, Chief Allen said, "He found her. Kid's staying down the street, at the Hortons', for the weekend."

He was not yet twenty with dyed platinum hair and a bright green headband. John walked towards him. The young man chewed on a fingernail, his back to the body and the activity going on. He seemed to be trying in vain to concentrate on the sun, now burning through trees.

"I'm Officer Jordan," John introduced himself.

"Pete Sanders," the young man said, easing his eyes in John's direction and extending his hand.

The hand of the youth was clammy, matching the wetness of John's. John joined him on the boulder. Though he could tell from the noises they were lifting her into the ambulance, he consciously stayed focused on the person next to him. Almost without realizing it, he'd made a decision to get to the bottom of this.

"First death?"

The young man nodded, giving John a wary glance. "I was taking the quick trail they—the Hortons, the people I'm staying with—suggested. They said over the rise was pretty this time of year with the apple trees all green."

"True. You saw her from a distance?"

"No," the young man's voice caught. He shook his head, trying to quell the trembling in his body. He took a deep breath. "No, I almost fell over her. I wasn't looking down. . . ."

It was a smooth path. John knew it well from having regularly walked Sami mornings, the old timber road that was now conservation land and could also serve as a shortcut from the main road to the top of the ridge near Yvette Peters's place. High school kids still tried to bring cars in and park at the top of the ridge. Given the time of year and the activity level at the police station, some succeeded. When returning home from working the night shift, John usually passed by here before turning onto his own road. You could catch the glimmer of a car's metallic sides on a full-moon night. Usually it was a couple of amorous teens trying to stretch the curfew on their parents. Harmless fun that he himself had tried at that age. Other than that, he and Sami and the occasional jogger took to the road in daytime.

"You tripped over her?" John asked. He couldn't say her name. She was still alive to him. She was walking and talking and laughing somewhere, hiding and playing a game that would soon be over.

"Almost. I stopped in time. I thought she was sleeping. I knelt down." He choked on his words and broke down. John waited until Sanders had regained his composure.

"If you'd feel more comfortable going home to change, we can take your statement at the station shortly," John murmured. He could hear the gurney being placed into the ambulance, the orders being made to lift, a little to the left. This he knew about, this he'd experienced at other scenes. Familiarity was a bland comfort as he tried to focus on what he had to do as an officer and try and forget what he wanted to do as a human being, as a man who had lost a beautiful woman. The youth nodded, and the two stood and again faced the scene.

The ambulance pulled away as a press car made its way to the clearing, a young, frenzied-looking man wearing glasses alighting. It was Steve Rideout, the reporter for the *Winslow Post*. A white chalk line made the shape of her body now, her crouched position etched on the earth until such time that the investigative team had covered their bases. A few of the investigators were poking around the bushes. John was about to open the door to the police car so that the runner could get in when the woods erupted with yelling.

"No! She's died and that's it!" Betty Turner screamed. "No autopsy!" She stood inches from Chief Allen while Walter, at Betty's side, shifted uncomfortably.

"It's required in cases like this," Allen responded, removing his cap to clear his forehead. John walked to them.

Betty threw her hands in the air and yelled about how it was finished, that there was no need to examine the body, that Emily had died of natural causes.

"Walter! Speak some sense into these people!" she screamed, throwing a hand to her eyes and wiping her face with her apron. "She was fragile! Always fragile!"

At Betty's prompting, Walter stepped up to Chief Allen, his glasses pushed into his nose. "Here now, Mr. Allen, this is not necessary, is it? This is upsetting my wife, as you can see. This is a shock. We simply don't want any further. . . ."

The unflappable Allen put up a hand. "There'll be an investigation and an autopsy, Mr. Turner. That's the law. If you wish to challenge this, you'll need a lawyer."

Betty burst into tears and leaned against Walter. "Keep on them, Walter! This is so unfair to our Emily. She didn't do anything, it's nothing! Nothing!"

The word "nothing" caught John. Over the years he'd noticed that what came out of people's mouths immediately following a tragedy revealed much about them. Such a word to indicate their daughter's death. "Nothing." These people were strange, a thought he'd held at bay over the years but that he found harder and harder to dismiss in his three months back in Winslow. He'd leave them to Chief Allen, knowing very well that legally there should be an autopsy, even though he himself, had he the choice, would have reacted exactly like Betty.

Betty was sobbing more quietly as Walter threatened Allen that he'd seek legal advice and that the police had no right to determine what to do with their daughter. Allen listened but didn't budge.

Steve Rideout approached him, but John referred him to another officer. He was not interested in delving into this with someone who'd be writing about her. He'd have to face enough difficulties.

He felt weak and wanted to sit down, but at the same time he couldn't stop moving around the scene. He neared the spot where she'd apparently collapsed, trying to weave a story out of what happened after he left the party. What had she said last to him? Where had she gone? How had they become separated? He'd followed her, but she'd gone outside and then he'd been interrupted by Yvette. Where was Yvette? Was she snug in bed and oblivious to all this? The woman needed to know, would be interested of course since Emily had been a guest last night, but more importantly might know where Emily went when she left the party. He wanted to talk with Yvette.

Allen conversed with the reporter. John passed them hurriedly and then went to question some of the investigators who were scouring the area for evidence of any foul play or pieces of Emily's possessions. They'd come up with nothing so far, not even a pocketbook or wallet. Apparently, if she did in fact leave the party and go home via this path, she carried nothing with her. Odd, thought John. He'd not yet met a woman who didn't carry some sort of handbag or wallet holder. Nor had she any key, although that was more explainable given that most residents of the town didn't lock doors and that she was close enough to simply walk the path. Apparently, given the estimate of the time of death, she'd been walking in semi-daylight.

He paused at the thought, and the tug at his gut renewed, harder this time. Had he walked Sami when he'd first woken, he or at least Sami might have heard something. Instead, lazy him, slipped back to sleep. He began to feel the well of emotion that had been surging from time to time, but this one felt as though it was going to break him. The drink, that was it. Had he not been such a lazy bastard and given into the bottle, he might have had his wits about him last night. Might have been able to save her.

He turned slowly from everyone and walked a few steps, towards the boulder where the runner had been, and stared up, squinting, feeling the sun pierce his fuzzed brain with its brilliance, reminding him of how much gray matter he'd destroyed by giving into his weakness, hearing his school teachers warn him that staring at the sun damaged his sight forever, hearing Emily's childhood giggle that rang out across the ridge when they'd run together to his house. He held now the ghost of her memory, already somewhere he knew not, nor perhaps would ever understand. And he'd had a chance to take her home last night. As the activity at the scene died, as car doors closed and people left, his eyes watered.

When he'd bit his lip hard enough to stop the quivering, he turned and noted that Chief Allen was the only one left. Allen meandered the area, ensuring that every task had been completed. Tall, athletic, with hints of gray at his dark-haired temples, Paul Allen had fifteen years on

John and had become in the last three months a close friend like John had never experienced. An Alaskan, Paul had married a Bostonian while on a whale-watch vacation off Cape Cod years ago and since then called New England his home. His vocation was maintaining the law, which he'd done faithfully and well in Winslow for the past twenty years, but his heart was at sea. He and his wife, Michelle, were planning a round-the-world cruise in three years when Paul retired. Now his tanned face and square, well-defined features stared at John through dark glasses.

He neared John and, in a fatherly gesture, placed a hand on John's shoulder. "Rough, isn't it?"

John nodded. The two men stood still and listened to the melodies of the many birds—robins, chickadees, finches, cardinals—who found the low brush perfect to hide nests and little eggs in. He stared up at the tall pines.

"Mighty strange. Sweet thing," Allen said. "You gonna be all right? Take time off if you need to."

John shook his head. "I'll head over to the Peters's place. After, I'll check back at the station."

Paul shaded his eyes with a hand and looked in the direction of the ridge. Beyond, but hidden from view, was the mansion occupied by Yvette Peters. "Take a good look around. Chances are the maids haven't been up yet to pick up the mess from last night. Hold all that work. I'll send over some investigators. Use your badge. If the lady of the house is up, spend some time with her." Paul's face clouded slightly. It had been years ago, but when he'd first come to town a vicious rumor had placed him as one of Yvette's many male interests. Michelle had almost left him before Yvette had spoken up and squelched the story herself. This being New England, where all stories both real and imagined have long lives, Paul's face reflected a hint of the hurt that had plagued him way back when. When John had first arrived, they'd confided over beers and the same look had crossed Allen's face.

"I'll call you." He started in the direction of the house as Allen went to his car, got in and spoke into the phone. Then the car turned and slowly traversed the dirt path in the direction of the main road.

John stood for a moment, listening to the sounds of a Sunday morning, his hurt growing now that he was alone. The woods enveloped him protectively, seeming to deny the fact that moments ago a body was in its midst. This had been their stomping grounds as kids. Ironically she had come to her end here.

"Johnny, throw me that stick," the little Emily called. "I'll pitch it into that mud pool." He saw her in his mind, stirring muddy earth after a rain shower, her skinny legs squatting on a boulder, her expression determined as was the case when she did anything with her whole being.

He had to get to Yvette's, he told himself, but he lingered. Somewhere he believed Emily was looking at him, still alive, playing hide-and-seek, searching for the dog and calling to John to follow her. The still of the woods spoke back to him, a summer still now, interrupted only by soft breezes, bird chirps, the occasional hum of a bee. The summer arrival they'd celebrated together last night. Dirty knees and earthy smells, Emily with her face powdered with dust, her white socks soiled, her thin arms reaching to him from her death place.

He whispered, "Why were you taken from me?"

With the whine of a police car siren in the distance, he shook his head and rubbed both eyes to clear them. Get your ass to Yvette's, he told himself. Try as he could to advance into a jog, his feet wouldn't cooperate. He trudged up the ridge, slowly and methodically, a funeral march. The beginnings of a chasm of pain took hold, a pain that would stay with him, he sensed, indefinitely.

Chapter Two

Yvette Peters's residence dominated one of two high ridges that cut through Winslow. On a clear day you could stand on her third-story wraparound porch and see Boston to the east and the hills of New Hampshire and Vermont to the northwest. The heart of a former Shaker village, the house had been the main structure, surrounded by other simpler but sturdy frame construction buildings for which the religious group had become known: solid simple lines, usually rectangular or square in shape, and all of wood timbered from the area. In their heyday during the late 1700s and early 1800s, the Shakers had populated the region in force. The dwellings were built with the communal lifestyle in mind, the oversized buildings having housed orphans and homeless adults as well as large families. The Shakers believed in equality of the sexes, communal living, and celibacy. They made for themselves a reputation of being industrious, faithful, and nonresistant.

Ironically, this residence had come to service the dalliances of the once-famous movie star. Born in France and, as a baby, immigrating with her parents in the 1920s, Yvette Peters had dreamed of being an actress since she could remember. As soon as she graduated from high school, she made her way from California's central valley to the night life of Las Vegas. She worked the bar scene and eventually landed a regular place as a dancer in a small cabaret at one of the up-and-coming casinos. Noticed by an agent of the Mayers' studio, she auditioned for a walk-on in a film that brought attention to the senior man himself, thus offering her—along with contemporaries Lauren Bacall and Bette Davis—spots in some of the big-time productions during the 1940s. One film, *Something Winning,* where she played the French lover of a soldier in World War II, had emerged to garner her critical acclaim for which she'd even been nominated an Academy Award.

Rather than commit herself to a promising acting career, however, she married a studio executive named Stuart Granger, the son of well-to-do New Englanders. Although she remained tied to the Hollywood life, her husband's worldwide travels took priority and she reveled in the title of "jet setter," flying to their home in the south of France for the summer, vacationing in the Swiss Alps for the New Year, and sharing time in autumn between their penthouse on Park Avenue in Manhattan and their getaway in the out-of-the-way town of Winslow, Massachusetts.

They'd chosen Winslow as a part-time residence partly due to the location of Stuart's financial advisors in Boston and partially to "get away from Hollywood," as she'd put it in an interview the *Post* had done just last year on the occasion of her solstice party. The marriage had survived only two years, but Yvette never severed the connection to Winslow and she continued to return to the house that through the divorce agreement became hers alone, a place where she claimed to have an ounce of anonymity and peace before returning to her international living style.

Once she divorced Stuart, Hollywood denounced her, preferring to keep Stuart in its good graces because of his vast fortune and influence. After all, Yvette had been a French immigrant, pushing drinks in Vegas and introduced to Hollywood only when Stuart had fallen for her Mediterranean smile and swaying hips. With him guiding the way, she'd made it to the screen. Without him, she'd faltered into the Hollywood of lost dreams and wasted finances that followed too many would-be stars and one-time success stories.

Yvette had never really moved beyond that stage of her life and an annual return to Winslow, where people still marveled at her presence and reveled in her tales of Clark Gable and Jimmy Stewart, gave her a needed dose of yesterday that allowed her to feel, in John's opinion, like she still mattered.

He stood at the marble steps leading to the mansion. All was quiet. The facade was made up of at least fifty windows, each the original glass with individual panes. Antique yellow-beige paint coated the house and small electric candles, the sign Yvette was in town, burned nonstop. The effect last night had been ethereal, guiding visitors up the walkway to the dream interior of thick personalized draperies, Italian marbled floors, lush and exotic furnishings. Each room carried a theme that could be placed back to the 1940s when the happy Granger couple had spent an entire year decorating with famed interior designers from the West Coast and New York, with an occasional visit by the revered Dolci of Milan, a personal friend of Yvette's from her stays in the south of France.

John reminded himself to get copies of the *Post's* coverage of those days. He'd commented to Yvette just last night how as a child he'd never really appreciated the work that went into making the house such a showcase. Now, he wanted to understand every inch of the house where Emily spent her final hours. He noted his chagrin at the sight now, whereas last night he'd been more or less upbeat. He'd called Jean, his former counselor in Manhattan, and explained his anxieties about his first foray socializing in the town since his return. She'd been encouraging and positive, prodding him to experiment with initiating conversations rather than playing the handsome wallflower who eyed women from a distance only to pounce at the eleventh hour and find them in his bed the next morning, the associated guilt overwhelming him so that he'd push them away before the relationship ever had a chance.

The feeling of doom descended in full force, nothing the expensive stonework or exquisite chandeliers could drive away. He gulped and put on his officer's face, reminding himself that he most likely wouldn't have to worry about Yvette fighting his interview at this hour. She was probably drugged to sleep. He wished his head was clearer.

He knocked at the door and was almost too soon greeted by Deborah, Yvette's personal maid. A stately fifty-year-old originally from Denmark, her blonde hair was arranged into an austere chignon at the nape of her neck, hair so white that it was hard to tell if it had grayed or was always that color. She gazed at John with sea-colored eyes that showed little save a questioning look. Dressed all in black, she could have passed for a Shaker, solemn and refusing to flaunt any bodily assets, though her ample chest was hard to avoid and the shapely legs had to have been prizes for more than one man over the years. John was unaware of any man in her life. It seemed she catered solely to Yvette's needs, to the degree she could also be considered a business manager. Yvette's every departure from Winslow was reported in detail in the *Post,* and Deborah was the spokesperson regarding travel arrangements and anticipated returns. He again made a mental note to review prior issues.

"Good morning. I'd like to speak with Ms. Peters, please," he said, noting her lower jaw tighten and feeling his own quiver of nerves at the anticipated conversation.

"Madam is asleep at this hour. Shall I set up an appointment for you?" she asked, her voice lilting and accented.

He chuckled to himself at her air of formality. Last night, Deborah, too, had indulged in the festivities that included the best champagnes, this being a big holiday for Scandinavians. Rather than serve at the event, she seemed to play the role of welcome committee *cum* conversationalist. Dressed in a pale pink suit, she introduced folks to one another and ensured gaiety prevailed. One of the out-of-town invitees, a white-haired man supposedly into investments at one of the Boston brokerage houses, had found her on more than one occasion to monopolize her time. John had seen them giggling like school children in a corner when he was leaving.

"I'd prefer to talk with her immediately. There's been a death."

His scrutiny was not without reward. Though she flinched visibly and her eyes widened, he noted also a slight nod of the head as if she acknowledged a truth, some invisible association ruled by her mind and confirmed by John's words. He had the impression she forced her reaction, but then instantly told himself to lay off. It was too soon for conclusions. He registered her movements for future reference.

"What?" she asked, her voice just above a whisper.

"Emily Turner was found dead in the woods near here."

Deborah closed her eyes and lowered her head. "Mercy," she whispered. She opened the door wider, giving John the room he needed to enter.

As Paul Allen had guessed, the house had not been put in order from the night before. John suspected that it was primarily because Deborah had been partying as well, she normally being the chief cook and bottle washer.

"Has there been any cleanup work done?" he asked, noting crystal champagne flutes with black or red stems in varying sizes on almost every available flat surface—side tables, the floor, the green marble mantle of the great room to their right, the mahogany banister of the wide staircase leading to the second floor, along the windowsills. Although in the minority, wine glasses and beer steins also took their rightful places.

Looking at the remains of the alcohol, he suddenly felt flushed. Deborah had made a point last night of telling him, when he'd stepped into the main kitchen and noted the stacked boxes marked "Champagne Brut," that they'd been flown in from Paris the week before. Yvette had friends who owned vineyards worldwide. He looked for a chair to sit down, but before he could his attention was diverted to the room beyond the great room.

Something caught his eye, a black outfit, someone moving along the windows, the shadow on the floor, gone as quickly as he'd seen it. As if aware of his observation, Deborah walked ahead of him, thus preventing a full view of that room.

"None," she said with firmness. "I let everyone sleep in."

"Was there someone there?" John asked, craning his neck.

"I doubt it. Would you like to have a look?" she asked.

They passed through the magnificent and open plan of the heart of the house as well as the main congregating room during the party last night. He marveled at its structure and beauty as the sun streamed through sheer white drapes. There was no home in Winslow like this one. The high ceiling and expanse of this room, which ran front to back and took up almost the entire side of the main house, though impressive, had ultimately simple lines. Square, with no visible beams or columns, the evidence of solid construction was hidden behind the off-white walls. In addition, whoever had done the decorating for Yvette had chosen to underplay any lavishness by keeping the basic lines of the Shaker style and complementing it with New England artwork and traditional accents such as wainscoting midway down the walls and a focus on the grand hearth made of fieldstone. A tapestry of colonials at a riverside spanned the Vermont slated-marble mantle on the fireplace. Blown-out beeswax candles sat still in the morning light, their precarious drippings solidified against the green marble.

The wide oak floorboard was new but well stained so as to impress the house's origins. Covering large areas of the floor were genuine Persian rugs with muted tones and soft cushioned support underneath. As they passed over them, John thought of taking his shoes off and sinking in. Deborah seemed oblivious to both the splendor, which had been at its best last night, and the clutter. In the next room, smaller but still able to accommodate at least fifty people comfortably, they saw more of the same scattering of half-full glasses, flutes, and mugs. In addition, three white leather chairs and a matching wraparound couch faced another fieldstone fireplace, still with the glowing embers of the small, controlled fire that had been blazing last night. Contrary to what John had thought, there was no one there.

It was here he and Emily had first spoken. He'd arrived after her, and she'd been talking with someone he didn't know, another of Yvette's many financial advisors as it turned out. Emily had found John's eyes instantly on his entering the room and he'd found it effortless to move past all the others who he did know and stop at her side, waiting for introductions while taking in her clothing and the methodical way she used her hands to express herself.

Deborah remained silent as he looked at everything in the room. She stood close to him; he could hear her paced breathing, and noticed the slight heaving of her chest which forced his eyes in that direction and his thoughts on what it would be like to be in bed with her, those large breasts grazing his chest, titillating him. Quickly he turned away, but she seemed to have noted his interest and kept her proximity as he made way for the corner, where he'd exchanged the first hello with Emily.

"I met a man last night, Scott Cheever," he said.

"Yes, a fine investment advisor. Yvette has used him for years. A close friend of the Granger side, he is."

"Where does he live?"

"All over the world," she said. "His offices are in Boston, Cheever and Associates."

John jotted the name down. He'd recently heard Cheever's name in the news regarding some merger. Cheever was in his thirties, something of a wonder kid as John recalled. Stanford and Yale man, family into the real estate business in one of the booming areas in Utah. Unlike John, he was tanned, worldly, and educated. Emily had been into a lively conversation with him until John arrived. A pang of jealousy struck. Had she stepped away from Cheever just to be polite to John? Her voice was friendly, but had she forced it?

She'd readily introduced them, and offered silence in order that Cheever and John could have whatever exchange seemed appropriate, but John had foregone hot stock tips or advice on the next leading mutual fund manager for Emily and her presence. Cheever had been pulled away by some alluring woman who'd claimed an interest in those topics. It was then they had talked.

"She seemed to be enjoying herself," Deborah said, her eyes on the exact place John and Emily had had their interchange. Deborah must have noticed them talking last night.

"Yes," John said, watching her more carefully. He sensed delay tactics. The more they talked of Emily, the less time there'd be to spend with Yvette, or to discover who might have been passing through this room. Deborah was watching him, eyes passively expectant.

"Would anyone have a need to go through here just now?" he asked, noting she turned so that he couldn't see her face. He studied the broad gold bandanna that kept her hair neatly in place. How long had Deborah been awake? Long enough to take care of her person. She was as immaculate as the night before.

"No. There are three hired maids, temporarily in service until Yvette leaves for Europe. You know she plans to spend the summer in France."

"Yes, she announced it last night," John said. "You don't find it possible that someone could have passed through here?"

Deborah shrugged her shoulders. "Look around, Mr. Jordan. Does it look like someone was here moments ago? There's the door," she said, pointing to the way they came in, "and one over there." The other one led to the patio, and had been the way he and Emily had gone through at one point. As it turned out, those were their final moments together.

"I'd like to speak to the maids."

"Certainly," she said. She looked at him, again with an odd expectancy, an almost "come hither" look now more evident, as if spending this short interval together had given her license to toy with his emotions. "Now?" she smiled.

"They should be prepared. Chief Allen will be sending investigators and, at that time, we'll want to take statements."

"Isn't this presumptuous?" She was now so close to him he could feel her breath on his face, a minty fresh smell.

"Hardly. Ms. Turner was last seen alive in this house."

"Surely there's no suspicions. . . ." Her accent had thickened and he was finding himself distracted by her. He envisioned a younger version of Deborah, white-blonde straight hair to her waist, topless and running along some beach, more than one male in her wake, teasing and playing in the waves. He would have placed bets on how she'd made her way into the United States, and made a note to check it out. He stepped back from her.

"I'm not assuming anything. My job is to ensure that every possible avenue is investigated. Where does the patio lead?" He'd not ventured beyond it last night. It had been dark beyond the bug lamps that outlined the pool and patio area.

"Servants' quarters, er, well, I mean, the two smaller guest houses."

She was correct. The guest houses had been the subject of a local publication on Shaker-style homes. The Shaker communities were made up of groupings of houses, not unlike modern-day developments except without the manicured lawns and two-car garages. "There were no lights coming from them last night." They were stepping onto the patio and he noted a rooftop through trees.

"No, no one had yet decided where to sleep. It was perhaps still too early to divide up the sleeping quarters when you were here."

He didn't need to look at her to know she was working on distracting him. They faced an Olympic-sized swimming pool beyond which a gravel path with lampposts at intervals led to the guest houses. She walked in front of him, her swaying hips in the direct line of his vision as they stepped nearer the buildings. There was no sound from the houses that faced them once they came to the other end of the path. In the silence, the sound of a car. He turned in the direction of the mansion.

"This may be the investigators," he said, turning back.

"No!" Deborah called. "It couldn't be." She hesitated. "They'd call first, no?" Her eyes questioned again, then they glimmered. "Someone else can let them in."

John looked at her. "I thought there was no one up yet."

She lowered her eyes and frowned. "By now, someone is awake."

They walked back, John several paces in front of Deborah. When they got through to the patio and inside the house, the sound of a car in the distance was clear. John quickly made his way back to the foyer where, from the windows that framed the oversized double-door entryway, he noticed that across the winding driveway a door to the five-car garage was closing slowly. To the sounds of Deborah muttering who in the world that might have been, he walked briskly to the garages. By then, the doors were firmly shut and there was no sign of anyone.

He circled the building, a single-story white structure with ample space for five cars and storage in its eaves. He peered into a side window and noted a maroon '48 Ford, one of the cars from the Fourth of July parades. Though she'd never been present, Yvette gave permission for it to be on display along with a white Bentley. They were always head-turners during the parade, usually garnering at least one of the prize ribbons.

There were two spots empty and a third space occupied by a gray Maserati. He'd seen Yvette being driven around town in that. What cars were missing? At least one was the Bentley. Deborah was at the front door watching him. He went to her. "What cars are usually kept in the garage?"

She peered over his shoulder, as if trying to see into the garages. "Ah, the Bentley?" She looked down at her feet. A strand of hair fell to her cheek. Irritated with its imposition, she looped it behind one ear. As she stalled, John studied her harder, his own stamina and ability to persist giving way to the sinking sensation that had been a part of him all morning, the creeping, excruciating realization that Emily was dead.

He didn't want to be here. He wanted to be back last night when he and Emily were talking. His vulnerable side had begun to manifest itself, throwing its strength against his professionalism and whispering to him that he could just walk away, leave this bitch who was covering up something, and say to hell with it all. Take another drink and be rid of the entire business.

He thirsted for a nice cool shot of whiskey, the gold smoothness almost a taste in his mouth. Before he knew it he was working out how he could slip away and get to his place in about ten minutes to find his car and drive to Ray's bar. All this in the moments when Deborah, silent and studying him for signs of what was going on in his mind, maintained a look that gradually grew triumphant as she noted he was quizzing her no more.

He couldn't talk. His throat constricted, he could think of one thing. Thirst. The drink. The damned, blasted drink. He felt his face flush and found that as she continued to stare, he grew less and less steady. She reached for him.

"You're feeling faint?" she asked, a hand now placed on his arm.

He shook his head to protest but she felt so cool, so reassuring, he wanted to embrace her. Then the dark feeling surged, a sense that the worst was yet to come. He knew this feeling, as it had been worked through between he and his therapist, but without her he was not able to quickly pick up on its manifestation and began allowing thoughts of a drink to rule.

"I'm okay," he whispered, knowing as he said it that she didn't believe him.

They walked slowly towards the mansion. A vehicle approached. It was a police car winding its way up the drive. Like a shot of medication, John's attention was momentarily averted. It was Chief Allen, his wife Michelle with him in the front seat.

Michelle. He smiled gratefully at her from a distance as the car slowed to a stop near them. Deborah let go of his arm as he stepped to open the door for Michelle. She emerged and embraced him without ceremony. A petite blonde with wide smile and athletic countenance, Michelle knew him well. They'd become fast friends through the chief and now that she was studying psychology at the state university, she was familiar with his issues, having been one of the best listeners John had ever met. John trusted her instinctively.

"Are you all right? I wanted to get to you as soon as I heard . . . ," she whispered, locking her arm in his.

Her body was such a comfort, but it loosened what reserve he had. Before Deborah could witness his tears, Michelle had guided him to the police car and moved into the back seat with him. Chief Allen resumed the discussion with Deborah, nodding to Michelle as if they'd already agreed her purpose in coming was to aid John.

John wiped sweat from his brow. "I've got the drink on my mind," he said to her, squeezing her hand.

She squeezed back and said, "Relax. Paul will deal with the maid. You need to relax, John."

She was right. He was pushing himself. This had been told to him many times. There was not a human alive who could day after day take the brunt of police work and all its blatant statements about human nature without having to take refuge in some sort of shelter. Over too many years, his had become alcohol and here were the triggers to his thirst yet again. The stress, the difficult personalities, the questions that led to more questions. This investigation had only begun and yet it would prove to be one of the most testing for him since he'd begun to try and tame his drinking habits. Who was he to think he could just walk away from the body and start investigating? That was what Michelle was saying now. He chose to focus on her words and block the rest out.

"Your boundaries are weak now, John." As they sat in the car, her husband and Deborah disappeared into the Peters'. Here was a strong woman, he noted, a woman who had she not been his close friend's wife might have caught his fancy. At the same time, she was missing those aspects he was typically drawn to in a woman. Her overly muscular legs spoke to many treks in the woods around Winslow and the mountains up north. Her tanned face was wrinkled from so much sun against which she didn't protect herself. Her bleached hair had seen too much peroxide and blended with too much harsh weather. Her eyes twinkled, though, and her touch was firm. A friendship firm. He knew why Paul loved her. The couple had probably developed their friendship first, or at least kept that as a priority over the years.

"I need something," he tried, knowing at a level she'd never allow him a drink.

"You'll be fine. You're not going into that house. Stay here with me. Paul will decide the next steps."

"Someone drove away," he muttered. "Jesus, it could have been someone who knows something."

"Don't worry. There's time enough," she said, but even so reached for the car phone to call Paul. When her husband picked up, she quickly related to him what John told her. In moments, Paul emerged from the house. He walked towards them wearing a very serious face.

"Yvette has left," he stated. "Already left for France."

"When is the flight scheduled?" Michelle asked.

"Later today out of New York. She left this morning," he said.

"Without Deborah?" Michelle asked.

Michelle and Paul looked at one another. "Good point," Paul said. "I've called the others to get over here to begin fingerprinting. We also need a list of everyone who was at the party." He made a few phone calls, requesting the investigative staff from both Winslow and the neighboring town of Leicester. "I'll wait until they get here. John, I want you to get back to the office and cover. Michelle will stay with you to help out. Honey, call Jason Strand at NYPD and have him find out about the Paris flights tonight. We don't want Yvette leaving the country. Also, see if they can find out if and when her itinerary might have changed."

John began to protest but Michelle suggested that John should listen right now and take it easy. John breathed deeply and tried to understand that the Allens were not only doing what was best for the investigation but what was best for John. It made him at once angry and docile. There had been too many nights they'd helped him, along with some nights he'd fought them. Those days were less frequent now. When Michelle told him to take it easy, he knew it was a control he had to obey without necessarily reacting to.

As Michelle drove away, John sat in the passenger seat, relieved. Part of him was needing to stay, but part of him was exhausted. She smiled reassuringly at him. "Shall we stop at the house to get Sami?"

He nodded, trying to grin and trying to understand. But all he could sense was the need for a drink, now stronger than his need last night for Emily. He gripped the handle of the car door, tightening with each breath. The haunting questions had returned, why the women and why the drink? Did he need to forever dismiss the two in order to really live?

Chapter Three

Sami was disgusted. As Michelle and John approached her, she snorted numerous times, digging at the ground and twirling such that she entangled herself in the rope that hung from the dog run more than she already had. As if to say, "Your return has been long overdue," she let Michelle pat her first then gave a glib nod to John. She used to do that when he returned home from all-night binges. She was doing it now for a reason. Her entire Sunday morning, usually a time for them to hike long distances, had been spent stuck in the backyard.

"Sami," he said, jostling with her. "Sorry, girl."

Michelle was fanning herself. "Hot one today. We were going to the beach until this happened." She caught herself and added, "She was a lovely person, wasn't she?"

Noting how the "she" was being used, he wondered if Michelle might be having a hard time, too. She and Emily had been schoolmates and, though not close friends, had assumed an amiable acquaintance when Emily returned from California. He recalled just last week when Michelle kidded him about asking Emily out for old-times' sake.

"More than lovely," he said. Forcing himself to think of something else, he then added, "You want a coffee?"

"We can get one at the station," she said, entirely in control. Of course, she also knew he'd get into his house and not want to leave, subject himself to his hermit status given the circumstance, pour a drink. It was another way he coped. Leaving him alone was one thing she would not do.

They returned to the car. Sami was already lounging in the back seat, fully aware that a meal and biscuits waited for her at the station. They drove in silence, passing the Turner property after a half mile. The house appeared inactive. Walter wasn't outside on his tractor, his usual position on the weekends and lately during the week as well. Nor was Betty at her flowers, something she did nonstop from spring's first breath until the destructive autumn frosts.

The pre-colonial, one of the outer Shaker buildings built at the same time as the original Peters property, was painted black, a color that lent to its austerity in spite of the myriad plants that graced the wide front lawn. At this time of year, the perennials were ceding their greenery to shots of other colors, giant red poppies, low-lying purple phlox, red Mrs. Bradshaws, pink hollyhocks, hostas preparing for their tall purple spikes, and peonies beginning to burst from round buds.

In spite of the display, this place gave John the creeps. It always had, with the way Walter lined up his tools after use, tallest to smallest along the hooks outside the barn—hoe, then rake, clippers, and the spade, the way even the dirt piles to be used in the gardens were just so, the constant focus on appearance. Like its inhabitants, the house boasted outward order. He detested its just-right distance from the road, walkways made of flagstone equidistant one from the other, the lamp lights at strategic places. Aside from the tractor being left on occasion in random spots across the property, not one other thing was ever out of place.

Even the wide barn door was ajar by exactly six inches. Betty had once complained to Walter that it was too heavy for her to push unless it was opened a bit. Therefore, Walter closed it shut only before retiring each night, and mornings he went promptly to open it well before she had to get to her car or her watering equipment. Over the almost forty years the couple had lived here, John guessed they'd spent over half their waking lives fixing and cleaning the place. Emily had been a prisoner of chores when she was a child. No wonder she left home at eighteen.

"They seem distraught," Michelle commented.

"Have you seen them?" John asked.

"They were at the station giving statements. Paul will be stopping by the house later. Looks like they've bypassed their yard work." Michelle knew well the couple's tendency for maniacal order. She, Paul, and John often joked about it, until Emily had returned and related to John how difficult her childhood had been. After that, they held their words.

The police station stood at the edge of town, a newly renovated three-story brick building that housed the offices, a small jail, and garages for the three police cars and the Jeep that came in handy in bad winter weather. It was a clinical and clean place, not unlike a hospital with its glassed-in office areas, tiled shiny floors, off-white walls, and a smell of the pine air freshener used by the night cleaning staff, a genial retired policeman.

Reporters milled at the front steps. John pushed his way past their questions and cameras, nodding with an unreadable expression. Inside, there were more people than usual. Surrounding Art Johnson were several young people John recognized as the medic team from the woods. Phones rang as Lucy Morrill, the regular secretary, answered and took messages. Still in her blue floral-print church dress, a spring bonnet perched atop her white hair, she'd come to assist. Michelle hopped to the phones as well, parking herself at a free reception desk and rummaging through the drawers for notepads. Pete Stanton, now in khakis and a white shirt, kept company with an officer John recognized from the next town.

John's desk was the first one behind the glass doors on the right, facing the main street and at an angle with the high school playing field. Some autumn afternoons when a game was in progress, he'd get out his binoculars from the top drawer and watch a few plays, reliving his own days playing for the Winslow Huskies. He moved lethargically to his desk, hearing Michelle, again on the phone as she checked in with her husband, telling him where they were, that John was doing okay. He tried not to think of how at times this "caregiving" of the Allens reminded him of being a child with babysitters and instead reminded himself that their diligence kept him gainfully employed.

It was the first time he'd been alone since the incident at the mansion. In spite of Michelle's melodic tones, he stood in a room that spoke to the fact that, as he found himself doing with every movement today, the last time he was here, Emily was alive. Her eyes blazed into his memory and he felt them on him, strangely reliving her gaze more than her words or her presence, like she was there with him somehow. He shook his head hard to blur the image but it seemed to rest on his senses like a drug unwilling to quit his system.

The thought forced him to the chair behind his desk. Creaking as it had since Paul pointed him to it on his first day on the job, a relic from old days when old Josh Whittaker ran the place, it was a classic oak swivel armchair with a dip in the seat for comfort. John could lean back and put his feet on the table, relaxing as if in a hammock. This time, he sunk into it wondering what to do next. So much to do and yet he was slipping into this inability to function he thought he'd overcome.

A knock against the open door forced him to look up. It was Art Johnson. "May I come in?"

In all the years John had known the man, which covered most of John's forty years, he'd never once heard Art speak in anything other than the most gracious, deferential tones as well as act in a gentlemanly fashion. An octogenarian and of the blue-blood stock that once owned the town, he had every right to seat himself without asking. Nevertheless, he waited for John's nod to proceed into the office. Art was a trained medical doctor, a general practitioner who moved into coronary work following World War II, when he'd been assigned the position in the Pacific. His passion for the study of the dead, he explained once to John, had behind it an interest in people living long and healthy lives. "If we find out why and how we die, my son," Art had said, "we can know what to expect and how to prevent the unnecessary."

It was these words that John thought of as Art shuffled towards the chair on the other side of John's desk. Having been to church and back with his wife Minnie before he was called to the body, Art wore his summer look, a pale blue seersucker suit with beige canvas shoes, a navy tie neatly sitting against his slightly paunchy belly. Though soiled only slightly from his foray in the woods, John noted the spot of blood on Art's sleeve. Art crossed his legs and placed both hands on his thighs.

"Any thoughts?" John asked, starting the conversation in an attempt to feel in control.

Art's wrinkled face was solemn. His usually merry blue eyes were large and soulful as he looked slowly up at John from his glasses that he'd begun wiping contemplatively with a handkerchief. He replaced them on his face, measuring each movement as if thinking through his words before speaking, a habit he was known for which, John thought, gave him an aura of wisdom. "Sudden."

They shared the silence, John nodding slowly, Art pursing his lips. In the background, Michelle giggled, enjoying a pleasantry with one of the medics.

"Meaning?" John began to feel panicked. "Sudden" didn't help him. He needed facts, details, gory details if necessary but the details of a death of a woman not yet forty. A woman to whom he had been very attracted.

"Not sure yet," Art said. "Need the full effort here, son."

"When will you begin?"

"Tomorrow first thing, it's looking like. Needed to rearrange a few things, but the sooner the better, I figure."

"What about the Turners?"

"They're filing to stop it but, you know if they go to those solicitors Higgins and Malloy, they won't get any kind of a notice before tomorrow night. Legally, I can start my work once the chief has okayed it."

"Betty seemed pretty adamant."

"She'll calm down. Then Walter will," Art said. He'd taken care of Betty's hot flashes and temper tantrums over the years. Everyone knew about her erratic emotions, a thing that was deemed due to her age and notions regarding post-menopausal women. Art called her "batty." "Walter does what Betty says, and Betty needs to calm down."

"They've lost a daughter," John said, looking down into his lap.

"And you've lost your little pal." The words were so soft John almost couldn't hear. When he returned his gaze, Art was giving him a kind, knowing look. "I remember the day years ago she got two stitches over her eyebrow. Must've been when you two were eight. Running wild over those boulders along Short's Creek. Slipped and fell she did, or at least you two claimed. I reckon you were chasing her, eh? Mighty cute thing she was back then, those braids and those big eyes."

They shared a smile as John nodded. "I've never been able to lie to you."

"Knowing the dead makes these things harder. We'll figure this out, but my take right now is she had some major shock, something that so shocked her, she was knocked down. Dead."

"Is that possible?"

"Unfortunately, even with a younger person it's possible, though not likely. Unless the autopsy reveals otherwise. Then again it may be something we can't be sure of." He took a deep breath. "You know, John, once a body's lying for too long, the secrets go out of it. That's why we've got to start right away and, as Min always reminds me, she needs to be put to rest."

John's phone rang. It was Allen. "How are you doing?" he asked.

John kept his eyes on Art's steady gaze, drew in a deep breath, and placed the phone on speaker so Art could hear. "Fine. I'm sitting here with Art. What's up?"

"Yvette Peters has been located at Kennedy Airport."

John listened, trying to quell the nagging sense that something terrible was going to happen. His body tensed as Paul detailed the encounter at the airport—Yvette outraged that her travel plans had been disrupted; who was the law that it could prevent a perfectly decent person from taking a holiday; she would return to Winslow and promptly see to it that her lawyers got involved in protecting her from invasions of privacy the likes of this.

John broke into a sweat that Art noticed because he handed John a handkerchief.

Last night, Yvette had waited before approaching him. Yvette Peters, her forced regal expression laid thick across her pushing-sixty-five-year-old face that had seen not a few plastic surgeries. Tight skin and the best makeup created an image that, had there been a filtered lens and the right lighting, would have made her look something closer to forty. Dressed in a red Cartier that clung to her still-curvaceous figure, she wore gold on every possible part of her body, her dyed blonde locks the perfect pageboy length, the look she'd carried since John could remember. Nails a crimson red, she'd stared at no one in particular, focusing her dark eyes on the huge beehive chimney and fireplace that marked one corner of the great room of her mansion. Next, she gave him that look, the one he recalled from years before, dark eyes penetrating and a slight curl to her lips. His entire body had the same reaction as back then, a numbness that spread from his heart through to his limbs. He wanted to walk out, but his body remained stuck in place.

A slow, knowing smile cracked and she studied his long legs, stopping fleetingly on his groin, letting him know how she knew him. He'd been caught off guard, but had it in him to acknowledge a greeting from a neighbor who'd come up to the punch bowl where he stood. Nevertheless he'd felt Yvette's eyes, the piercing black look that years before had triumphed over his youthful wariness.

Back then, he'd been unaware that his body would have an effect on women, unaware that the feelings that emerged as he discovered his own sexuality would interfere with his better judgment from that point on.

It had been one of her solstice parties, one that Emily was not present for, she having left the winter before for California. Not unlike last night's affair, that party also boasted the finest foods, the best catered service and even, given Yvette was not as far removed from Hollywood back then, some well-known Broadway and film personalities. The music had been a combination of classical and jazz, with recordings made especially for Yvette by Nat King Cole and Ella Fitzgerald.

She had cornered him once he'd become sufficiently drunk, not too late into the evening but late enough so that most minds present were equally dulled by alcohol and the proffered drugs that remained discreetly available for those in the know. Most guests had paired off or were in the process of making way to the surrounding houses and bedrooms with someone they hoped would eventually end up in their arms.

Other, less libidinal types were slouched on couches and settees, regaling in the seemingly endless supply of sumptuous canapés and the most expensive wines and alcohol.

He remembered the notes from "Ramblin' Rose," King Cole's voice softly and luxuriously sending messages of letting go, of not holding onto something that needed letting go. Why I love you, no one knows. He remembered feeling sad that Emily was gone and wondering did she want to go because she wanted to get away from him?

Yvette's fingernails skimmed his arm, her eyes mesmerized, beckoning him to her and then slipping her hand in his arm, walking him upstairs to her darkened bedroom. The late hour had only a hint of light left, and the shadows from the moon cast figures on the white satin sheets. She led him to the side of the bed, then stood behind him, unbuttoning his shirt slowly. He felt himself harden and closed his eyes, wordless, helpless in his way to prevent what was happening. She undressed him and by then he wanted to have her, wanted to explore her according to her whispered suggestions. He heard her zipper, the silk dress slipping to the floor and then felt her naked breasts against his back. She pushed him first to the bed and turned him and took care of him promptly, sighing as he, exhausted, gave into her curious hands and active tongue.

When he lay spent, she placed herself on top of him, roused him again, differently and deftly, and then gave herself up to him, losing herself in a fury of cries and grips. The imprint of her dug-in nails on his back remained for months afterwards.

They crawled into bed and he slept for some time before waking. When he did, she was no longer there. The room had returned to an antiseptic, orderly place. Her dress was gone and his clothes lay neatly folded on a chair, a glass of water by the side table. The house was still. A clock showed 4 A.M. He got up, went to the window. He was nauseated from too much drinking, and his head spun from the events. Where was she? An odd longing overtook him, like she should not have left without telling him, that the evening's outcome was for him and her together to decide. She was nowhere to be seen, and he guessed her to be in another room asleep. Of the many rooms upstairs, he had no idea which one might be it, so he dressed and made his way down the stairs and out the door.

It was years before he called what happened rape. Years of feeling bad and not knowing why, of seeking women's bodies and getting away with having them but nothing further. Even those who were interested in more, in what he learned was a healthy relationship, never got far with him. He'd smile and never call them. Yvette had taken control. For five years following that first time, she arranged to have him regularly in her house, in her bed, in her body. He responded, not understanding, trying to sort the sense of invasion against the curious pull of being one with a woman, this woman who frightened and excited him.

Chapter Four

Late spring 1958

John opened his eyes. His dog Jeepers licked his hand that hung over one side of the bed. The house was still. The trees made shadows against the white curtains. A breeze rustled them and he thought he heard a car.

"Mommy," he said softly. The room next door where she slept was dark. Usually there was a night-light on in the tiny bathroom that separated them. Tonight, there was none. He focused his eyes on the opening. "Mommy," he said louder.

He'd received an oversized wall clock for his most recent birthday. Black hands with white gloves pointed to the time, and the face had eyes, nose, and a big smile. The numbers were luminescent, something he'd been so excited about that he'd run to a closet to watch them light up, leaving his birthday party for over twenty minutes to marvel at its light and the gentle tick tick that from that point forward had been a comfort when he was trying to fall asleep. Now it read some hour very late because the hands were past the twelve. He'd not yet mastered telling time, but knew that it was a long while before dawn and a long time since his mother had put him to bed.

"Mommy!" he cried, sitting up and pulling Jeepers up onto the bed. The cocker spaniel was thrilled to get away with something for which she was usually punished and made several circles on the puffy covers before settling against the pillow and one of John's exposed arms. John hugged the dog.

His mother wasn't in her room. She would have come by now. He lay listening to the clock, its sound becoming louder in the silence. He wondered if she was on the couch. Sometimes she was fast asleep there, a cigarette burning precariously at the edge of a cigarette holder, or worse, down to ashes between her fingers, and an empty glass of something that had a sweet sour smell. He would get up and wake her, then help her to bed. Though she would sleep past lunchtime those days, she would be so affectionate and grateful on discovering he'd helped her to bed.

"Sweetie, you're my shining star," Darcy Jordan would whisper, her gray eyes red-rimmed and clouded, her hands often shaking as she reached for him and explained that "Mommy's had a late night because she worked so hard and needed to take some medicine to help her relax before going to bed. It was strong, John, so strong it put me right out!"

John recalled nodding and telling her he hoped she felt up to going to work that day. She'd assure him she was fine and that the "medicine" had helped her feel better. "Just like new, Sweetie," she'd rasp, lighting a cigarette.

He pulled his feet over the side of the bed and felt the cool night air through his toes. While in town buying popsicles at Doc McDougal's with his friend Emily, he'd overheard several adults buzzing about the latest news. Yvette Peters the movie star was having a party. John had asked his mom if he could go but she'd only laughed, a bitter laugh he'd not heard from her since his father died.

"Surely children would be bored at that sort of place. I wouldn't let you go anyway. We're just plain folks and that house has ritzy parties." She'd blown a strand of hair from her eyes and carried on with her sweeping. "If I go, it will be to work anyway." Darcy had recently been employed by Yvette to assist with any major affairs. This would be a post–Academy Award party and there was a promise of some well-known stars like Roy Rogers, a name brought up by one of the ten-year-olds at McDougal's.

Easing over the bed side, he pulled his pajama top tighter around him. "Jeepers, come," he whispered, waiting for her to hop down and patter to the door. He tiptoed to the hallway, flicking on the switch that was right outside his door. "Mommy," he called, eyeing the living room sofa feet from him, its back to him.

The house was compact, a single-floor square structure dating back to the Shaker days but unfortunately one of the buildings that had been overlooked when the town declared tracts of land off-limits to development. The bylaws allowed for funding to preserve the dwellings on these tracts. During that time, the Jordans' house had been hidden in brush and trees with no road to speak of leading to it. Officially part of Yvette's property, she'd rented it out to the Jordans when Darcy's husband died. Prior to that, they'd lived at the top of a triple-decker in the center of town. After getting help from Yvette moving in, Darcy had cleaned it as best she could, and some of the townsfolk from the Catholic Church had donated furniture. Over the years the once-sturdy construction had fallen into ill repair with little insulation, rotting floors, and walls infested with termites. However, Darcy made the most of it, using the large fieldstone fireplace to keep the house warm and the dated gas stove to cook on. The dirt road that led to the nearest main road several miles away was the only way to get in and out of the property by car, so it was quiet and they were left to themselves for the most part.

Initially, John had been thrilled because he could roam as he pleased without supervision, and he'd quickly made friends with Emily Turner, who lived in a nearby house. They had begun to investigate the woods, brooks, and fields with Jeepers and had already declared a few "secret" hiding places their own. Emily was returning first thing tomorrow so they could get to Short's Creek to catch pollywogs before church.

Now, however, the knowledge of being miles from the nearest neighbor left him frightened. His mother wasn't in the living room. He padded to the kitchen, calling her with a tentative voice.

He shouted once more. She wasn't anywhere. The shuffling of his feet the only sound. Jeepers whimpered, sniffing the kitchen floor for crumbs and finding a single potato chip, a casualty from John's snack earlier in the day. As she crackled and chewed it, John watched her golden coat lighting the center of the small room consisting of a large and noisy refrigerator, their gas stove that normally would have cheered him because it emanated much-needed heat on those nippy spring nights, and the sink with dishes piled high. His mother didn't keep up the house the way she kept up the Peters's place, and John often drank from the cups he'd used the day before. The stale smell of cigarette butts rising to his nose, he turned towards the kitchen table. It was cluttered with dirtied ashtrays and newspapers. A table lamp with a low-wattage bulb burned.

He stood on the chair and peeked out the window, tears forming. Where was she? Was she all right? Why didn't she take him with her? He scrambled down, rushing to the bedroom on the off chance he'd missed her there.

Flicking the light on, he saw the rumpled blue bedcovers and smelled the same stale smoke that permeated the blankets and spoke to nights his mother sat in bed and smoked, her eyes blank and uncaring. She was thinking of his father, she'd tell John if he asked. "Thinking, thinking, Sweetie." It wasn't long after saying those words she'd burst into uncontrolled sobs and he'd hold her tight. Sometimes he held her for a very long time.

His mother had a faded blue quilt night jacket someone from the church had given her. Sitting in bed, the lights soft against her skin that once had been so clear but now had grown drawn with dark circles and shadows, she used to resemble other mothers, prim and dutiful, that is, when she didn't have a cigarette hanging out of her mouth. He'd pretend they lived just like the other kids in school, that his mom was at home all day waiting for him to come in from play so she could cook him dinner.

Now, the night jacket was thrown to the floor, open and exposing the torn silk lining. He'd seen it that way this morning. Her room was about half the size of his own with an even narrower closet. Her few outfits he knew well – the pink shirtwaist and the blue two-piece suit for church were hanging in the closet, and a pink neckerchief lay on the floor. She usually wore it with the dress. Otherwise she wore what she was in tonight, a white summer smock and dark slacks.

Sobbing, he cried out her name, aimlessly wandering the rooms until he returned to his own, curled into a ball, and fell into a deep sleep that gave rise to a nightmare. His mother had come to tuck him in and she was covered in blood, her reading glasses on and cracked as she stared at him with bloodied veins in her eyes, hands that reached out to touch him, squeeze him around the neck, choking, choking him until he woke with a loud, long scream that wracked him to the core.

"Mommy!" he cried, his voice breaking with sobs. He ran into the kitchen. The telephone. He could call someone. He climbed onto the kitchen table next to which the wall telephone hung. They shared a party line with six other neighbors. John had never used it, only watched when his mother picked up the receiver and held it to her ear, speaking into the mouthpiece that was attached to the box on the wall. Some nights his mother would joke when the neighbors' lines rang instead of theirs – two fast rings for the Turners, one for the Hortons. Even the Peters's residence was a part of this system.

"That nice Mr. Walter Turner is probably calling back to his family in England," she often said, a faraway look in her eye that John recognized as her desire to leave the town, but it was invariably followed by downcast eyes, as if to ascertain she was its prisoner yet.

He reached for the hand piece but accidentally slipped due to the newspapers underfoot, causing himself and the phone piece to fall to the floor. After that, everything was a jumble. His face burst with tears and cries at the same time he heard voices in the phone, voices that would haunt him thereafter, a gruff-sounding one, then a questioning, laughing one.

"Mommy! I want my Mommy!" he screamed repeatedly until there was no sound coming from the phone, until his throat hurt and he sobbed quietly, faint with fatigue and fright and crumpled on the floor, Jeepers sniffing periodically around him, letting out helpless little whines. The eerie silence broke his hysterics. He stared at the black cone-shaped device with the single wire line trailing back to the wall attachment and then crawled towards Jeepers, holding him tight and sobbing quietly into the dog's soft fur. They lay on the cold linoleum floor, as John repeated a chant that he would recall with a shiver well into adulthood. "Please come home, Mommy, please come home!"

His mother told him that God was always listening. "God hears our pleas, John, Sweetie, God is always around us." During that long night, he held firm to his chant and believed the words of his mother because otherwise there was nothing but the dark night and the empty, scary house. Jeepers slept first and then John fell jerkily into a slumber that remained, finally, undisturbed until morning.

He heard her before he saw her. Her feet scraping on the doormat outside woke him as daylight streamed through the windows. "John!" she called and caught herself with a big intake of breath when she saw her son and Jeepers crouched in the corner.

He jumped up and ran to her, folding himself into her body and crying out, "Where were you, Mommy?"

"Why, child, I was out for a morning walk!"

"But you were gone!" His blue eyes widened.

"Hush! Of course I wasn't! I'd never leave you!" she whispered into the top of his head that was pulled tight against her chest. He could smell a perfume he didn't recognize and noted the tiny blue and yellow flowers that his face was pressed up against. This was a dress he'd not seen on her before. Her hands were clean and soapy-smelling and he wanted to hold her forever, but her words disturbed him.

"No, you weren't. I woke up," he pouted, trying to piece together what she was saying.

"Sweetie, now, c'mere! There!" she said, patting his head and straightening his pajama tops. "You must have had a nightmare. Look, you walked right into this kitchen all by yourself! You sleepwalk, you know. Now, get back into that room of yours and finish your sleep." She led him towards his room, the swishing of her dress sounding so comforting to him, her hands firm on his shoulders. He looked up, white-blonde bangs in his eyes, and studied her as they stepped past the living room and its disarray into his room, where the sight of the bed reminded him of his long night.

As she tucked him in, she hummed quietly. Lipstick was fresh on her well-rounded lips and she had a glimmer in her eyes he'd not seen in a long time, since well before his father left.

"I called for you. I went into your room and looked on the couch," he said.

Darcy Jordan busied herself folding his clothes from the day before and placing them just so on the top of his dresser. "Now, silly boy, you get some sleep. These clothes don't look too bad, so you can wear them today, too. Mustn't dirty them either. Otherwise, we'll have to hitch a ride to Bubble-It this week and I'd like not to."

Her brown hair hung straight to her shoulders and her normally drawn face had a certain clarity to it. She smiled as she moved about, and looked in his small, smoke-stained mirror more than once to check that no hairs were out of place.

Though the perfume smell dominated, he thought he detected that odd, empty-glass smell but wasn't sure because it seemed to be different than usual. Then there was the smoke breath. His mother was made of so many smells.

Silenced by her insistence, his wide eyes, about the only thing visible now from under the blankets, followed her until she stood in the doorway. She winked and said, "Now, I'll wake you in time for church. Get some sleep." Her fingers went to her pouting lips and she blew him a kiss. "Luv you!" She disappeared behind the closed door.

From her room, he heard her continued music, in a voice so lovely he found it hard to believe it was the same woman who most of the time used her vocal cords to cry. He hadn't dreamed this, had he? The unhooked phone was still on the floor. He rolled over and closed his eyes. Jeepers padded nervously around the room. She was used to being out by daylight and this infirmity irritated her.

He got out of bed. His thigh was sore from having slept on the hard floor. He let her out and listened for his mother. Her voice was softer now, she'd moved to the kitchen. The snap of the lit match, the pouff of the stove's burner catching, the flutter of his mother's hands as she waved the match fire out. He walked quietly out of his room.

A rap at the door brought his mother to the screened door. "Oh, hello!" she exclaimed to someone she was very glad to see. He thought of his dad.

It was a man. In the passage that led from the living room to the kitchen, he stood watching his mother in the doorway, fascinated by her hips that moved one way then the other, then cocked against one side of the door, her shapely and thin legs crossed at the calves, one hand curved against her hip bone, her head thrown back in a loud, hearty laugh.

He craned his neck but could see no one. The voice was vaguely familiar. "Little one asleep?" he asked.

A shiver went through John. They were talking about him. He stepped back into the living room to hide from view, still able to hear.

"Sure. Thinks he caught me out at night, the little twerp," she giggled coyly. John felt as though someone had smacked him.

"Great imaginations," said the man. "Mine, too. They're all trouble. Not worth the time, I say. But you, now you're another story."

His mother laughed. "Get along. It's church day and all. God's watching!" The sound of the screen door closing should have been sound enough for him to run, but he stood. Frightened and stunned at his mother's choice of words, denying at the same time, he wondered over why she'd say such a thing. He thought perhaps he'd heard wrong. Except he wanted to cry and punch someone at the same time.

As his thoughts raced through his already-spent body, he realized too late he'd not left his position as eavesdropper. In no time, she stood facing him. Her eyes, a mixture of surprise and disappointment, quickly grew dark with anger.

"John Jordan, you get back into that bed immediately!" she yelled. This time her hands were rough, pushing and shoving him, poking as she yelled, "Who in the hell are you to listen to grownups? When did you have permission to do that, you little runt? Why, if your father hadn't dumped you on me . . ."

He felt himself lift away, completely removed from the scene. His body was shoved onto the bed but by then he was far, far away from her words and her screams. He was out somewhere with Emily, out in the woods playing catch-the-fireflies. She was so much fun with her braids and her endless laugh. They were running, hands clasped together, each claiming they'd caught not one but two, each wild about reaching some nameless place where they'd let the bugs go but still be able to maintain they had caught one more than the other.

The door to the room slammed shut and he stared at the white ceiling with the crack down the middle. It was time to get up and play with Emily.

He waited until he knew his mother was in the bathroom, the tub running and she again humming her happy tune. The hands of the clock said 7 A.M. now. It was two hours before church and an hour before she'd come back. She had to do her wash-up and, he figured, because of her upbeat spirits, she'd give herself more time, and even perhaps one of those drinks before brushing her teeth and getting dressed for church.

There was time to find Emily. He pulled at the folded clothes and dressed, his face feeling hot with something more than the dripping perspiration. Maybe he could tell Emily. She wouldn't make fun of him or pretend it didn't happen.

He heard the familiar sound of a rock on his window, their signal to come play. Pulling back the curtains, he looked out onto the backyard, the drooping plants that needed water, the expanse of weeds and grass that needed mowing, beyond to the petite gamine who stared at him with wide eyes.

She twirled a braid in one hand, then waved at him to follow her, waiting only another split second before taking off and disappearing behind the clump of aged and dying apple trees, beyond which was the woods and their playland. He opened the window. Their weights thumped as he tried to get it as high as he could before slipping through it and down onto the soft earth. He ran after her and, as his feet hit the ground one after the other, he tried to put the night before behind him and think of this sunny day and this person he could trust who was several hundred yards ahead of him, and that they'd have some time together before he had to face the truth and then deny it.

41

Chapter Five

Betty Turner placed a hand on her chest and drew in an exaggerated breath. "Walter, help me!" she cried with eyes on her husband who rushed to her side. John, Michelle, and Paul watched Betty gasp as Walter led her to a nearby chair. Two officers were already upstairs in Emily's room. The snap of a camera clipped the silence.

Betty closed her eyes and raised her hand, her wrist across her brow. "There, there, luv," Walter said, helping her wipe her forehead. "We'll get you some help." He glanced at John. "She needs a doctor."

"Art Johnson can be here shortly," John said.

"Not him! She needs a professional man!" Walter scowled.

John was about to protest when he felt Michelle's hand on his arm. "Walter, what is wrong?" she asked, moving closer. They'd come to see if there was any change of heart about the autopsy.

"She's bleedin' tired and stressed out!" he said, stroking her brown curls. "Woman's had a shock, you know. We need a doctor!"

Paul answered, "Let's call an ambulance, then. Get her to the hospital." He picked up the phone and dialed 911, summoning the nearest ambulance to the Turner address.

"Not that!" Betty said, sitting straight and pressing the front of her flower-print shirt. "It's far too expensive. . . ." She shot a look at Walter.

"Of course, darling, we're not going to do such a thing. You need your rest. Come, I'll get you to bed. A nice cup of tea and a rest, that's what you need."

The others sat and watched the Turners shuffle towards the kitchen on the other side of the house, making their way up the narrow staircase that divided the older part of the home from the more recent construction. Walter repeated comforting words as they stepped into a room and then closed the door, after which not a sound could be heard.

John, Michelle, and Paul exchanged glances. Paul stood up from the couch that was opposite an oversized fieldstone fireplace, walked to the hearth, and picked up the poker. He stirred the ashes that gave rise to puffs of smoke.

"Was it chilly last night?" he asked.

John followed Paul's movements, trying to piece together the latest behavior of the Turners. "Rained in the early hours. Must've been a chill."

The house was a testament to the attention the couple paid to it. It was over two hundred years old and retained much of the dated charms like the double fireplace with two open hearths at corners to one another, exposed natural beams, and a beehive chimney that exploded into the entryway so that any newcomer was forced to acknowledge its presence. At the same time, the newer wing was spacious and modern with floor-to-ceiling glass sliding doors, skylights, a kitchen with new appliances, and a family room equipped with the latest entertainment gadgets. Wide pine boards stretched across the floors with the exception of the kitchen that boasted Vermont green slate throughout. The upstairs hallway was visible from the downstairs as were the doors to the many bedrooms that were off of its hallway. Every colored glass bottle, hanging straw basket, gleaming antique chest or side table spoke to a diligent effort to preserve the past and utilize today's technology for the best in creature comforts.

"They use all those rooms for themselves?" Paul asked, looking up on hearing a sob emanate from Betty and Walter's room.

"The upstairs section of the barn is for guests," Michelle said, "but I seem to recall Betty mentioning just last summer that the arrival of an unexpected van of Canadians required they use a few rooms upstairs."

The shutting of a car door veered the attention of all three towards one of the paned windows. Outside, a young woman alighted from a blue Ford. Dressed in jeans and a white sweatshirt, she wore her brown hair in a ponytail tied back by a bright red and black knot. She reached into the back seat to pull out a knapsack and then walked to the patio outside the kitchen, where a breezeway brought her to the side door. Walter hurried down the stairs as the other three moved towards the kitchen to see who it was.

Walter's voice was charged. "There's no room at the moment, I regret to say."

"My name is Rain Danforth. Is this not the Turner guest house?" she asked. Her voice was clear and vibrant. John noted its quiet command, a polite softness mingled with calm assuredness. He moved past Michelle to get a better view. With wide, brown-rimmed glasses placed at the end of her nose, the woman stared directly into Walter's eyes.

Walter's back prevented a full view as he answered, "Yes."

"I've come to see Emily," she said.

Michelle's intake of breath was the only sound.

Walter shifted his weight uncomfortably. "There must be a mistake," he began, looking in the direction of the staircase. Betty had not made an appearance. He grumbled and, as if by some unseen cue, allowed Rain to enter. Without another word, he went outside.

Staring from one to another, an awkward moment of silence passed until Michelle finally said to Rain, "You came to see Emily."

Rain nodded. "She told me I could stay here, at the Turners, if I ever came out East. Is she here?"

"She's dead," Michelle said.

For an instant, Rain's face maintained its expectant look, her lips pouting slightly, her eyes gazing directly at Michelle. Then, her eyes narrowed in an expression of incomprehension and she turned her head to the side, as if questioning what she'd just heard.

"I'm sorry," Michelle said. "Her body was found early this morning."

"What happened?"

"We don't know yet," Paul Allen said. "There will be an autopsy."

The silence continued and John almost involuntarily moved towards Rain, wanting to touch, to comfort, at the same time unsure of what would happen next. Oddly, Rain didn't break down and cry. Instead, she paused and then seemed to resume her original stance and composure, as if some internal signal had gone off. Her eyes darted to where Walter had disappeared.

"They must be upset."

The silence that followed seemed to answer for Rain an as-yet unspoken question. She nodded, then looked at John.

"There's a garden here. In the back Emily told me about. May I see it?"

Michelle and Paul exchanged puzzled looks as John replied, "Sure. This way." The two left out the same door Walter had.

They fell into an easy discussion. John updated Rain on the details of the discovery of the body, the party the night before. She was attentive, pensive, but not emotional. Her eyes often fell downwards, as if while John talked she were reminded of something Emily had said or done.

45

They crossed the terrace and headed to where Walter was bent over the path near the roses.

Walter ignored them, continuing to methodically dig around the bushes, eyeing one by one the flat pieces of slate that awaited placement along the walkway. His hands were dirty, so dirty John couldn't see the fingernails or the true color of his skin.

"Okay, Walter?" he asked.

Walter grunted and didn't look up.

"Do you have any idea about what happened last night?" John asked. "She must have said something to you or Betty, during the day, before going out?"

Walter gave him a sidelong glance, and another more sarcastic grunt escaped. "We don't keep after our daughter like watchdogs, you know."

John began to circle the area, distancing himself from the other two, looking up at the sky then down at the ground. His muscular legs were comfortably hidden under his jeans, and he noted the sensation that ran through his body as he glanced Rain's way. He wanted to ask her to go for a walk, wanted to get away from Walter and wander the countryside. Instead, he faced Walter again.

"You must have had a sense of whether or not she was on the property."

Walter picked up a piece of slate and ran his hands around the sharp edges, rubbing it hard.

"Be careful, you might hurt yourself," Rain said.

The comment seemed to encourage rather than discourage him and he stabbed the ground with the sharpest edge, flattening the loosened soil and placing the stone just so. "Ask Betty. She's the one who minds the comings and goings. Ask her if the bed was slept in, or if there was a glass of half-drunk milk on the counter that morning." He stopped his work, lifted one knee, and looked to the horizon. "Or perhaps if there was any blood on the staircase . . ."

"I'm not suggesting anything foul, I'm trying to understand what happened last night," John said. "She was here last, was she not?"

"She was a grown woman. You're asking me if I was baby-sitting her, like she was a two-year-old."

"Walter," John said, stepping towards him, trying to catch his eye as he'd resumed his stone picking. "You or Betty must have had a notion of her goings-on. Plus, this place is so remote. In such a small town, I'd think it almost impossible to NOT know what someone is up to. But the odd thing here is, no one seems to even have seen her at all once she left the party!"

"This is remote all right," Walter said. "It's the back end of nowhere, as my lovely Betty says."

Rain knelt down beside him, handed him a piece of slate.

"That's not right for this spot," he said, tossing the rock. "Too small, it'll crack at the first pressure of a human foot."

"You do masonry a lot?" she asked.

His gaze settled on the rock he'd just placed. "No. Used to be an engineer. This isn't my idea of living. Not even at retirement and doing these bloody rural retirement things. Betty laughs at me. Everyone laughs at me."

Rain said, "You seem to take to it so well. Emily must have had loads of questions for you, about the land here. I mean, once she returned. She was always talking about getting back to Winslow and researching the town's origins in more depth." She motioned with her hands to display the distant hills just visible over the far ridge, beyond the Peters's property. "She was so curious, always after the bottom line, if you will."

"She was a damn cheeky one," Walter muttered. "Didn't know her place."

Rain glanced at John and held back words that seemed on the edge of her tongue.

"Never stopped. Drove us batty. Especially Betty."

"Not you?"

"I keep to myself." He began to flatten ground for another piece of slate.

In a sudden spurt of energy, he slammed the slate into the ground sideways. Now it stuck in the ground the wrong way. "Give up! She's gone, dead! What the hell does it matter anymore? Everyone else has given up!"

"I'll never give up," John said quietly.

"You'll have to, young man," replied Walter, sliding a glance John's way.

"No one can make me."

Walter looked at him finally, a long, evil stare. "You'd be surprised what people can make a person do, lad." He turned away. "Leave me now."

John had come up behind Rain and touched her shoulder. She turned around, facing him with luminescent gray eyes filled with tears. They both walked away, in the direction of the orchid house at the far corner

47

of the tended yard area. John felt Walter's eyes on his back as they walked, his silent curiosity giving into a yell.

"Nothing of your mind over there, now," Walter said.

Rain turned and asked, "May we wander around?"

Walter shrugged and returned to his work. Rain headed towards the orchids, already visible because of oversized windows that let in plenty of light. It was a small shed and the door to it was bolted. She circled it. John watched her, standing some five feet away.

"They enjoy orchids," Rain said. "Emily told me about this." Her eyes ran up and down the large windows, studying the flowers, some streaked with bright oranges, the white speckled with black ones, the dark purple veins against pale petals, all exquisitely arranged on shelving that provided ample lighting for all the flowers. Rain's back was to John. She was still, her head slightly lowered. He wondered if he should move closer or further away and then she turned, slowly at first, then picked up her pace until she was next to him.

He caught a whiff of her perfume, something musk, with a hint of jasmine. Her face was pale. He'd have guessed her from the north rather than sunny California. She kept her eyes on the building.

"Emily had a problem with this place," she whispered. "Nightmares."

"This?" John asked, pointing to the shed.

"The whole estate, guest house, whatever. Yes, and this," she pointed. Then she turned to him. "She told me about you. About how you went steady as kids."

"How did you know her?"

"Emily took one of my psychology classes. I'm a therapist."

John nodded. "I see. Had a good one in Manhattan myself. Was Emily studying for that?"

"No. She was intensely curious about the topic, though, and often spoke of her parents. I feel as though I know them."

"Not a happy couple."

"Emily said they were sick."

"Sick how?"

"Codependent is the popular term. Not in the obvious way, as I understand it—alcohol- or drug-dependent. They're dependent on one another. One does, the other reacts, sometimes with resentment, sometimes with silence, sometimes in anger. It's all very subtle and so routine for them that they don't realize what's going on. Then they wake up the next morning and try to forget the fact they don't understand why they reacted the way they did. They preserve peace at all costs, even when it means their sanity."

John felt icy all over. He kept his gaze on Rain, who had stopped talking and was staring at him.

"Are you okay?" she asked.

"I just had a moment there, some sort of wave of something. It's been happening since all this. . . ."

She grinned. "I understand. Anyway, I came to visit Emily and to tell her something she'd asked me to look into. Now, unfortunately, she'll never know."

"What is that?"

Rain hesitated, studied him some more, then whispered, "Emily was a twin."

Chapter Six

Behind Rain, Walter continued his work. Afternoon shadows had moved across the lawn. John's ears still rang from Rain's statement. She was looking at him expectantly.

"Are you sure?" he asked.

"Apparently Emily came across a birth certificate, though it wasn't authenticated. She was curious and unable to get information from Betty and Walter, except their denial that she was a twin."

"What was on the birth certificate?"

"It was very odd," Rain said. "Emily called the town clerk's office in the central valley town where she was born. The clerk she spoke with pulled out a copy that had Walter and Betty's name on it but the name of a child other than Emily, with the same birth date. When Emily said she was looking for the name Emily, the clerk checked the records and came up with the correct one. Emily decided to drive to the town clerk's office that day but, once she arrived, was unable to get anyone to help her find the second birth certificate. The clerk she'd spoken to on the phone was not on duty and no one could find another copy. Helene was the other name."

John watched Walter stand and brush dirt from his knees. Was the man listening or trying to? He was only about twenty feet away. Soft as Rain's voice was, he might have caught a word or two. He nodded to Rain and directed his gaze towards Walter. Rain picked up on the hint and was silent.

John muttered, "The morning after his daughter dies and he's tending his garden. . . ."

"What seems to be the problem here?" Rain asked. "His wife is ill and he's not cooperating with the police?"

John shrugged and signaled Rain in the direction of the house. Since they'd left, two cars had pulled up, another police car and the little white

Fiesta John recognized as Art Johnson's. He led Rain towards the house, passing an oblivious Walter who continued to pound the earth with the sharp edges of the slate.

Inside, officers were well into taking fingerprints, in spite of the sobs coming from Betty's room, her protests regarding this invasion of privacy. However, this time her cries to Walter went unanswered. Michelle had made tea and, on seeing John and Rain, poured two more cups.

"Art's trying to convince Betty to let the autopsy go through, also says she's fine. Nothing a good night's sleep and some aspirins won't help," Michelle reported. Her face was drawn. She glanced periodically to her husband who was directing the investigators and discussing how to line up all the partygoers for interviews.

Rain and Michelle began talking about California and John took the opportunity to do what he'd thought about doing on entering the house, going to Emily's room. He stepped quietly past Betty's room and down the long hall from where he could see the heads of people below. Her room was around the corner in the oldest section of the house. A small room with eaves, he knew it as soon as he stepped inside.

Calling it "The Fortress," she'd described it to him hundreds of times. Each time she rearranged furniture or added something, he got another full report. A pale green spread and matching pillows covered the head of the queen-sized bed, a four-poster dated from colonial times. Frilly slipcovers decorated the lower border. He stared at the pillow in the center; it was rumpled as if someone had just gotten out of bed. The sheets were pulled back. A white lace nightgown lay crumpled on the floor. She had slept here last night, unless the bed had gone unmade from two nights ago, which he doubted given the fastidious demands of her parents. He stepped to the nightgown and, though he knew he shouldn't, picked it up. It was a full-length silk nightdress with spaghetti straps and delicate lace around the chest. Her scent was still on it, that hint of fresh air mixed with a cologne she'd bought years ago when on a trip to Europe. She'd told him she used it only for special occasions, so it would last forever. She'd worn it last night. This garment smelled the same. He let the gown drop to the floor.

The murmurs from downstairs droned on as he looked around, pain and alarm filling him. It was an ordered room—two bookcases floor to ceiling to his left, a small writing table at the one window near the eaves, a rocking chair. A book stood on her bedside table, a psychology book by Alice Miller. She'd been reading, which was not unlike her. The bookmark, pressed plastic with dried lavender flowers, stuck out from the halfway mark.

He went to the window and took a deep breath, then turned to face the room and see how the daylight hit her bed, how the sun most probably streaked in as soon as it had risen. He looked outside and saw the orchid house. There they'd made love for the first time. It had been a hot summer night and they'd been alone all day, taking long walks and discussing their dream of marrying at eighteen and John becoming a landowner. With land, they'd be able to have a working organic farm and Emily could grow herbs and fresh vegetables. John would run the farm and also develop land in the area. They'd start small and bit by bit own most of the region. It would mean wheeling and dealing with that land-hog Stuart Granger, but they'd do it.

She'd been so lovely in her cutoffs and white T-shirt. He could see the outline of her small breasts stark against the material. He'd been aroused before, but this time he knew he'd not be able to allow her to leave him tonight. He wanted to stay with her, sleep with her, and they had.

He returned to the present. Now the room was empty, save faint scents of the woman he loved. No headway had been made in uncovering clues to her murder. Perhaps in this room, but what? Her bureau had nothing on it, save a picture of the nearby mountaintop, one he and she had climbed as kids. Curiously, family photos—like what Betty chose to hang on the walls, staircase, and any available shelf space downstairs—were absent. He recalled why she called it the "Fortress."

"Because it's my protection," she had said, her eyes playful yet serious. He never got more from her than that, except he knew her to spend hours there and, when asked what she was up to, she'd reply that she'd been reading. He noted the books lined in the case, the piles neatly stacked on the floor, and made a mental note to get to the closets. Any money there were more books, more books than clothing. Her dress was always simple. Jeans in varying forms—skirts, dresses, pants, shirts. She'd mentioned it made life easy, no decisions other than when to clean them. She'd been like that even at age ten, when jeans were for farmers and hippies in San Francisco, not a growing preteen. Betty had always given her trouble, but on that issue Emily prevailed.

Again, the notion of such a fancy nightdress struck him. He'd always imagined her wearing an oversized T-shirt to bed.

Had she woken up and dressed, run outside? To simply fall down and die? Was she followed? What made her get up in the first place? Why hadn't she taken a car? Had Betty and Walter heard her leave? Come home?

She'd left the party relatively early, while there were still many guests. She'd been found dead wearing the same clothing she wore at the party.

He heard footsteps behind him. It was Scott Cheever, the acquaintance of Stuart Granger who had been at the party. His tanned features offset his wide, blue eyes. A pretty boy used to getting anything he wanted.

"Scott," he said, extending his hand.

"Pleased to meet you. We met last night," Scott said, self-assured and with an ease that kept John's distrust in the forefront of his thoughts. Scott's white golf shirt and forest-green slacks gave away where he'd been earlier.

"Interrupt your game?" John asked, his eyes now falling on the room, on Emily's nightdress. Somehow this man standing here made John want to step outside, close the door, and not let this stranger see the "Fortress." It was her domain, no one else's. Yet, in minutes others would come to check it out, to rip apart the bookcases, to disturb her clothing. Like what would happen to her body. Someone would cut into it and invade it to try and reveal truths. Truths he sensed went back further than last night.

Scott chuckled and appeared not to note the irony in John's voice. "Early start to the day, yes. However, I heard the news on the radio. Mr. Granger is concerned."

"That's why you're here?" John hadn't thought Granger would be interested. Emily was not the one with all the land, Granger's only reason for being. Her parents were. There was no conceivable reason that there'd be anyone associated with Granger Enterprises near at hand. The fight for land purchase had died a painfully slow death at the last town meeting, and even Granger's millions couldn't convince the town they needed more single-family homes, regardless of the attractive options presented for sophisticated septic design and extra funding from the state. Following that meeting, John had begun to wonder if Granger hadn't lost his touch. Scott Cheever ran his own financial consulting firm, Cheever and Associates, and had become over the years Granger's money man. John should take advantage of the moment to find out more about the elusive Granger. Instead, in an attempt to divert Cheever's wandering gaze, he stared directly into Cheever's eyes.

"If I can be of any assistance with questions and, yes, if you will, help out with any feedback regarding Mr. Granger and his concerns."

Cheever's voice was even and tempered with a haughtiness that John took for snobbism. He never liked the smooth, clean-cut types.

"Where did you go after the party?"

"I left with my wife around 1 A.M. We drove to our townhouse in Cambridge and went to bed. Must have been around 2 A.M. by then."

"Your wife can corroborate this?" John asked, not remembering Cheever having been with one woman all evening. Instead, Cheever had time-sliced with many women, and in the end had also tried to get to Emily except John had been there. What had he wanted from her?

"Certainly. Magrite is at home now. I didn't want to disturb her leaving so early for the club, but she's ready to be interviewed. We've spoken already on this."

I'm sure you have, thought John. "Magrite. Is her last name Cheever?" He took out his notepad.

Without missing a beat, Cheever didn't let John's taunt hit him broadside. "Certainly. We've been together for years. A charming girl. Ran her own interior design studio in Manhattan prior to 'taking to the country' in order to be my wife." His chuckle, a guttural, feigned one, had begun to wear on John. He made a note to investigate his past.

"You know Deborah, Yvette's aide?"

Cheever's eyes twinkled in an unabashed acknowledgment—man to man—that he knew Deborah in many ways. "Fine assistant," he said. "Takes good care of Yvette."

"Did you leave the party with her?" John asked, deciding to risk the rebuttal.

Cheever's eyes narrowed. "You must be mistaken. Deborah is an older woman, Jordan."

"I didn't get an answer," John said, steadying his gaze even though his heart had begun to race.

Cheever cleared his throat and took some lozenges from his pocket, popping one into his mouth, thereby giving himself time. He replied quietly, "Of course not. Ms. Deborah is a lovely person. Sane and dedicated."

"Sane?" John asked.

"You know, together," Scott said. "I really must be going. The reason I stopped up, aside from the need to get a gander at the lovely Emily's room, was to let you know that I am here to cooperate, but I must leave for London shortly. If you need to see me, I'd appreciate a visit tomorrow morning by 10 A.M. I've had my secretary block off an hour. Will that suffice?"

John nodded. "Of course. Your attention is . . . commendable. However, be forewarned that if you're needed beyond tomorrow's interview, you will not be allowed to leave the country."

They stared at one another, Cheever breaking it with a glance at his golf shoes. "My, my, will it go on that long? I wonder about Emily to begin with. Wasn't she unstable during her youth? I seem to have heard that from not a few people around town. Of course, it might be exaggeration. Have you heard anything like this?"

The beginnings of vicious rumors, John thought. How interesting. "Never," he answered.

Cheever shrugged.

Just then the clatter of pots and pans rose from the downstairs. The two men went to the hall from where they could see Walter scurrying from the sink to the butcher-block work aisle, carrying lettuce and bread and other lunch preparations with him. As he hummed a tune, he called to Betty.

"Luv! Come now! It's time for a bite to eat. It'll do you good. Come then!" His accent was thick, and it appeared he was oblivious to the people surrounding him. While officers began the tedious job of fingerprinting, placing the white powder on furniture, he scowled and scolded but did nothing to prevent them from continuing their work.

"Now, watch the frames on the pictures. Silver, you know. Dates back to the 1940s, that one," he said, nodding at an eight-by-eleven on the wall near the foot of the stairs.

John and Cheever made their way downstairs. An officer was dusting a frame with a picture of Betty and Walter arm in arm at the Golden Gate Bridge. The wind was blowing, and each was a younger version of themselves, Betty with shoulder-length brown hair and her trademark print dress and handbag, Walter in a dark jacket and his glasses low, making his nose appear bigger than it was.

"Someone take that for you?" John asked.

"Mmm?" Walter asked absently. Then, looking up, he said, "Oh, yes, yes. Young man nearby. Betty asked him to do it. I'd have not handed the camera to him otherwise. Filthy hippie he was."

"You were there when, twenty years ago?"

"Thirty," Walter answered. "Visiting. Should have stayed, we should have. . . ."

Betty coughed from the top of the stairs. All eyes watched her slowly make her way down. Rain approached her.

"Let me help," Rain said, reaching for Betty's extended arm.

Betty allowed Rain to guide her down the stairs. "Walter, dear, now don't go to any trouble. I'm hardly famished, you know." She stopped to watch the officer dust the photo. Her brows creased as she noted him wiping the dust away, leaving streaks. "Must you do this?" she asked in a whisper.

John answered for the officer. "Routine, Mrs. Turner."

Betty stared at John as if for the first time in years. Her eyes had dilated as if it were night and, as she fiddled with the string on her nightgown that stuck out from her cranberry-colored terrycloth robe, her hands shook.

"Young man, you knew her way back when," she whispered as if to a stranger.

John kept his eyes on her, ignoring Cheever's reminder to call as soon as possible and noting his hurried exit without as much as a word goodbye to anyone including the Turners. Such familiarity from someone who had presumably never been to the house, at least not in the recent past.

"We played together," John said.

Betty's eyes took on a faraway look. "I remember now. She'd run away on me, leave whatever she was doing to go play. At first I worried so, your mother and all." Her look was embarrassed and then switched back to her clouded one. "Forgive me."

John nodded. In spite of the fact she was dumping on his mother, he feigned understanding cop.

"But it was something about which Emily never listened. She'd simply run away, calling after your dog. Jeepers. You see?" she chuckled. "I remember. Isn't he buried somewhere between our house and yours?"

"Next to the old apple orchard. The one no longer used," John said.

"Ah, yes," she whispered. "Lovely dog, so gentle and fast! Why, Emily had a hard time keeping up! She'd say you had races with the dog. Did you have races?"

"At times." He was aware of Rain at his side. She was studying Betty intently. "Emily was a fast runner."

Betty's face pinched in pain. She blew her nose. "Oh, but she wasn't supposed to run like that! She was so fragile!"

John wanted to protest that Emily was stronger than he at that age. He remembered how she'd hit the softball when the kids would play downtown summer evenings. How her steady hand, good eye, and strong follow-through would never settle for less than a double, regardless of who pitched. Something silenced him. If her mother had this view of her, let it come out. At least she was talking.

He noted Rain stepping unobtrusively up the stairs.

"Fragile?"

"Like a China doll. I used to call her that when we'd sing to sleep at night. Did you know she sang well, too?"

"She did," John said. "We'd do 'Row, Row, Row Your Boat' for hours. She always kept up."

Betty emitted a sob and rushed to John for comfort. He felt the weight of the woman, her pressing against him as she cried unabashed into his chest. John looked to Walter, who looked up at them with a blank expression.

"Oh, my my my," Betty cried. "Why why? I'm so upset."

"It's okay," John said, trying to comfort.

"But she might have been here if. . . ."

"Need your vitamins and energy, luv," Walter interrupted. "I've made you pastrami on rye, your favorite." He took the knife and with a swift crack at the bread sliced it into two equal halves. He invited no one to join them, simply put the finishing touches on his own and then cut it the same way. He began eating before Betty sat down.

Betty's hand dug into John's shoulder then released. She wiped the tears and straightened herself out, moving quickly away from John and even giving him an annoyed look as if it were he who closed in on her. "I beg your pardon," she whispered ever so genteel-like. With a brush of her curls back from her creased forehead, she made for Walter, who stood and showed her the nearest stool to him.

"Now, then, sit. Eat," he ordered, nodding John's way as if to let him know she was going to be just fine. "We've a big day ahead. Tomorrow, too."

Rain appeared behind John. "I'd like to help in any way. . . ."

"Not necessary," Walter said as he munched on his sandwich, a crumb hanging precariously at the corner of his mouth before he irritably wiped it away. Betty stared at her sandwich.

"What about funeral arrangements?" Michelle asked, having overheard the conversation from the living area.

"Can't very well do much there now, can we, what with the coroner all over the place? Keeping us from our daughter," Walter said. Betty began to cry softly.

"You identified her," John said. "There's still work to do." He couldn't bring himself to say the word "autopsy."

Walter looked up. "Young man. If the cut-up job that's envisioned by Art Johnson is what you're referring to . . ."

Betty placed her head into her hands and began to sob loudly. "God, no! God, no!"

Walter protectively reached for her. "Look now what you've done."

Rain intervened, walking to Betty and, in spite of Walter's blocking her, reached out and embraced the woman. "It's okay."

They rocked back and forth, Betty sobbing uncontrolled for a long while. The investigators continued their work and Paul Allen could be heard in the next room giving orders to downtown. It was odd and uncomfortable. Methodical, business-like motions to gather evidence and move the investigation forward seemingly buffered the realization of what they were as yet unable to face. Yet at the same time the activity seemed to keep everyone from breaking the regimented behavior demonstrated until now. Everyone present knew Emily. There had to be more than this mechanical motion, and Betty had been the first to break the ice.

Rain comforted her. "Can I get you anything?"

Betty tried to regain her composure, accepting a handkerchief from Rain and blowing her nose. Walter resumed eating his lunch.

"I know this is hard for you," Rain began. Her eyes were red-rimmed and John thought she must have been crying upstairs. Had she been to Emily's room? "But you must understand, Betty, that the police need to take steps in cases like this."

"Like what? Emily dropped dead," Walter said. "She was a fragile child."

Rain continued to address Betty. "You would want to know, wouldn't you?"

Betty looked anguished. Her eyes directed at Rain, she seemed to be seeking answers that she knew wouldn't be found. "I, I, want. . . ."

"We want to bury our daughter, luv, now don't we?" Walter asked, pulling Betty from Rain.

The couple whispered words of comfort as the room grew silent. All the investigators had moved upstairs to continue the work.

"Yes. I can't bear the thought of her tiny body. . . ." Betty again lost her composure. Rain maintained her supportive position next to her and, again, in spite of Walter, prevailed.

"An autopsy is the best way to determine what happened. I'm sure you know that every step will be taken to ensure she's handled appropriately. You loved her very much didn't you, Betty?"

Betty began nodding off into space, eyes wide and expressionless. Walter stood and cleared the dishes, loudly placing the glassware in the sink and running the water. Betty took on her trance-like state again, fading back to the inaccessible woman she'd been on coming down the stairs.

Walter dumped the dishes in the sink and began wiping the countertops, muttering slowly then louder and louder still. "What in God's name is a cut-up job going to prove? I've said it once and I'll say it again," his voice boomed, "No autopsy! I'll get me a blithering solicitor if I have to!"

Jarred from her reverie, Betty reached for Rain's hand and patted it. "We don't have to agree, do we?"

Rain opened her mouth to speak but Chief Allen intervened. "I'm afraid you have no choice but to allow it. This is a homicide until determined otherwise. Under the law, this calls for an autopsy."

"No one wants to do this unnecessarily," Rain said, still addressing Betty. "Perhaps you need a little time."

"Perhaps we need a lot of time without people crawling around our home!" Walter said. "How long is this invasion going to go on?" He glared at Allen.

"Until we finish all the rooms, and the barn," Allen said.

"The barn! What the hell does the barn matter?" Walter asked.

Rain and John listened as Walter ranted about he barn being off limits because he said so. Rain had succeeded in calming Betty somewhat. She sat studying Rain's profile as if she were the only person in the room.

"Lovely eyes," she said. "Gray?"

Rain nodded and smiled. "Betty, how would you like to talk tomorrow, just you and me?"

Betty looked at her husband. "What?"

"I'm a therapist and it might help to talk about all this."

"What! Now you're calling my wife crazy! I'll have none of this nonsense," Walter said. "She's my wife and I decide what's right for her."

Betty nodded reaching for Walter's hand. "Of course, dear. I agree. There's no need to talk with you." She let out a nervous giggle. "Of course, chats over tea would be nice."

Rain backed off. "Of course."

Walter had stacked the dishes in the dishwasher and had put the kettle on to boil. Rain continued to sit beside Betty, almost as if she did then Betty might have a change of heart. Of course, it was the only place Rain had to go unless invited elsewhere and she probably had made up her mind to make the most of it. Good idea, actually, John reasoned. With her on-site like this, Betty and Walter could be observed better, and he sensed Rain would be very cooperative. Her slender body curved subtly under her loose clothing. One leg touched the floor and made a pencil shape, the other bent on a rung of the stool just so. Her hair lay straight across her shoulders, a symmetry of sorts that went well with her long nose and her constant gaze. If anyone could make headway convincing the Turners they should agree to the autopsy, it wouldn't be someone from town, least of all the cops. Perhaps this newcomer who knew their daughter was the right recipe for keeping this couple on the up and up, and inviting the free flow of information.

His sense was that they were withholding information. Why? He'd asked that a lot in the background of his thoughts all day and what he had to come up with as far as an answer was Emily and her youth, the years he and she played together. Those times she fearfully ran to him, always with some story of her father's temper tantrum or her mother's foolish whining, always with terror in her eyes, almost as if the actions of her parents, although trivial in their detail, dredged up some horror story, the plot about which she had no idea. She'd cling to him and, though he enjoyed the feel of her hands on his arms or her hand in his, he'd wonder what else was there? What else drove her to run from these people? Did she even know? If she did, then what kept her from sharing it with John? And if she didn't, what was it?

For as sure as John knew his name, he also knew that this event was now without the involvement of her parents. Emily's life had been so protected, and freed only those times she fled to John and asked him to play with her. He wondered now if the reason she asked him to play was so she could block out what had just happened to her. So protected from living and so protected from growing. Each time she said good-bye to John, her eyes took on a similar far-away look to that of her mother now, a look that said, I have to retreat into my own world because if I face what I must face, then I'll snap so I have to fake something in its place.

Chapter Seven

Summer 1958

*H*e *remembered that day better than any other of his childhood, and that night even more vividly. His mother had left him at Josh Sander's birthday party after they'd walked the entire five miles, Darcy having been too proud to ask for a ride. They'd not had the money to buy Josh a gift, which Josh almost blurted out until his mother caught him and scolded him. John hadn't worn the right clothes either, not the little shorts and matching short-sleeve tops that the kids would also wear to school. He was in his same clothes from school, overalls and a pink shirt that had been his mother's and that she'd taken in for him. Darcy had not stayed but the other parents had and they seemed to enjoy themselves as much as the kids. There was food galore — hamburgers and hot dogs, potato chips and cups of Hoodsies, plus an oversized rectangular cake and tiny baseball players on a chocolate playing field. The kids played games and John, being the fastest runner, won at tag.*

After it was over John, trying to imitate the other kids' manners and behavior, had thanked Mrs. Sander for the nice time. His mother hadn't shown up to take him home, though, and Mr. Sander had offered him a ride. John felt funny driving in the big blue Ford with this man he hardly knew who kept making nice talk about Winslow and the coming summer.

"Will you go away for a vacation?" Mr. Sander asked, his large hands on the wheel, his eyes on the road.

"Dunno, sir," John had replied, knowing full well there were no such plans.

Had Mr. Sander shown a glance of pity his way? Even at his age, John sensed people studying him for reasons other than those they studied his classmates. He knew he was different; he knew he and his mother were poorer than others; he knew his mother was the subject of gossip, but he really didn't understand it.

However, the reality of his situation had begun to sink in. He was used to his mother's nightly absences and had learned not to ask her about them or comment when she returned in the early hours. He was still terrified waking up to an empty house and, had it not been for Jeepers, he didn't know what he'd have done. His recourse was to seek out the dog, bring her up on the bed and hug tight, so tight the ribs of the animal were comfortably a part of John's embrace. For hours he lay in bed, listening to the night sounds, the coyotes in the fields, the cadence of the crickets, the occasional bellow of a bullfrog from Short's Creek. He'd tell himself his mother was in the next room sleeping and that she wasn't hearing his calls because she'd worked so hard for Mrs. Peters and that in the morning everything would be fine. But this didn't help him sleep. The clock ticked and the sounds continued. He'd drift to sleep but not before hearing his mother coming in through the screened-in porch. Usually she was humming, usually she sounded happy.

She never checked on him. He'd hear her go to the bathroom, belching and splashing water, still humming. Then she'd noisily go to her room, bumping into not a few pieces of furniture, holding momentary conversations with them, and finally plopping onto the bed. It wasn't long before the house returned to the same silence as before her return. It would be noontime before they woke.

"My shining star," Darcy would say, peeking into his room. "Isn't it time for you to get up? You're already very late for school!"

Nights when she'd be out during the school week, John paid the price by walking into class late. There were snickers from his friends and disapproving stares from the teacher. In the schoolyard, some kids taunted him about what his mother did nights. He was unable to stand up to the confrontations, which earned him a reputation of being a sissy. Some of the tougher crowd in the fourth and fifth grades would take to shoving him around. The verbal taunts hurt more than the gibes, and he knew at some point there'd be either his self-respect or theirs to pay. He bided his time. He'd have to prepare before taking them on.

In another, very important way, one evening that summer marked a turning point. It was a night like most others when Darcy was out. Because the humidity had been unrelenting that week, all the windows were open, accepting the occasional early morning breezes and lending traces of relief to the eventual beating sunshine of later in the day. John was feeling hot and uncomfortable, unable to hold onto Jeepers as usual because she would pant loudly and John would begin to sweat more than usual. He took off his pajama top and lay flat on his back, legs spread, hoping she'd return. As it had for the last two nights, thunder rumbled in the distant hills, and he could tell the summer storm would come and go, dropping blinding sheets of rain for minutes, stirring up even more humidity than before. An endless cycle.

Thunder was welcome, John had decided. Though Jeepers would shiver, John would feel better that God was up there placing the lightning bolts just so in the sky, rolling those bowling balls in heaven, like his mother always described to him when she used to tuck him in. God was watching Winslow, and therefore there was a chance God was watching over John Jordan.

This night, the radio predicted, would bring the cold front in and with it the relief everyone had been waiting for. Now, the calm before the storm was upon them and not an animal made a sound. John sat through the eerie stillness and soon after felt a cool breeze blowing, portending the coming storm.

He got out of bed, went to the kitchen, and closed the door. He tried to shut the windows too but, after days in the same position expanding the wood, they had stuck. Back in his bedroom, he decided that he'd leave his window open and let the rain come in. Though the house was old, there were lightning rods on it. Yvette had done this for his mother when they'd moved in, at the insistence of Walter Turner.

By now, John knew that the man Darcy was with was Walter and by now he'd also talked about this with Emily. Just that afternoon, they'd sat on the big rock overlooking the bend at Short's Creek and decided that Walter and Darcy were making birthday plans for Betty, and hopefully Emily and John as well. They'd all get together to surprise Betty and it would be a great big party.

"But my mom isn't very happy this summer," Emily said reflectively. Her tiny arms waved as she spoke and she primly pushed a braid off of her shoulder. "She cries a lot. I think she's sick."

John would nod. "My mom cries a lot too, cries and laughs. It's weird."

"But my daddy is happy, always humming. I see him humming in the garden. He comes home from work and goes right to the garden. He's even let me help him pick tomatoes," she said. "He never used to let me pick tomatoes."

"Do you get the biggest ones or leave those for pickling?"

She giggled. "I pick the biggest and then ask Mom to slice them for me, so I can be the only one to eat them. Yesterday I found one this big!" The fingers of both hands met at the tips and made a ball. She peered through the hole she'd made and stared with her big eyes at John. It was his turn to giggle.

"Em, do you want to be a parent?"

Emily began making invisible drawings on the rock. "I don't think so. I don't think it would be fun."

"Why?" he asked.

"Because, my mom and dad fight a lot and it scares me. They fight about . . . about . . . your mom."

"But my mom is friends with your mom and dad."

"Yeah," she said slowly, still making wide circles on the rock, her eyes averting his. "But I think my mom is mad at your mom."

"Oh." He thought of when he and his mother were walking to church and how Betty had come out and told Darcy she was no longer welcome to cross the property. Darcy had given Betty a sly look, then curtsied very dramatically. It had made Betty shake her head and turn on her heels for the house. When John had asked his mother why she did that, she'd only sworn and told him it was none of his business.

"I guess parents are just hard to understand," Emily said. "I don't want to be hard to understand."

They stood and ran to the creek, getting their sneakers and socks soaked as they chased imaginary trout and ran from man-eating bloodsuckers.

Now the thunder cracked followed by a bright bolt of light, one that lit up the land outside and in John's room. The wind was steady, and he counted only seconds between the lightning and the thunder. "At Peters's property soon," he reasoned, pulling Jeepers close. He closed his eyes and felt the cool, welcome air. Suddenly a shriek cut through the night air. John sat up in bed. It was a woman's scream followed soon after by another crack of thunder. The scream had melted in with the storm. He listened again for the sound that seemed to come from the Turners'. This afternoon, he and Emily had not made their usual thunderstorm agreement, that if either of them got scared they'd run to the other's house. For Emily, who'd beaten a path to his bedroom from her house many a time, it would be easy because his room was on the first floor. For John, it was more of a challenge because he'd have to step around Walter's electric triggers that when tripped lit up the entire property. He'd then throw a rock at her window, the signal for her to descend the staircase and get out before the lights all went on. It had never come to that, neither of them had dared leave the house at night, but as John sat there listening for another piercing female scream, which was what he'd decided it was, he thought Emily might just appear.

As minutes passed and the storm intensified, his sense of accuracy dulled and he wondered had the sound been a coyote or the wind. Still his heart was racing, if not for the strange sounds, for the approaching storm. Where was his mother? Why was she doing this? He was scared and she wasn't there. She couldn't be far away. Why didn't she come?

The rain began. Heavy drops turned into torrents. In minutes, the leaf-stuffed gutters gave off the spill freely, flooding the dry earth and creating pools where none had been before. Cracks of thunder and lightning opened the skies more as endless sheets of water drenched the area.

He murmured his Bible song about peace and love, how God was there, but the words rang hollow. He wanted his mother. Strangely, the music of the wind and rain coupled with Jeepers slow, steady breathing took his mind off his worries, and John felt a need to close his eyes. Slowly, gradually, gratefully he drifted into a slumber he'd not wake from until his mother shook him violently some time later.

"Get up!" she yelled. "Get up, child!"

It was the nightmare coming true. His mother's bloodied face stared at him, bloodshot eyes and her putrid breath on him. She pulled at his bare shoulders that moments before had been relaxed in sleep.

"Whaaa!" he heard a cry come from him.

"Get me a cold cloth!" she yelled, falling onto his bed. He touched her cheek and felt something warm and sticky.

Jumping from the bed, he made for the bathroom. The switch didn't work. "Mom, no lights!"

"I know! I know! Get candles! Get me a cold cloth first!"

He was running in circles, tripping over Jeepers, the dull morning light his only guide to finding a clean towel and some candles.

The towel he managed to find and dampen, but he couldn't find candles. He brought the cloth to Darcy, who covered her face and began to whimper. In the pale light he saw blood all over her dress, the yellow and blue flowers, and in her hands were the crumpled clothes he'd not seen all summer, the white smock and dark slacks. They too were covered in blood.

"Mommy, what happened?"

Darcy sobbed at length, rocking and holding the cloth to her face. She didn't lower it for some time. When she did, John recoiled in horror.

Her entire face was bloated and black and blue. He couldn't see her eyes for the puffiness, and the dried blood stuck clumps of hair together. Her cheek had sustained a hard blow and bulged when she opened her mouth to speak. She was missing one of her front teeth.

"Mom!" He reached for her and rocked in her arms, but her touch was lifeless, a limp hand hung over his shoulder. "I'll call Dr. Johnson!"

"No! Johnny, be a good boy and put more water on this towel, bring it back, then leave me."

He did as he was told, quickly adapting to his mother's requirement to not make a fuss. Still, he kept thinking of how Art Johnson worked miracles on cuts and scrapes. But something was different here; this wasn't a case of cuts and scrapes. A wound on his mother's neck continued to spill blood. The daylight had intensified and now he could see Darcy clearly. She'd been hit, beaten very hard.

"Mommy, what happened? What's all that blood coming from your throat?"

Darcy's eyes were closed and her head moved slowly one way, then another. It was her moaning that alerted John to her state of semiconsciousness, a low, mournful tone that droned on and then grew silent only to revive after a time, reaction to the pain that seemed to come from parts of her body in varying intensity.

The blood spilled from her throat, and as the dawn's light intensified John had trouble finding more clean towels. All over the house, pink- and red-stained rags sat, small clumps giving away the seriousness of Darcy's injuries. Try as he might to convince her to see Art, she refused, whispering threats of punishment if John got on the phone.

John silently sat by her side, watching her fade from and return to consciousness. He didn't know if she should be allowed to sleep or not. A year back, he'd fallen in the schoolyard and the teachers were adamant that he not fall asleep, even though that was the only thing he wanted to do. Now he wondered should he be allowing Darcy to doze. She seemed to be sleeping comfortably at one point, and he debated trying to get Art on the phone, but decided to heed his mother's request by keeping vigil at her side.

There was a faint rap on the windowpane and he saw Emily standing there, her nose pressed to the glass. He looked down at his mother who was sleeping, then made way to the window.

"Em!"

"Your mother, is she all right?" Emily asked, seeing Darcy lying on the bed. "What's all that blood?"

She'd noticed the stained towels in his hand. He let them drop. "Nothing."

"Can I come in? I'm frightened." Her wide eyes were very sad and her face was pale, a much different version than the one he'd seen the day before at Short's Creek.

He nodded, "I'll get the door."

He went to the kitchen and let Emily in. The door had been forced open during the night, probably by Darcy since John had locked it earlier. Drops of blood dotted the linoleum and a smear of it was on the telephone.

"What happened?" Emily asked, her eyes wide in horror.

"She's been hurt," John said. "But she won't let me call Art Johnson. Emily, will you go get him? Will you run to town and find him?" He looked fearfully towards the bedroom hoping Darcy wouldn't hear.

Emily thought a moment. "My dad and mom had a bad fight this morning. My dad said he'd kill your mom if she ever stepped in our house again."

John looked perplexed. "Why?"

Emily shrugged. "My mom told my dad she was leaving him. That she was 'fed up'. John, I don't want my mom to leave my dad."

John looked at her with concern but could only think about his own mother. "Can you get Art?"

Emily looked at the phone. "Can we call?"

John noticed the phone dangling off the receiver. "I guess, if we're quiet."

They dialed the number and Art answered. He promised he'd be by within the hour. John returned to his mother's room with Emily. The two kept watch until Art's arrival. When the doctor saw all the blood, his face showed the same surprise and concern that Emily's had. Art was a wise, kind man. He maintained his composure. Since his return from the Pacific and World War II, where he got his medical training during the goriest situations, he'd been the town general practitioner and had served with diligence and discretion. He'd gained much respect from the residents. Except Darcy. For whatever reason Darcy was suspicious of him. But John was glad he was there. Art ushered Emily and John to the living room, made them some chocolate milk and asked that they be quiet until he finished.

When he finally emerged from the bedroom, his face was drawn. He walked over to John, sat down beside him. "Did you know where your mother was last night, son?"

"No sir. She's out nights . . . some nights."

"Did you see the dirt on her nails?"

"Dirt?"

Art opened his closed hand to reveal dirt. "Under her nails. Seems she was digging. She's got raw fingers from digging." His look was reflective. "Your mom needs to sleep now. I've given her something for the pain. When she wakes up, call me."

"She didn't want you here, sir," John said.

Art nodded. "I see. Well, I'll make me a trip back here in a couple of hours, how's that? She'll still be sleeping but I can make sure she's doing all right. She took several stitches in her throat. You say you don't know where she was?"

John shook his head. Then Art beckoned Emily to him and patted the empty space on the couch beside him. Emily dutifully went there and gazed into his eyes.

"Do you know where Mrs. Jordan was last night?"

The silence revealed nothing to John, except he never forgot those moments, the sweat pouring down Emily's cheek and Art's eyes taking on a sadness he'd never see again on the physician's face. Emily shook her head.

"No, sir."

He patted the top of her head. "Your folks okay?"

"Yes, sir."

"They go out last night?"

"My dad did, for a while. Mom was pruning the orchids. It's time to clone them."

Art nodded. "Give them my regards. Take care, you two. John, watch over your mother. She's had severe injuries but she'll be okay." He got up and, like an old man — although Art was still in his early thirties — shuffled to the kitchen to again take in the bloody scene. He let himself out and the kids heard the car slowly drive away.

That night was the last night Darcy Jordan left her son alone. When she woke up, she fought Art's assistance but eventually relented to taking painkillers to dull the hurt and to allow the healing to begin. She never told John what happened that night, except to say, "Momma has been very silly running into trees and getting all cut up." John didn't really know what to believe so he believed her, but never went around telling anyone that his mother had been hurt running in the woods.

Her work at the Peters' was curtailed, and for several weeks she had no work until Art Johnson found her a day job cleaning offices in the downtown area. She proved reliable, always returning home in time for John's return from school. She even did her best to help him with homework. There were still nights when she got drunk, for that was what John learned her "medicine" to be, but her presence was preferred to her absence. He was no longer alone nights. This helped him feel comfortable enough to start paying more attention in school and allowed him to be stronger about the taunting in the schoolyard.

Emily and he grew closer, but each knew that something definitive had happened the night of the thunderstorm, for her parents never allowed her to play with John again and Darcy never mentioned that "nice Mr. Turner." The Jordans never walked past the Turner house and, because Darcy was no longer a part of the Peters's place, there was never an opportunity to run into the Turners.

Emily and John kept up their secret playing and meeting, but hidden behind their laughter and their activity was the knowledge that something beyond their comprehension would keep their families separate for a long time, perhaps forever.

Art Johnson never mentioned the incident to John. John would go for physicals — Darcy would, too — and they were treated as he treated everyone, with not a mention of the past, just the suggestions for good health for the future. John thought that one day he might ask Art what his thoughts were about that night, but he knew at the same time there'd probably be no words coming from the man. With the healing of Darcy Jordan's wounds, the incident passed.

Chapter Eight

Betty and Rain walked towards the orchid house. John was at a loss what to do. Should he join them? Or should he stay with Walter? Did Paul have other work for him? What about Yvette? Already hours had passed and there were still many guests and hired help to interview.

Rain looked his way, a thoughtful, sensitive stare. Then she turned, put an arm around Betty and the two closed the door behind them.

John returned to the house. Paul suggested he stop by Yvette's. If she wasn't back yet from New York, she would be shortly. He should stay until her return, watch over the place and start interviewing the help. Paul and Michelle would remain to await results of Rain's conversation with Betty and wrap up.

On his way to Yvette's, John stopped by Art's office in town, a small, two-room place that hadn't changed much in over thirty years. A waiting room with three chairs and a desk with computer and typewriter for his secretary, his own small office with wall pictures of his kids from their younger years, a large mahogany desk that was his father's before him, and a long adjustable table where he ministered to his patients.

"John, you look tired," Art said, peering over his half-moon glasses and away from a large encyclopedia. "Any developments?"

"Turners still refuse the autopsy. What if we can't get anywhere?"

Art sat back in his armchair, swiveled it to look out the window that was behind him. The downtown traffic was moderate this afternoon. He watched a few cars go by.

"The law's on the side of the victim. There'll be one, all right," he said.

John studied the elderly man and noted the glazed look in his usually cheery eyes. "Art, what do you know?"

Art turned his way. He studied John a long time. With a slow, measured movement he turned to his desk, folded his hands, and stared at the blotter that contained pictures dating back to the fifties. His three sons and daughters, pictures of patients post-op, pictures of him with families of the deceased. Having spent occasional summers helping out with the cleaning and answering of phones in the office, they were familiar sights to John.

"There's a lot of stories, John. About the Turners, I mean. It's been many years but I recall there were issues over Emily from way back. You know yourself she was uncomfortable living in that house. People, you know, they marry and then some of them don't get along but stay together for years. Back in my day it wasn't the thing to leave a marriage. You stuck it out. Those two stuck it out, but I'd say they'd have been better off separating. They never liked one another. You have to like one another."

"Like you and Min?" John asked.

Art smiled. "Like me and Min." He chuckled. "Although I must say some of the time things get, shall we say, charged, but by and large, I'd have a big gap in my life without her, yes."

"Rain told me today that Emily found out that she was a twin."

Art was silent. His eyes bored holes through John. "And?"

"That's all we know. Apparently, she was looking in the town where her birth was recorded, in California."

Art stared down, nodding. "There was a twin."

"You knew?"

"I knew of a twin. That there was one, that it was a girl, that she never made it to celebrate her first year."

"What happened?"

"Illness of some sort. Betty and Walter were shaken. After the birth of the twins, Betty and Walter came out from California with them."

"How come Emily never knew?"

"She wasn't told because Walter didn't want her to feel deprived in any way. Betty wanted to tell her and came to me to discuss it."

"What did you recommend?"

"I thought she should do as she felt, perhaps wait until Emily was older but not hide the truth over time."

"Was Betty comfortable with that?"

Art hesitated, then began, "Betty has always been very jumpy, on edge. Her behavior today is remarkable given her temperament. I would have thought she'd have had a nervous breakdown by now. It's very odd, but the two of them have a strange, stabilizing effect on one another. She tells Walter what to do, especially when he starts ranting and raving, being negative, which he does frequently as you know. He treats her like his favored prize. He worships her, is with her constantly. Was Betty comfortable? Truthfully, I doubt she's ever been comfortable. Odd, those two . . ."

"Why odd?" John asked, knowing where he wanted to go. The entire town, including Art, knew them to have horrific fights. When Emily was a child she was too often in the line of fire of a pot or pan, and worse a glass vase. Once, the day after a fight, Emily came to school with five stitches above her eye.

"It's a tumultuous relationship as well. I believe the psychotherapists call it passive aggression. I wouldn't know too much about those things." He seemed to fade into the past, his eyes glazed over even more, and he turned to look reflectively out the window. "The dirt under Emily's fingernails, the dirt today, was not the same dirt surrounding her body."

"How could you tell?"

"I garden. When you garden, you're aware of the ground. I've lived here over seventy years, bought three different homes, three different gardens. Know the land. It was hard clay under her fingernails. The soil in the woods is more acidic, pine needles and rocky, more porous. She'd been somewhere before that."

"Can you prove it?"

"If we study the soil samples, yes. Otherwise, it's my word against anyone else's."

"Meaning, she was somewhere, digging or in the earth somehow, before she walked into the woods and then collapsed," John said, realizing how hard the word "died" was for him to say.

"I believe so."

"Rain is with Betty now, talking with her."

"Good," Art said.

"Art, where is the child buried, Emily's sister?"

"California, I believe. They left Winslow shortly before her death, returned to California for a vacation. After she died, they buried her out there before returning back East. You know Betty was originally from California. Now, I have a question for you. You and Emily were very close. Do you think Emily ever suspected anything about a twin before she left Winslow to live in California?"

John studied the parquet floor. It gleamed back at him, almost outlining his own shape. A car passed quickly, too quickly. Had he been on the street, he'd have stopped it for speeding. The image that came to his mind was the night his mother was beaten. He recalled Emily's trembling body. What had she said?

"Emily was always afraid of those two," John said. "I can think of many times when she alluded to their cruelty. Right now though, I can't think of any conversation we had about her being a twin. She used to joke about being a tomboy, but that's it."

Art nodded. "Think it over. Sometimes a memory lapse returns on us." He stood and went to John, placed a hand on his shoulder and led him to the door. "Call me if anything develops. I'd like to start working on Emily tomorrow first thing. Unless there's word from a lawyer, there's nothing to stop me. You understand."

"Sure," John said, shaking Art's hand. "I'll keep you posted."

He left and drove out of town, along the winding country miles back towards his house. Though he wanted to stop and feed Sami, he kept going, reminding himself to not linger at the Peters's.

When he arrived, a black Jaguar was parked in the driveway. The front door was answered by a maid he recognized from last night's party. She was in her twenties with a pale face and harried look, as if she were overworked and under pressure to keep on going. Hesitatingly, she asked who he was, then let him in after John displayed his badge.

Deborah appeared not long after. As she stood in the hallway trying to make excuses for Yvette being unavailable, the owner appeared at the top of the stairs. John's eyes rose to the woman and their eyes locked.

Dressed in a red silk robe, she slowly walked down the winding staircase, a cigarette burning from a holder her fingers toyed with as she moved. Her face was made up, vermilion lipstick and rouge he could see from the distance that separated them. A shiver ran through him and he felt himself paste a phony, blank look on his face.

"My, my, what a surprise! You of all people!" Yvette said, eyeing his body up and down. "Well, you look a little worn out but other than that splendid!" She reached him and pinched his cheek. "You missed me, I hear! How awful, this young woman Emily. Such a thing to happen at her age!"

John refrained from comment. She took his arm.

"Come, let's sit in a cozier room."

They walked towards a small library at the opposite side of the house from where most of the partygoers had been, a room full of books with a maid quietly dusting them off. Deborah followed to turn a few lights on and shoo the maid out.

"Can I get you anything, madam?" she asked Yvette.

The collection of booze and wine was visible from a glassed-in armoire. "No, darling, we'll be fine. Unless Mr. Jordan wishes something without alcohol." Turning to him she flashed her dark eyes. "You're not on duty, are you?"

"I am."

"Pity!" she called out theatrically. "Foolish me thought this was a visit from an old friend!"

She sat on a dark red ottoman, patted the seat beside her. "Come, sit here."

"I'll sit here," he said, moving to a high-back chair that matched the upholstery of the ottoman. Yvette stood, moved to the liqueurs and poured herself a creme de menthe and mineral water. The green liquid shivered as she passed John and the crystal hit the ceiling, creating dancing lights above them until Yvette was seated.

"Darling, you've found out what happened to that poor creature?"

"Not yet. What do you know, Ms. Peters?" he asked, trying to focus on her words and her demeanor and not the leg she exposed from her robe, crossing it provocatively and letting her slippers come to the tip of her toes whereby she could balance one as she rocked her leg back and forth.

"I know she was a devious little child. You both were," her voice was smooth, lolling, teasing.

"You knew us back then?"

"I knew of your nasty deeds. The trampled flowers in my garden from your dog. The footprints all over the yard the summer a new lawn was put in. You were very curious about my property, weren't you? I figured after a few years that it was you two. Used to sneak around."

"Where were you this morning at approximately 5 A.M.?" he asked.

"In bed," she whispered, taking a sip and licking her lips suggestively.

"Was there a reason you left early this morning?"

Yvette's eyebrows raised in surprise. "Why, I announced last night at the party that I'd be leaving for the south of France."

"You had tickets for tomorrow. One of the officers checked it out. You canceled the flight scheduled for next week, booking another for today instead."

"I had to get there sooner. A friend from Spain was passing through the area where I live and wanted to stop by. We talked recently and I decided to change my plans. I'm not allowed to?"

"Certainly. It was odd that you changed them at such a time, 6 A.M.?"

Yvette masked an angry glare by turning it quickly into a smile. She laughed. "Oh, my, you don't understand about the time differences, do you? Six A.M. this morning is noon on the continent, darling. I receive calls at all hours! Why, that's why my life is so exciting! Never a dull moment."

"Your friends on the continent don't consider the hour over here before calling?"

She laughed again, sipping before answering. "As I said, Mr. Jordan, it was a last-minute engagement I didn't want to miss."

"May I have the name of your Spanish friend?"

She shook her head, paused, then laughed. "Do you speak Spanish? My dear friend Marguerite will have trouble giving you information otherwise. She doesn't speak a word of English!"

"I didn't realize you were fluent in Spanish."

Yvette threw her head back. The creases in her neck gave away her age. She laughed for a long time. "Such an investigator! My dear associate Deborah is gifted in seven languages. What I struggle with, she helps out! It's simple! Now, if you don't have any further questions, I'm going to ring for hors d'oeuvres. Won't you join me for some pate de fois gras? It's fresh from the continent, left over from the party. We never got to it!"

Before he had a chance to decline, she was on the intercom with Deborah, ordering what sounded like a full meal. Then, she stepped towards him and touched his cheek. Standing over him, she stroked.

"You're as handsome as ever. I've missed you," she whispered.

John felt his body tighten. He suddenly realized the mistake in coming here unaccompanied. Her hand touched his shoulder. She was staring into his eyes and he found himself unable to move away from her gaze. What was it about her? He detested her, for what she'd done so many years before, for the hold she had now.

The sound of someone approaching saved him. Yvette quickly moved to the far side of the room and answered the ring. "Come in!" she called.

The maid entered and began to make up a table in the corner, laying down white cloth, placing the sterling silver covers hiding the food on it, then leaving after ensuring there would be nothing else.

Yvette sought out some of the pate and bread, then returned to the ottoman. John's breathing was shallow as he tried to compose himself.

"She was a difficult child. I also had trouble with her since her return, you know," Yvette said. She was busy chewing her food and seemed to have switched her role from one of seductress to reporter.

"No, I didn't know that."

"Stealing."

"How so?" John asked, trying to recall any conversations that he'd had with Emily about her association with Yvette. As far as he knew, they were acquaintances through Betty and Walter.

"Oh, really she was trouble if I do say. Always borrowing money. Her parents were constantly approaching me. . . ."

"But she wasn't in Winslow for many years."

"Oh, but she was in contact with her parents. Always out of work, always destitute. She ended up getting over $150,000 from me, through Betty's pleading of course, and then not paying me back! What do you imagine! I felt awful having to keep requesting it, and of course I know Betty and Walter are incapable of paying it back." She sighed. "So now, I guess it's too late. . . ."

She munched, not looking at John.

"Can you give evidence of this?"

Indignant, she rose, moved towards him. "Are you calling me a liar? Of course I can! You can also go next door and ask those two! Really, Mr. Jordan, how could you! Now, if you'll excuse me, I've an appointment with my hairdresser. Is there anything else?"

A volatile woman and John was alone with her. Deciding to play it safe, he said, "Please remain here for the next several days. We'll need to talk with you further. If you or anyone in your employ has any information, please call the police station."

Yvette headed towards the door and then turned, giving him a seductive look. "May I also stop by your cute little cottage to give information?" Not waiting for an answer, she disappeared into the hallway, calling for someone to see him out.

He left and returned to the house, where Rain was waiting outside, playing with Sami. He found himself appreciating her light skin, the whiteness against her jeans, the sturdy countenance she projected. She was laughing and running in circles.

Breathless, she called out, "Sami's hungry!"

He smiled. "Let's get her inside and feed her then. They followed the dog inside and John quickly placed food in her dish. Rain settled at the butcher-block kitchen table.

"Nice table," she said, running her fingers along the wood's grain.

"Thanks, made it myself."

Rain looked at him, an appreciation in her smile. Then she turned serious. "Betty has agreed to the autopsy."

John moved to the table and sat down across from her. "How did that come about?"

"We went to the orchid house. That place does something strange to her. She became melancholy, more so than you and I or the others. She showed me all the flowers, explaining how each had started, how she'd grown them from cuttings, cloning. She is so proud of them. Spends hours at a time there when she's not working around the house. She began to cry. I suppose it had to do with the death, her feelings pouring out. I let her cry. She then regained her composure, enough to continue her description of the orchids. I know a little about them, and told her of types I saw once in Hawaii. She knew of them, seemed to know about all of the species. I asked her had she traveled to find them and she said 'No,' that she'd read about them, and then she and Walter decided what they wanted to grow.

"She calls them children, talks to them. I think for a while she didn't realize I was there. She became almost cheerful, stepping about from one plant to another and singing softly, talking gently. 'Little one, how are you today?' she said once." Rain drew in her breath, looked at John.

"Then she became quiet, kept looking at me fearfully. I've seen this in patients. They dip in and out of a state where, because reality is so painful, they're happier in their imaginary world—like Betty with her orchids—but are regularly forced to take a look at the real world and break down.

"She cried in my arms then, sobbing but not really saying much, sobbing like one does in deep grief. This makes sense of course, her daughter was alive yesterday and now is dead. I told her this but she didn't seem to appreciate the message. Then it was very strange, she said something she wouldn't repeat afterwards but sounded like 'no hours.'"

"No hours?" John asked. "What do you think it means?"

"I'm not sure. I'm not even sure if that's what she said. She then sat still, quiet, with her eyes open. I began talking then, gently and softly, encouraging her to understand that people wanted to help, that everyone was upset about Emily, that in the long run it was best all around for an autopsy. She seemed to understand that knowing the answers would help over time, help to understand, and even heal. We talked about Betty and Walter healing, getting over the death in a good way, but she didn't respond to that, even denied it was required. Said Walter was fine, that she would be, too, in time.

"I sensed she was feeling good with me but the mention of Walter brought her defenses up, like she had something to hide, whereas before — with the orchids and by talking one on one — she was gradually getting comfortable. Then the wall went up. She started toying with the orchids again.

"She did, however, agree that what I said made sense, that in the long run it would be best. She said she'd talk with Walter, and doubted there'd be any lawyer. She half-joked and said they couldn't afford one anyway. Then she did something strange, but for someone like this very predictable.

"She withdrew into the person who would walk back to her house to be with Walter. She became pleasant and polite, no tears. She arranged the flowers a final time, began chatting about nothing much in particular, and her face took on a business-like, serious look.

"I've also seen this in patients," Rain said.

John nodded. "My therapist discussed this sort of behavior. In fact, it's in all of us."

"True," Rain said. "We protect ourselves from feeling."

He stared at her, the wide gray eyes staring back with a factual, interested look. What did she think of him, he wondered? Based on what she'd just told him, she had to be very perceptive. He smiled at her. She smiled back.

"So it looks as though Art can do his job tomorrow," John said, his voice fading, the image of Emily lying on a slab hitting him.

"Another thing, John," Rain said. "The book in Emily's room. The one it seemed she was reading. It was by a famous Swiss psychologist. An expert in parental abuse of children."

John's face clouded. "Why would she be reading that?"

"She often talked with me about her family, in generalities of course. I was not her therapist once we became friends. There was trouble from her parents, grave trouble. I think it's something we shouldn't ignore as this case moves forward."

He stood and moved to the gas stove, an oversized job that bulged in the tiny kitchen, but with a cast iron top and the old moveable burner covers with long black handles. He lit a match and placed it near the pilot, the puff of the ignition gave way to a blue dancing flame. He put an old kettle over it and checked to see that there was water.

A strange sensation filled him. He felt Rain's eyes on his back, his body. What was she thinking? She slipped into silences, he noticed. If he turned, they'd stare and he was nervous about that, about staring into her eyes and giving his thoughts away. Her insight jarred him and he was in no mood for being jarred. He heard her settle into the chair, could tell she'd shifted her legs, perhaps crossed them.

He began to think about a glass of bourbon, or a neat Jack Daniels at Ray's bar. The taste smacked across his lips as his tongue made them wet. What was she doing here anyway? How had they come to be together? This wasn't his style, nor was it an arrangement with which he was at all comfortable.

The kettle rattled some as the heat did its thing. Cups, tea bags. He moved an arm to the upper cupboard and opened, stared at the cans and half-filled sugar and flour bags, hardly used, most likely with worms or worse inside. Such a bachelor pad! A tin of tea bags from at least a year ago hid in the back, and he reached for it and occupied himself with opening it when he heard her behind him.

"Can I help?" she asked.

Her voice was silken and floating, like those rare summer breezes on a sweltering afternoon. You want more and more but they've already passed, not to return for a while. He forced a smile and turned.

She stared unabashed into his eyes. So up-front, so direct. She neither seduced nor acted dumb. She was who she was. Jeans and, today, a crisp white T-shirt. It took effort to keep his eyes from her small yet firm chest.

Behind her was the sink. "Cups. Over there are clean ones on the rack," he said, his voice barely a whisper.

She moved away as a bead of sweat slipped down one of his cheeks. The kettle began to scream at him and without thinking he placed his bare hand on its handle. Its impact temporarily swayed his thoughts— the slam of the kettle back on the burner, Rain's startled movement towards him, the cool hand on his forearm.

"You okay?" she asked.

He chuckled and shook his head, wiped his brow, and accepted a hand towel she offered. "Stupid."

"You were miles away," she whispered.

Damn woman, he thought. Got his number already. Next thing she'll have figured he lusts for her as much as a drink and this tea thing will all be a big farce. The cursing resounded in his head, the sounds of his youth and the mother who fed his brain with her anger. The damn fault of the rest of the world was why she was who she was and they were so stuck and miserable.

They settled at the table. "Tell me more about Emily in California," John said.

Rain adjusted her chair. "Anything in particular?"

"How did she live? Was she well off?"

Rain tried to suppress a giggle. "Well, if sharing a four-room house with five other women is well off, I suppose she qualified! No, in fact, she lived very frugally. I met her after she'd settled in the valley."

"The valley?"

"The central valley, northern California. There are a lot of farms, believe it or not. It's not that part of California that receives all the press. I taught a few semesters at the state university at Sacramento. That's where we met. She expressed interest in talking with me outside of class. Turns out she wanted therapy but couldn't afford it."

"Yvette told me she borrowed $150,000 from her."

"Not that I was aware of," said Rain. "She didn't focus much on money, but she wasn't wasteful or extravagant either. No, I don't think she was ever into money like that, unless she kept it very quiet."

"Did you talk with her about money?"

Rain gave him another of her steady stares. "You know she was my patient. It might be difficult if not impossible for me to tell you everything she said. I'd need to evaluate it under the circumstances. Patient privilege and all."

"Even though she's dead?" He heard himself say the words, but they rang insincere, as if he were an actor reciting lines.

Rain thought a moment. "As I say, I'd have to evaluate it. I'd need some time, and also want to discuss this with some of my colleagues."

He nodded, studied the tea in his cup, the bronze liquid and the curl of smoke reaching his nostrils. He was tired, and was either going to seduce this woman or have a drink. Afraid to look into her eyes for fear of what she'd see, he studied his cup as if it were a most important object.

She wasn't falling for it, though. Her hand reached to him and her cool fingers grasped one of his hands. They sat in silence, he afraid to look at her, she patiently giving support. This silence was strange for him, different, a type of invasion of privacy he couldn't protest in spite of his discomfort. He realized then how blearing tired he was and felt his eyelids droop. Closing them, though, gave birth to yet another image of Emily. This time she was a young child and her face was clouded with tears.

"It was a summer day like most of them," he began, "Emily had come over to play and done her regular knock-knock on the window. She did that because we weren't allowed to get together anymore, so she couldn't come to the front door. Normally she wore her hair in a couple of braids or one long one down her back. This time, she had her hair all chopped off, uneven with some bald patches showing. Real short. She looked like a boy.

"I laughed at first, until I noticed her tears. When I asked her what happened, she only said that her mother went 'a little crazy with the scissors.' I told her I didn't believe her, that she looked like someone had gone after her with a hatchet or something.

"I can still see the look on her face," he said, eyes closing. "She was horrified, staring at me as though I were some nightmare she'd wakened from only to realize the nightmare was continuing. Over and over I apologized. 'Em, I'm sorry, so sorry,' I said. 'I didn't mean to make fun of you.'

"She kept kicking the ground and wiping tears, but she neither explained herself or moved away from me. I could tell she was angry but she was also frightened. Of what, I didn't know. Eventually, she stopped crying and we took a walk to the woods. I never asked her about it and she never told me what really happened. For a while, until her hair grew back some, kids made fun of her at school, too. I felt bad for her. She had a great head of hair, lots of it."

Rain nodded. "She told me that story, too."

John looked at her and felt a tug at his heart. The sun had set and dusk was moving quickly towards darkness. Rain's face glowed in the dying light and her eyes glistened. Her hand was still resting on his. Though he wanted to turn his over and clasp fingers with her, he refrained.

"Did she describe how Betty had cut her hair, what led up to it?"

Rain's silence placed him on guard once again.

"Patient privilege?" he asked.

Rain nodded. "As I said, perhaps this can be discussed more fully, but I need to look into a few things first."

Sami began whimpering to go out. Rain stood to go open the door before John could protest. He hadn't wanted her to move.

"There she goes," said Rain, peering out the door and around the corner. "She made a beeline for the back of the house."

"She's been doing that all day," John said, standing. "I suppose I should check it out."

"I'll go with you," Rain said.

They went out the front door and around to the back, where Sami furiously sniffed by John's bedroom window.

"What's she on to?" he asked. "Sami! Off!" His command met on deaf ears. Sami continued to paw the window ledge, whining and shaking her head. "Oh, all right, let's have a look." He looked at Rain. "I need a flashlight to see, it's probably nothing but a mole. There's lots of them around here. Can't grow tulips. They eat the bulbs."

He left and came back with a high-powered flashlight. Shining the beam at his window, he quickly found the source of Sami's concern. Rain drew near.

"Blood," she said, confirming his suspicions. She reached to touch.

"No!" he exclaimed. "Leave it!" He tugged at her arm and moved closer to the sill, shining the light on what appeared to be multiple drops of blood. In a corner of one of the windowpanes, a crack had begun to pierce the glass. In Sami's mouth was a piece of cloth. John took it from the animal.

The threads hung from what was a piece of jeans. He rubbed and then looked at Rain who, as he, had quickly discerned the owner.

His head had slowly begun to shake. Emily had made it to his house last night. She had come the old route, their childhood secret way. He felt his fingers clasp around the material, crunch it in his fist. He felt his ruddy knuckles, his big hands closing in on a piece of the gentle child he had grown to love. Rain was whispering something about touching it, but he continued to massage the swatch, uncaring. The image of an injured Emily clawing at his window, begging for help. The bang on the windowpane that had disturbed his sleep. She had come to him for help.

"John, are you okay?"

One of those points in your life, a drinking buddy had once said, when you see your faults in Technicolor. John's rainbow had blood, and the blue of her jeans skirt. He'd let her go to her death by being, as usual, lazy and unresponsive.

"John, what is it?"

He slowly turned his head to face Rain. Sami had stopped sniffing and moved to a corner of the yard where apparently a hole had become the escape for a small critter. She barked loudly.

Rain's hand went to the material. "What is this?"

John had already made his decision. His lips pressed together, he marched back to the house, entered the front door, and stood watching Rain approach, stop and wait.

"Does this mean it's time for me to go?"

Her eyes were incredible. On another occasion, he might allow curiosity to rule, invite her back in and get it on with her.

"It's time to go." He looked down and focused on her feet, black walking boots with big heels that, after an unnamed stretch of time, turned and stepped from the house without further discussion. Car door shutting, engine starting. The crunch of tires on the dirt road. The hollow emptiness that meant he was alone.

There was nothing to drink in his house, that he'd ensured after Emily's body was found. No need to perform the furious search of days past for some drop in some lingering bottle. No need to unwrap Christmas gifts left unopened that contained what he was looking for. His house was dry. Ray's bar was ten minutes' drive. Ray would give him just one. He didn't want to go to town, though. He grabbed his keys and drove away. Carlin's Bar and Grill was twenty minutes away, but he'd be undisturbed there. The help changed regularly and they'd not remember him from that summer years before when he broke the front glass display. Or he could drive far away, but that would be trouble. He'd have, at some point, to drive back. Carlin's.

Her jeans material was still embedded in his fist as he drove. Was she wet and pleading as she tried to pry his window open? Had she called to him? "John, open up, please!" Had she lost her strength, made a final effort to reach him by hitting the pane and slicing her fingers on the cracked part? He imagined the scene. She had reached the window and, loud and clear so that he could hear, called out. Then she'd placed her fingers as he'd taught her, under the wood of the first row of panes and pushed. She wouldn't have known he'd replaced the windows on returning to Winslow. She wouldn't have known the lock was more secure. She'd have struggled and she'd have strained herself. Unable to raise the window, she'd have banged it, and the foolish cheap glass he'd bought had cracked and hurt her. Worse, he'd not waken fully enough to realize she was there. He'd turned over and ignored her.

The road was a gray mass in front of him. He instructed himself, turn right at the red barn, a long passage past fields and the big rotting barn that had fallen this winter due to snow, into the next town. Sami was outside on her own. Steady along the turns, this road is full of potholes.

The town had a single main street. Sunday church and quick errands for the paper and dog food had become Sunday afternoon dinner and television baseball in this working-class town. Save the errant teens smoking and wearing their baggy clothes, the town had the hang-dog look he expected. He grew impatient at the T-intersection, where so much oncoming traffic allowed few cars from John's road to pull out. Diagonally across and next to the self-serve gas station was Carlin's, set back from the road with the predictable yellow door lamps glowing. At any hour they burned, suggesting the dark interior and the darker mechanisms to forgetfulness.

He parked behind the building, where no one from the road could easily see his car. Inside, two men sat at the bar, deep in discussion. An elderly man with unkempt white beard, who John recognized as Main Street's loitering townie, read the newspaper in a corner booth, the fingers of one hand protectively around a half-filled glass of golden brew.

A fleeting sense of fear rose from John's toes to the base of his neck. He was doing something wrong. He should close the door and get out pronto. This act was a familiar one, however, and it was already too late. The greeting was sent his way from the man behind the bar. He sat, ordered a double.

Down, down into his feelings, numbing, holding him suspended. Pleasant. Fiery. Filling. She wasn't dead and she wasn't near. She'd become just another woman who had invaded his space. She had no right to do that. As soon as that happened, misery would follow. He sought other thoughts, the television and the baseball game. Men playing men. Distraction. Not much, he'd told the bartender on being asked what he was up to.

"Understand there's been a murder," the man said. He was balding, about forty. His face had the ragged look of fatigue that came from hours of physical labor punctuated daily by a dose of drinks.

John nodded. "Yep." He'd not thought of word spreading, of the next town over knowing. Why hadn't he figured this?

"Murder for sure?"

John looked away. None of your fuckin' business, he wanted to say. A sip helped. His insides comforted him, warmed him, embraced him as he'd wanted embracing less than twenty-four hours ago. Evening of the first day. All days would be counted from last night. Before and after. He'd recall what he might of this drinking session, but one thing would be clear. It was the next day. The day after. The night approached. He'd step into the memories of what he lived through having her at his side. Or would he? There was a way to stay away. There were several ways to keep those thoughts from surfacing. Several escapes, yes there were. Yes indeed.

Rarely did a woman enter Carlin's unaccompanied. Sunday nights especially. The last woman John recalled who let herself loose was the young blonde wife of a local contractor. Failing to find her husband at the bar, she entertained herself by entertaining the men. One minute, her arm draped seductively over fat George, the owner of the town's dump trucks, another minute rubbing the stomach of one of her husband's high school buddies, her eyes fixed unabashed between his legs. She left in the company of a competing builder, eyes glazed, shirt unbuttoned to her waist. John had actually straightened up to the bar when she'd passed him. That night, however, he'd made plans. He wondered if the couple were still married. He wanted a tramp tonight. But who?

Two more drinks. He was raising his hand to signal a third when she walked in. The blonde head made straight for him. How fortunate, he heard himself remark as he tried to run fingers down her cheekbones. Michelle took hold of his hand.

"C'mon, you," she suggested, pressing into his shoulder to show him the direction of the door. He snuggled up to her leather jacket, trying to embrace, but she directed him more forcefully so that he was sideways on the bar stool, a foot on the floor, ready to detach himself from the seat.

He blubbered about not wanting to leave, let me at least finish this drink. They were in the car, moving in the darkness. Headlights flashing into his eyes. Her warm body, her voice suggesting a good night's sleep. At his place, Sami welcomed him with a tackle so that he almost fell to the ground, but he used Michelle. Cowered into her warmth, felt her breasts and muttered something about putting him to bed, would she?

Her words were tempered with the discipline that formed the bones of her body. He pawed her as they made way to his bedroom.

"You wanna put me to bed like a baby, baby?" he slurred. "Then let me cuddle with you."

She repeated his name, this time ordering, the next time assuring. He wanted to rape her, throw her onto the bed, but his hands and feet jellied as she led him, forcing him in the direction of his room. He felt strong but wasn't making headway. This woman was all around him and he wanted her naked on his bed. Fuck who her husband was.

His head fell onto the pillows. She hoisted his booted foot and it was then he went for that blonde head, pulling it towards him and locking his mouth on hers. Her fingernails jammed his forearms and he used the pain to direct her to him, pressing her breasts to his chest and chuckling, rubbing, pressing too hard. A sharp blow in his calf stirred him. He loosened his grip and she slid from him, slapped him. The dazed look he gave her must have convinced her he'd come to his senses because she paused, stared at him as she gasped for breath.

"Cut the shit," she ordered, her eyes on fire, her chest heaving.

He went for the gray-green material of her shirt, buttoned so as to leave skin showing. His determined hand slit through the material, her bra, too, leaving her chest exposed.

"C'mere," he gurgled.

Again the sting of her hand against his face threw him back on the bed. A third slug and he went into blackness.

When he woke, it was dark and the house was silent. Pain seared through his forehead, pounding each cell with a reminder of his indulgences. A light was on in the living room. The standing lamp he'd fixed for his mother following his first electrical wiring shop class in high school. The clock read 4 A.M.

His wobbly feet on the hard wood would not cooperate. Twice he fell back on the bed, but forced himself to keep trying. Without aspirins he was a dead man. Slowly he scuffed across the floor. She was curled up on the couch and covered with an old point blanket, the pillows propping her to a sitting position, but her eyes were closed and her breathing ensured a deep sleep. He moved to the light and snapped it off.

Passing her, he advanced to the kitchen, found an aspirin bottle in the cupboard. After downing five, he returned to the couch where he wedged his way into a vacant spot, ensuring he didn't touch her or disturb her.

The collar of her blouse was visible and he noted the rip that disappeared under the blanket.

"God damn me, lady. I'm fuckin' sorry," he whispered, wiping hair from his brow and gazing at her sweet form. He'd have to explain himself to Paul, apologize directly to Michelle. Although, damn it, he wasn't quite sure why. Something about her lying here reminded him of something he'd done last night, aside from getting drunk. Wasted, he corrected himself.

The chirp of a bird. Dawn approached. Summer now. God, his head ached. He watched Michelle, her features still hidden in the darkness, her creamy hand that lay outside the blanket curled so that the metal of her wedding band shone. He waited. The medicine would take time, and then wouldn't quite clear things up. He was in for a slow, dull day.

Sami sniffed his feet. He took her to the door and let her out. The cool air blanketed his face and he gulped it in, wishing for clearheadedness, closing his eyes with the pain in his left temple. Even the word "alcohol" could not be brought to the fore of his thinking. Too painful all around. He shut the screen door gently so as not to disturb.

Outside, Sami growled and took off into the woods. Readjusting himself on the couch, he thought of skunks, babies just making their way into the world. Sami would make quick work of them. It was that time of year.

The brief respite of waking and facing the day suddenly clouded to reality. Emily. The material of her clothing. He looked down at his fist. What happened to the jeans? He pinched his temples, trying to pull them together as if that might aid in lessening the pain or inviting memory. No luck.

Had he dropped it? Was it in his car? What did this mean? He wanted to retrace his steps. Carlin's. Too far away. If he started the car, she'd waken. Plus, the place was closed now. Had Michelle taken the material from him?

Horror generated from the base of his spine and curled up to his hurting head. No, this wasn't happening. The reality. The fact he was now, what was he now? The dead woman had made it to his house. What was that? Who would believe he didn't hear her pleas? How could he explain that his longtime friend had called for help, tried to get into his place even, and he didn't react or was unaware? What was in store?

He looked to Michelle. The Allens would help. He shouldn't overreact. Night makes you think the worst. He massaged his forehead. If he'd been a praying man, he'd be on his knees. Sami whined outside the door. Again he shuffled to the door, let the dog in and instructed her to sit.

Once back on the couch, Sami settled at his feet. Michelle stirred, her eyes opened. For a second, they widened, expressing last night's fear, then gave way to recognition. Closing them, she curled to one side, pulled the blanket over her. "What time is it?"

"'Round four-thirty," he said, wide awake with guilt and wishing for her alertness, envious of her innocence, her ability to take care of her need for sleep. Simple requirements for which he'd trade his situation in a heartbeat. He thought he heard her groan, but then the returned paced breathing ensured she'd fallen back to sleep. Not in the mood for talking.

Daylight was making everything gray now, more discernible. It wouldn't be long before he'd have to start talking, explaining. He was frightened. A coldness had invaded his blood and he wanted a blanket, too, wanted to hide from what was in store.

Coffee? No, too much effort, too much noise. Where are you now, Emily? Your body is in the county morgue, but where are you now? Where did you go? Can you reach me? Can you help me understand what happened?

Wasn't it that the dead didn't leave the earth immediately? That they lingered depending on their state of mind at time of death? Had Emily's spirit flown to heaven right away? Or was she circling the town, still trying to piece together those pieces she never quite grasped of her life? Was she a troubled soul?

The silence that answered induced discomfort. With his thinking had come the hope she might answer, miraculously appear and assure him he was innocent, that he'd done her no harm, not like he'd done to himself last night.

And what about Michelle? The slow, uneasy sensation that they'd struggled on the bed grew into a realization. What else had occurred? He was such a weak, incomprehensible slob, he didn't deserve to live but he was too damn cowardly to take his own life. That would be an option. Walk outside with a dagger and plunge it into his heart. Let them find him, too. Let the funerals follow one another. That way, people would always think of them at the same time, and wonder about their connection. Just as he had all his life.

Michelle was staring at him. He blinked as he noted her right eye, swollen, with a terrible blackness surrounding it. He hadn't hurt her like that, had he?

"'Chelle," he said, placing his hand gently on her wedged legs.

"You okay?" she asked, moving a hand to her eye, rubbing, then wincing.

"I'll get a cloth," he said, heading for the kitchen.

He found a clean dish towel, ran cold water on it, and returned to hand it to her. Her eyes closed with relief as the cloth touched her forehead, covering the injured eye.

"John, where's the material?"

The words sliced the quiet. About to deny he ever had anything to do with material, he caught himself. "Material," he said.

"Can you retrace your steps? Can you tell me what you did last night before getting to Carlin's?"

"Sure, sure I can." He stood and paced the floor, his steps echoing on the wood floor, so much as to cause the dull pounding in his head to intensify. He moved to the space rug where his steps were silenced then stopped, sat on the couch. "I had it. I had it for the ride. No, I didn't. I didn't have it inside Carlin's. . . . I . . ."

He couldn't pretend with this woman. Whatever he said she'd know the truth instantly. He placed his face into his hands.

"I don't know what I did with it, Michelle."

Expecting her reassuring arm to cross his shoulders, he startled to another level of alertness once he realized she had no intention of comforting him right now. She remained still on the other side of the couch, neither condemning or condoning. The weariness was draining, his body ached, and now he was being scrutinized as the dumbass he really was.

"You realize this may be evidence," she said. "Rain told me what Sami discovered. Paul will be here soon with one of his people. They'll have to run a thorough check of this house."

It was coming now. The Inquisition. He'd be hauled into the jailhouse and kept there. He'd not be able to proceed with the investigation. He'd be a suspect. Moving to her, he grasped her shoulders.

"Don't let this happen, Michelle! I didn't do anything! She came to the window but, but I was out of it. As usual. You know how I get! You know what I do, my filthy habits. I was stone cold out most of the night!"

"Did you drink at the party?"

"No!"

They stared at one another. He wished he were her. Anyone but himself. Map my soul onto yours so I don't have to be who I am, he wanted to cry out.

"Then why were you out cold?" she asked.

"I got home. Late. I was not in the mood for sleeping. You know how it is."

"No, John, I don't know how it is."

Was she being difficult, giving him a taste of what was to come at the station later today? Or was she simply telling the truth. Her voice was even and noncommittal.

"Look," she said, "Just tell the truth. I believe you wouldn't hurt Emily."

He stared at her injuries. Shit. How could this woman say such a thing when her entire body revealed his violence? How would this go over?

"What we need to do now is get to the bottom of what happened last night to Emily. She came here, she came for help, John. That I believe. You'd never hurt her. Ever."

Eased into thinking less harshly about himself, he lay back on the couch. "I'm scared, Michelle."

"It's scary. But listen to Paul, listen to me. Try and work with us, John."

"I am. I do."

"No, you don't. You took off last night to get drunk. You can't do that! Not now! You can't behave like you did last night in your bedroom. Look at my face! Look what you did!"

He shook his head, refusing to confront the bashed, blackened eye. She drew his face to her so he had no choice.

"Look!"

Such a mess. Such a beautiful, messed-up face. She deserved better. She had better. What the hell was she doing here? "Why didn't Paul come to Carlin's?" he asked lamely.

"I wish I knew. Now." She replaced the towel over her eye and eased onto the pillows. "John. Get yourself together. Go wash up. Paul will be here soon."

He reached for her hand. She covered it with hers. "Go, John. Go get dressed."

As he made way to the bathroom, Sami dutifully followed. He closed the door, leaving her on the other side eyeing him expectantly. Another strange schedule for the dog today.

He splashed cold water on his face and turned the shower on high, waited for the steam to fill the small space. The water was scalding as he stood under it. Envisioning the dismal jailhouse, he told himself that this may be his last comfortable wash in some time. What was going to happen to him? How would it be from today on? He placed his head under the shower head wishing the heat would beat his brain to a pulp. Someone come and do away with me.

His mother used to knock on the door when he was washing. "John, hurry!" She'd always be late for something, waking each day forgetting her commitments. Once he had listed them out for her on the refrigerator, trying to help her understand what it meant to be on time, but she never paid any attention to his list. Invariably, they were rushing mornings. He never had time to just stand under the shower and luxuriate in its heat, in the comfort of the water pelting his back, his chest, his hands as they reached to his face to rub away the tears. The only place to hide from her was here, under the shower head, away from her voice, her incessant whiny voice.

Michelle was on the other side waiting. Waiting to bring him to the station. There would be questions to answer now. He would stay under the shower. He would take his time, let the water pound at his hurting head, at his hurting body, at his miserable hurting heart.

Chapter Nine

"Where is Granger now?" Paul asked, his unreadable face trained on the floor. They sat across from one another in Paul's office at the station.

"Dunno."

"We'll need to find him," Paul mumbled. It was late afternoon. Earlier, John had accompanied Michelle to the station and waited for Paul to show up. The offices empty at that hour, he stood and stared John down as Michelle, her eye blackened and her blouse ripped, explained what had happened the night before. John wanted to dissolve into the floor with the look Paul gave him, a look at once impassive and utterly knowing. It would take all Paul had to keep silent, to move about the station mechanically and to address the issue at hand, and he had. His face was drawn and Michelle had remained inordinately silent. It felt like the walking dead. John felt no need to speak, whatever he said would be inappropriate. He'd already apologized many times to Michelle, and now realized that the regrettable way she returned her gaze each time he spoke should clue him in. She didn't care. They were just words. Her face was blown up like a balloon and her clothes torn, signaling his insistence on having her. No regard to her marriage, or his own sense of dignity, wherever those qualities lay hidden.

Paul took John's statement about the discovery of what was presumed to be Emily's blood, the missing swatch of jeans that had matched a missing piece of her skirt that had been removed from her body. Paul also informed them that the land the body was found on belonged to the Granger estate. A small tract separated the Turners' property from Yvette's and extended to the low-lying hills that were part of what had been targeted for development. It would only be appropriate to disclose to Granger what had happened, and also to see if any light could be shed on the reason that Emily might have been at that spot when she died.

John shook his head. "I always thought the land was Yvette's."

Paul, worn and moving a lot slower than he had the day before, flattened a land map that had rolled at the corners. He pointed. "That was surveyed almost forty years ago. Apparently, some hundred years ago or so before, there was a stream running through there that was thought to be a good source of fresh water. That's why, when Granger left Yvette, he retained that land. Water is always an attraction, even if it's a small brook. The guy probably had visions even then of developing the land."

"When?" John asked, saying anything to keep the conversation away from the recent past, Emily, or Michelle.

"Back when he bought the land. Art told me last night that in the thirties, Granger's father bought up most of the land in this town, with the intent of selling off parcels, as had some of his cronies in places closer to Boston—Dover, Sherborn—those towns that border the Charles River. Theory was that it made sense to have land near water. Now," Paul chuckled, "water's a problem." He was referring to the latest state legislation regarding the requirement that septic systems be installed over fifty feet from natural water sources.

"Anyway," Paul continued, "Stuart Granger most likely intended to follow through with his old man's ideas. Keeping the land to himself meant profit down the road. It was probably surveyed for their divorce agreement."

"Do we really need to find Granger?" John asked. "He must be old by now. I heard someone else was running the business."

Paul nodded. The family had slipped into a mystifying state of unknown over the years. Gone were the lavish parties—the divorce and Yvette's ownership of the big house took care of that—gone were the newspaper articles following Granger's every move.

"Last I heard, he'd taken ill. Art was called in for a time, to his penthouse on Beacon Hill. Something undetermined. Something Granger didn't want in the press. Art speculated it might have been something contagious or terminal and the family didn't want to give the allusion that Granger might pass on. He never did as far as I know. Makes sense to check it out. We should find someone other than Yvette who can address any legal matters that arise from having discovered a dead body on the property."

John nodded. The team of medics and police had been trespassing, but he doubted that would be an issue. More important was the understanding of where Granger was, or at least how far away he'd been from Winslow over the weekend. Most likely, he'd want things kept quiet. Chances were he wasn't giving up his quest to develop yet. He'd be back, with more lawyers and fancy ideas. A corpse uncovered on one's property placed a damper on any attempts to market the wonders of New England autumns, falling leaves, and crisp, cool days hiking in the country.

"Art says he was moved to New York, supposedly to get expert medical assistance," Paul continued.

"Seems odd, given Boston has the best of the best," John murmured.

Paul nodded. For the first time in a stretch their eyes met, Paul's regard betraying only slight distraction. John groaned inside. Take me to a field and shoot me.

As if hearing him, Paul drew a quick grin to one side of his mouth, almost teasing. Paul Allen would keep John in the thick of things today. First, it would make John miserable due to his thumping head. Second, it might, just might, make John think a bit longer about taking another drink with Paul's wife and assuming anything other than her friendship. John was certain Paul had already spoken his mind to Michelle about her ever coming to John's aid again.

How to ruin a friendship, by John Jordan. He hunched lower over the map.

"Can you manage to get yourself to the *Post*? Ask for old issues starting from the forties. Whatever you can find on Granger. Be thorough. It'll take you a while but today's quiet. School closing and all."

This week the schools closed for the summer and most residents began the exodus to the Cape or the north shore, the mountains, anywhere but here. By July 4, there were few if any regular residents. Campers and tourists passing through taking advantage of guest houses and bed and breakfasts were about the only witnesses to the local parade. The town seemed too small to hold the interest of any but the most die-hard residents and the elderly for the holiday.

John agreed to get to the *Post*. He wondered about his ability to concentrate but ruled against putting this idea forth. Paul was not in the mood for objections.

He would walk. No driving. No distraction. The day had dawned glorious and even as he trudged behind Michelle and Paul as they left his home some hours before, he'd taken a second to breathe deep. Fresh, cool summer air, with just a hint of new plants and buds. There was nothing like the unmistakable smell of life renewing itself.

He made his way down Main Street, in the direction of the last remaining Victorian-style house that had not been renovated with a storefront. The *Post* had maintained its original facade, misleading those in search of it for the first time and pleasing most visitors with its Addams' family-style dominance. John used to have nightmares about it, now he headed for it as if to a refuge. At least he'd be able to avoid Paul Allen's indescribable gaze.

From the small desk that served as the reception area, Joanie Michaels nodded to him. Joanie was eighty-five if she was a day, with white curls decorating her forehead and her pink flowered shirt looking to be the style she wore when John was a kid asking her to look at back newspaper issues for a Cub Scout activity. This time, though, he wasn't researching the Shakers.

She gave him a sympathetic smile. "John, dear, how are you?" she asked, throwing John's stomach into a tailspin. The first person to greet him warmly today. His guilt made him feel nauseated. He refrained from answering, tipped his baseball cap instead.

Joanie would be well aware of the incident over the weekend. Her husband, an auxiliary fireman, had been at the scene in the woods. As she probably had since they married over fifty-five years ago, she would have waited up for him. His return was never guaranteed, she would tell everyone, especially when there was a fire.

He requested the key to the old editions room and headed to the windowless basement space, where for hours one could pour over anything that the *Post* had in print. As he settled in an old armchair and flicked on a green-shaded table lamp, he realized this was the best place for his aching body and shamed heart. Some sort of protective womb, without the mother part. He thought he'd start with 1940 and work his way up. Ever since 1910, the paper was produced once a week, on Tuesdays. If he read quickly, a daunting task under the circumstances, he'd get through World War II by at least noontime.

Some ten minutes later, stacks of plastic-wrapped newspapers piled at his side, he dove in. After the first article about a snowstorm blocking access roads to town, however, his thoughts wandered. Pain seared through his temples. He stared at the papers. Boring news of a boring town, a little dot on the world with its dilemmas and laws like any small town, blown out of proportion because life was so dull you needed to create your own news from no news at all. He rested his head, just for a minute, on his forearms and closed his eyes. Dark shadows laced with Emily's eyes crossing his mind as he drifted, free from aspirin and coffee, to the only place he had the strength to support.

He dreamt of his mother, of her desperate eyes and blood-stained clothes, of her nonchalance and her voice, first the whine and then the comforting lull of her singing. A broken tree branch crossed his face, slapping his eyes with sharp points and tough bark. A woman was screaming at him, pulling him into a yellow moon, laughing as she moved.

His arm jerked, waking him abruptly. He was panting, sweating. Glancing around, he was still in the quiet room. Someone from above crossed the length of the floor, and the hum of a distant machine assured business as usual. Probably nowhere near quitting time. He turned the page of the paper, but as cobwebs clogged his brain, he felt a tremendous thirst and went to the water fountain outside, wiping his lips with the back of his hand after taking a long, cool drink. It was just what he needed.

Before sitting down to his work, he returned to the stacks. He'd start with her birthday. What the hell. Dead June of this year, born 1952. My girl. I outlived you. What did you do with our ring? He surprised himself by his recall of the silver snake ring they'd found in the woods, an item he'd long ago forgotten. A hiker had left it on a rock. She'd slipped it onto her swearing finger and laughed. He'd told her it was theirs, because they'd both found it and then she'd placed her lips on his. His hand had found her knee, so soft and smooth and his fingers had made their way to her thick white socks. It was the first time the thought of seeing her naked had emerged. It took many more years for this thought to materialize. Had she kept the ring?

For what seemed a long time, he engrossed himself in the news but, finding nothing on Emily during that year, he soon tired. He revisited the stacks and returned with the 1953 issues. Nothing, except the July issue was missing. He noted that and resumed his reading, finding the birth notice for himself that year.

Darcy and McKinley Jordan are the proud parents of a boy, John James. 6 lbs., 8 oz. They live on Brook Run.

John's fingers trembled as he touched the black print, touching first the name of his father, the closest he'd ever get to the stranger he never knew, would never know. McKinley, or "Mac" as Darcy referred to him, drowned in the Squannacook River several miles down the road. Fishing, or so they said. Over the years, John concluded his father had been drinking, but nothing was ever said. He flipped to 1954 and found the obituary. RIP. He suppressed the urge to rip up the page.

Next, he tried to focus on Granger, but his mind continued to wander. His thoughts veered to Emily. Once again, as he'd felt since the body was found, he sensed her presence. Close, so close he wanted to reach out and yet his rational side took over suddenly and coaxed him back. Strange. When someone was dead, she was dead. That was that. Or was it? Or was it simply this awful hangover?

"Finished?"

John wheeled around at the voice. Paul stared at him, that already too-familiar gaze bearing down on him once again.

"Uh, sort of. Not," he said lamely, shuffling pages and stacking the issues again. "Not much here."

"Did you find anything about Granger?" Paul asked, nearing. He was already studying the issues. "1954 already?"

John looked quickly at Paul, then resigned himself to the inevitable. "No. I started there."

"Why? Granger made his first purchase in the forties!" Paul's voice was charged.

"I wanted to read up on Emily."

"Was Emily buying land, too?" Paul asked sarcastically.

John didn't dare look at the man's face. Not only had John tried to screw his wife the night before, he wasn't even following orders now. Shit. Give up, Jordan. You're nailed.

Paul nudged him. "Well?"

The feel of a rough hand juggled whatever sense of self he had. Warped though it was at this point, he would allow no one to rough him up. Reflexively, he shoved Paul's hand aside. Paul in turn grabbed John's shoulder and without mercy pulled his shoulders straight.

"Look, you. Get your act together, man! You've been asked to do something here! What the hell have you been up to for the last three hours?"

It couldn't be three hours had passed. John stared dumbly at Paul.

Paul exhaled loudly, as if he'd taken a huge drag of a cigarette. "The autopsy has completed. Let's go."

The news helped his body get into gear. He stood soldier-like. God, Emily was now dissected. He began to breathe deeply, with each breath reminding himself she felt nothing. It was nothing for her now. He fumbled with the papers but managed to replace them as neatly as they'd been arranged, turn off the light, and lock the door behind them.

Upstairs, he thanked Joanie and followed Paul out the door, eyes on the broad shoulders and navy shirt, repeating to himself, "Just follow. Don't screw up. Just follow."

He kept wondering what it was he'd wanted to ask Joanie.

＊　＊　＊

Earlier that day, when they'd assembled at the station, John had seen Art Johnson's car buzz past the station heading in the direction of the county hospital. Six A.M. or so it had been. John had felt angry then, angry that he couldn't go with Art.

As they drove to the station, Paul was silent, almost, John thought, on purpose. Whatever Paul knew he wasn't letting on. John decided to keep his own counsel also.

There, Art was waiting for them, a manila envelope in his hand, his legs crossed and his face trained on the view outside. It took no more than a few minutes to relay the news. No sign of struggle, no punctures, no gunshots, nothing to indicate an attacker. Her heart had stopped and she had apparently fallen.

John toyed with a Styrofoam cup, picking bits of it off and throwing them into the nearby trash bin. Paul paced the office area, one side then to the next.

"It looks like Betty had a point, gentlemen. Emily Turner was fragile. Acute coronary trauma. In other words, heart attack." Art removed his glasses, looked up from the papers to the men.

"Just like that?" Paul asked.

"It's possible, Paul. There have been documented cases of people who, for no apparent reason, drop dead. On further investigation, the death was considered due to heart failure."

"How?"

"Extreme emotion. Fright is not an uncommon culprit. In recent times, some studies point to a clear connection between emotional stress and cardiac vulnerability. This causes life-threatening arrhythmias." He paused, then continued. "Others say, voodoo and the like."

"C'mon!" John blurted, standing. "That's ridiculous! There were no wounds at all?"

Art shook his head. "No. However," he turned a page over gently, "there was evidence of old bruises on her arm and back. Probably due to a childhood injury. Perhaps . . ."

"What old injury?" John asked. Paul stepped closer to him. "She didn't have injuries."

"You weren't with her over the last ten years, were you?" Paul's tone was unmistakably laced with the earlier sarcasm. John shut his mouth and sat down again, wondering if the injuries could have been more recent than childhood.

Art added, "Scars and scar tissue remained. Somehow she'd been injured with something sharp, but that was years ago. There was no indication of recent injuries, I'm afraid."

"This notion of fright," Paul said, "what exactly does that mean?"

"I've not seen this myself, but I did refer to some of my medical books after Emily's report came out. It can be construed that a person dies of fright. Just like that. They're so traumatized. . . ."

"Bullshit!" John yelled out.

Paul dug fingers into John's shoulder. "Cool it. Listen, man!"

Art continued. ". . . so traumatized they die right then and there. It happens. Whether or not she had a history of a weak heart, we'd have to look into that."

"Are you aware of any childhood illnesses?" Paul asked.

Art shook his head. "No, she was a pretty active girl, and a sprite young lady as I recall. No, can't say that I do."

"We'll have to look further then," Paul concluded. "Her history while she lived out west. Perhaps Rain could help." He removed his hand from John's shoulder. "Can you have a talk with Rain?"

John nodded without standing. He was still waiting for more from Art, but as Art slowly closed the file and replaced the papers in the envelope, it was clear that there was no more to relate from the autopsy. He tried to block out the image of her body slit and quartered down the front on some morgue slab. Weak heart? Impossible. He didn't believe it.

Paul, increasingly impatient, nodded to Art. "Thanks, Art. Can you look into her records? Anything from the hospital. Anything other doctors might be aware of. Her former injuries might shed some light. John, talk with Rain."

John stood, nodded.

"Now, understood?" Paul asked.

John masked a glare that was making its way to his face. Michelle wasn't going to bear a grudge, why would this guy?

He exited with Art. The two made their way to the parking lot. The evening air was thick, as though a storm brewed in the hills. The distant hills had blended with the sky into the haze that marked humidity's return to the region.

Art took a deep breath. "Take it slow, my friend. This should not wear you down." The old man glanced warily, then placed a firm hand on John's shoulder.

"She wasn't hurt as a child, was she, Art?"

Art's silence seemed to betray his reservations. He was staring at the invisible hills just like John. "What frightened Emily? Do you recall?"

The question startled John. He thought of her face, the look of pure terror that sometimes crossed it, but that look was often muddled into a smile, a joke, a tease that got them on track. Always, when they met, he saw it first, and then when they parted. He never asked her why.

"Remember when my mom was hurt, Art? Emily had come to the house. She had this look that was scary. Like she'd seen a ghost. But we didn't talk much that night. Matter of fact, we didn't talk much about our families from that night on. Seemed it was off limits as a topic." John shook off his still fuzzy head. "I don't get it."

Art patted John's shoulder. "Get some rest. In the morning, we can talk again."

John watched the Fiesta back out then turn onto the road. He envied Art going home to a cooked meal and a woman with whom he could converse. Then Rain came to mind. She might be able to help, though his mind was slow. His head was pounding and his mouth was dry. He returned to the station, placed a call to the Turners' and left a message for her to meet him at Ray's bar. They'd go somewhere and grab a bite to eat. Before all this, he'd be preparing to go for a run. It was the perfect evening, to clear his head, to help him prepare the right questions. Rain was a no-nonsense woman and would respond to his questions provided they were intelligent and thought-provoking, not the mindless chatter of a drunk too lost in his mess to know what to do. He also wondered what she'd discovered today.

✳ ✳ ✳

Climbing the ridge and maintaining a jog was a challenge. Gray slate that used to be mined from the area formed most of the incline that led to the top, causing him to slip until he finally moved to the grassy edges of the paths. From here, a panorama of western Massachusetts spread before him, rolling hills that turned different shades depending on the time of day. Wonder filled him. It was this, his destination, where he could stare out at the blue and clear his head with the freshness of nature bombarding him, as he had for years. Puffing, he finally found the path at the top that followed the ridge along the west side. The sun was lowering, but had slipped behind clouds, and so there were only gold-red rays slicing the dark clouds at the moment. The quiet preceding a storm reigned, but not as heavily as to warn of an actual storm. He'd be fine for another hour or so.

He stopped at the clearing that provided the best view of the town below. It could have been any picture-perfect New England town, complete with its white steeple church and gazebo on the common. To the left of the general store was the cemetery. He calculated. Shit, thirty years tomorrow his mother was buried there. He zeroed in on the slate gray and thin piece of stone under which she was buried. They placed her in the Protestant cemetery. The Catholics had required money and he'd had none.

Priding himself on his ability to admit to himself she was a tragedy, he drew in deep breaths and bent down, trying to block out the day she, too, was discovered in the woods. In her case, the animals had reached her and had their feast. At least Emily had been left alone, and he'd been able to view her in death as he'd always imagined she'd look lying in bed beside him, still, pale, a work of art, his woman no matter what everyone else thought. Darcy, on the other hand, had lost most of her face and stomach parts. Her insides had been torn up and there was only her fingernails, painted the vermilion red she adored. "I love that deep dark red, honey." The nail polish identified her. Eyeballs gone, face torn away, body blue and bloated in places. A horrifying statement to human deprivation and abuse, like her life had been. John had screamed it was a bear, but Art had hushed him saying there weren't bears for miles, that it was coyotes. He kept pointing to the cuts, measuring their depth and the width of the claw marks. John had continued his screaming and later, they told him, he'd blacked out.

Darcy had been killed by animals, everyone in town said. The obituary had presented her death as an unfortunate accident. No one had mentioned, at least in John's presence, what they thought had really happened. In some ways, John had wished someone had had the courage to discuss it with him. He'd have told them his mother was so drunk, she passed out and her fate was her own doing that night. No one knew better than he what his mother on the drink was like.

He hated her, too. He hated her now as he never had. She'd left him and left a mess behind. Her damned reputation most of all. No matter who he ran into in town after that, he could read their shame betrayed as sympathy and wanted to vomit. Only Art refrained from comment or facial expression. Art because Art had seen enough in his life to know that life was the thing to be treasured. John was alive, his mother was not;

therefore, John deserved his respect. Unfortunately Art was in the minority. Others, too ashamed or embarrassed for John, gave away their feelings via sympathetic comments or plain snubs. He had already toughened up, though, many, many years before. It was as though all of Darcy Jordan's life with her son was spent preparing him for the big, final, conclusive embarrassment. She couldn't hold her drink and it got the best of her. John inherited her shame and her reputation. Why the hell had he returned to this town?

Somewhere deep down, as he stared at her stone in the distance, he felt compelled to wonder yet again about that night. How strange his two women of significance had died in the woods, victims of what? Of the night? Of drink? Or what actually? Emily was not a drinker. His mother was a pathetic soul but not inclined to stupidity. Nevertheless, the recent events seemed to be unfolding as they had when Darcy was found dead. Nothing that can be done, no sign of attack, no apparent reason other than the woman herself.

He kicked the ground. Was Emily's death meant to go without answers, too? Tomorrow or the day after she'd be buried. With her, the secrets?

Something was up. He wasn't sure what, he wasn't sure who could help him but he knew there was more. There was Granger, there was Yvette, both had lived here a long time, both were capable of hiding behind their money. There was Darcy, even, and her nights out. What had she shared with Walter those days? He was a little kid back then. Adults would not have told him much.

He shook his head so much that it rang. Stupid. That was years ago. Walter was silent and obviously so was Darcy. Connection? Not possible. Emily had left for a new life. She had returned, though. Why? He thought of Rain and dinner tonight. It forced his legs in the opposite direction, back down from where he came, jogging slowly, each step causing his ears to ring but keeping him oddly balanced as well.

The sun was setting in streams of gold and red, the light reflected off the trees. He'd have another hour to wash and dress. He'd take her for pizza in the next town. The place there had good vegetarian. He sensed she'd enjoy that.

※　※　※

She was dressed in a black shift with a slit up the back, all the way up beyond her knees. From the front, it was conservative, fitted and coming close up to the base of her neck with wide straps. But the back, the part he'd see as she walked in front of him on entering the restaurant, the part that he'd see when helping her into his car, was the slit and her bare legs. Slip-on black heels and toes painted a tropical pink. Her hair was wound in a knot at the top of her head. She looked cool and beautiful.

They drove for fifteen minutes and she asked him questions about the roads they were on. How old, why they were named the name of the town you weren't in, the town you were on the way to, what determined where the sidewalks would be, why the town centers had only churches and graveyards, why, why, why.

It was good, the chatter, the informational flow. For the first time in two days, he almost could say he was relaxed, but didn't trust himself still. He must not drink. He must not drink.

"I can't drink tonight, Rain," he said quietly after he'd turned the ignition off and they sat outside a small pizza joint. The lights were low and a pink sign flashed "Antonio Bataldi's." "Bats" for short, John had explained while they drove, as they entered the small, dimly lit establishment that smelled of garlic and roasted tomatoes. The best pizza around, crisp and not oily. Bat himself did the cooking. Still didn't speak a word of English. Forced every redneck in the area to understand "buongiorno!"

Rain had chuckled very sensually. John knew he would be in trouble if he didn't come straight with her up-front.

"I was drinking the other night and. . . ."

"Michelle told me. It's okay," she said, her eyes on the menu. "Let's have soda water tonight. Perhaps espresso after dinner?"

He couldn't detect any eye makeup. Her eyes glimmered in the candlelight, their gray now a shade of navy blue. He exhaled with relief and studied the menu as well.

They ordered a large vegetarian and an antipasto to split between them. She ate heartily, recalling the trattorias of Italy that she'd experienced as a college student. At one point, tomato sauce dribbling from her mouth, she laughed. "There was this old man in Brindisi—we were stuck there waiting for the train to Rome—who made a pass at my friend Alicia. Man, he was so forward! Kissed her right on the lips. A married old fart with a swarthy smile. We laughed the whole way back to Rome, all of us except Alicia!"

She giggled again, then grew solemn. "John, I did some asking around about Granger."

John stopped chewing. He settled against the leather of the booth.

Rain continued, "Michelle told me about the land where Emily was found. I talked with the Turners. Betty mentioned Stuart Granger and his illness. Walter grew jumpy and began changing the subject but Betty hushed him by saying it didn't matter anymore anyway. She said that he was still alive, that he was living in Manhattan, or just outside. That he was still very ill but living the life of a recluse."

"Did she tell you what his illness was?" John asked.

"No, she implied he was dying, made reference to the will he'd left behind, how much money there would be. When she said that, though, Walter spilled some tea and she went to attend to that. It was all over their rug by the fireplace and he was fussing so. She seemed very distraught by the spill also. I take it those two are very anal about their possessions."

"Or Walter was trying to distract you."

Rain chewed thoughtfully. "Perhaps. I don't trust him but at times he's simply a lamentable old coot."

"It would make sense to get to New York," John said.

Rain shook her head. The silver barrette holding her hair up glistened. "First, there's an old guy who used to attend to him here. Art was first but then I guess that didn't last long. Apparently, Granger didn't want help from the locals. The old guy was an immigrant who lives in the next town, Harley is it?"

"Yes, Harley. Smaller than Winslow. Working class."

"Interesting," she said. "You New Englanders and your categories."

He smiled. "I noticed that, too, but only on returning from New York, where categories are more along the financial lines. . . ."

"Anyway, the name is Malmkoviz. Peter Malmkoviz. He used to be a butler long ago at, guess where? Yvette's."

"I must have seen him," John said.

"Want to join me tomorrow in Harley?" she asked.

He nodded, stuffing back what he really wanted her to join him in.

Chapter Ten

Harley was, in reality, a section of another town located ten miles from Winslow. Arrived at by taking the westbound road out of Winslow, it was essentially a stop along the old Boston-to-Vermont rail line. Marked by a single-story train depot along abandoned tracks, the tired-looking building hinted former grandiosity with its mansard roofing, ornate wrought-iron benches, and a sculpted water fountain. Rusted machinery dotted the cracked cement platform, tie rods spread out helter-skelter across the tracks, piping and even old furniture lay strewn about as if someone had abandoned them in haste. The tracks were barely visible underneath sprouting weeds and grass.

Not far from the station, Rain and John found Malmkoviz's home, located on a tidy plot of land at the end of a dirt road. Trimmed evergreen shrubs bordered the front yard. Here and there along the walkway small rhododendron bushes let drop wilted petals that only weeks before had most likely been glorious. The ranch-style home was painted a pale blue slate with white trim windows. Flower beds at the base of the front of the house had been tilled and watered awaiting the blooming of perennials that already announced their small green buds. An elegant wind chime whispered its solid, hollow tones from a corner of the small front porch.

They rang the doorbell once and promptly steps were heard from inside. A small man with white hair answered the door. Peering from gold spectacles, he adjusted them, studied his visitors in a prim, questioning manner before saying, "Yes?"

Rain answered with a wide smile. "We'd like to speak with Peter Malmkoviz, please."

"I'm Peter," he said, responding with a slight accent, clearly admiring Rain and her fresh-washed look in pale blue blouse and white jeans.

Rain introduced herself and John and the reason for their visit. Peter lingered over John, studying him in a knowing fashion that made John shift from left to right uneasily. Returning his gaze to Rain, he motioned to them. "Come in," he said pleasantly.

The small front hallway gleamed with white marbled tiles, and an iron coat rack stood against French doors. Outdoor footwear—Wellies, mud boots, hiking shoes—stood at attention atop brown paper that covered a block of the tiles to prevent splattering. Malmkoviz, who wore summer slacks and a crisp white polo shirt, led them to the left room, which appeared to serve both as an office and sitting room off of which was a small solarium with exotic plants.

"Sit, please," he said, moving towards the solarium to close the doors. "I was just touching up the orchids. They're so sensitive once the heat picks up in the summer!"

He smiled again and seated himself in a embroidered armchair with matching footrest that was close to the fireplace, a copy of the Sunday *New York Times* in a neat pile on the floor. Rain and John settled on a couch made of a solid rose-colored material that enhanced the tones in Peter's chair. Above the fireplace, an oil painting of flowers looked to be an original.

"So, I understand there was an unfortunate incident in Winslow," Peter said. His sparkling blue eyes fixed on John.

"Yes, unfortunate," John said, adjusting himself in the chair. Something was giving rise to an inordinate discomfort. His feet tingled and he felt like running out the door. "We're trying to get what information we can on the properties where the woman, the body, was found." He switched his gaze to the fog settling on the glass of the solarium doors.

"The land where she was discovered belonged to Mr. Stuart Granger," Rain offered. "We understand you took care of him for a while during his illness."

Was Malmkoviz nervous now or not? A slight adjustment of his back against the chair gave rise to the question in John's mind. He stopped looking at John and turned to Rain, but this time his face held a tinge of gray.

"Poor Stuart," he said, his voice raising an octave or two.

Rain and John shared a startled look.

"I felt so bad for him. One day he was walking and talking and running a multibillion-dollar business, the next he was bedridden."

"What with?" Rain asked.

Rather than answer, Malmkoviz nodded, as if they'd already discussed this point. "Poor, poor man. I'd get him out in the fresh air. He came here, you know, every morning the chauffeur dropped him off, wheeled him up the front, brought him right into this room. I'd take over. Wheel him into the solarium for a good part of the morning, while I did my own chores and all." He glanced proudly at the shining hardwood floors and squeaky clean windows. Then, he stood and went to his stereo system that covered an entire wall along the back of the study, pushed the button and beautiful, soft classical music began to play.

"Shubert," he whispered to the equipment, almost as if his guests were not present. He glanced back at them. "Apologies, I wasn't . . . my manners." He returned to his chair, crossed his legs. His folded hands were gripped tight. John noted the white knuckles.

"After I'd complete my chores, I'd wheel him to the dining room. I adore cooking and he loved to eat, so that was the big part of the day. We had marvelous meals, we did. There was a rack of lamb. . . ." Again, Malmkoviz drifted into his own thoughts, his eyes dropping to view the swept-out fireplace. "Yes, it was lamb. I was going to say the medley of salmon and sturgeon, that was a good one, too, but, really, if I had to choose, it would be the rack of lamb. Actually I made it more than once. You have to use fresh rosemary, though, no matter what anyone tells you. . . ."

He stopped, looked up. "Oh, I'm so sorry. You must think I'm daft! Well, I suppose at eighty-three. . . ." He looked to Rain.

"You're not eighty-three!" she exclaimed.

A grin crossed his thin lips and John saw a vision of the man as a younger gentleman, slim, on the small side but with a fit body, polished manners, and a dapper dresser. What was Malmkoviz doing here? He seemed the type to be in New York, or some other large artistic metropolitan center.

"I am, but, my dear, it gets harder and harder to keep up. . . . You know. No, you couldn't! You're so young! So lovely, if I may be so bold." His eyes traveled to her leather bag then back to her face. He stared expectantly at her.

Rain smiled. "You were saying, you cooked for Mr. Granger."

"I did. Would you like to see my kitchen? I'm very proud of it, the latest utensils. Well, not the latest, they're actually years old, but the best. Copper!" His eyes glimmered. He raised himself to the standing position. "Shall we?"

John and Rain stood and followed him to the long hall that led to the back of the house, stepping on marbled floors and slowing down to view what appeared to be original works of art hanging in gold frames on the walls. Malmkoviz seemed not to notice the priceless objects. His footing was sure and he moved swiftly.

A brightly lit, yellow kitchen that ran the entire length of the back of the house boasted floor-to-ceiling windows along the widest outside wall. Stainless steel cooking equipment, fans, cutting blocks, knives lined largest to smallest, and gleaming copper pots hanging from the ceiling met their eyes. Malmkoviz went to the stove and turned on the burner to warm water. "Tea? I only purchase the best, from a little tea shop outside St. Albans, Vermont. Get up there twice a year. Tea from India. There's nothing like a good Darjeeling. Really good, not like those monstrous things in the grocery store that come in packets." He busied himself pulling down white china tea cups and saucers from the cupboards, arranging biscuits from an oversized tin on the counter into a matching serving plate, and then motioning them to the chairs at the butcher-block table that gave view to what appeared to be a garden that took up the entire backyard. Rain marveled at the scene as Malmkoviz pointed out the section he used for perennials and the garden area.

"What was his problem?" John asked.

Peter, whose back was to them, turned. "What?"

Then, as if realizing John's question, he answered. "Oh, Mr. Granger. Well, Mr. Granger was ill, yes he was. It was a condition not unlike Alzheimer's. He was very weak most of the time and forgetful. It started slowly, I even recall our first few weeks together wondering what the problem actually was! He was alert, walking with a cane and very interested in my flowers."

Peter joined them at the table and stirred his tea, reflectively staring out at his gardens.

"Little did I know that he was not typically someone who enjoyed flowers. Oh, if you saw his many properties, you might say so, but planting and managing the grounds was not his doing. He had many employees, you know. Some were yard people, others worked inside his estates. Anyway, he had many gardeners. I would ask him about flowers and he'd not have a clue, and I'd been past his estate in Winslow enough to know there were many beautiful flowers in the gardens, to say nothing of his tropical collection."

Peter nodded towards the solarium. "That's where I got many of mine, you know. He had them sent over when I mentioned my interest in tropical plants. The very next day! He watched me arrange them and it was then I realized his faculties were not all there. He kept repeating himself and, when I'd correct him about a type of flower, he'd sit and stare.

"Still, he was a gentle person. It wasn't until I had a chance to get out on my own and visit with friends in Boston that I discovered his reputation for being a very difficult, hard-driving businessman. How had it come about that he was with me so docile, I wondered?"

He stirred and stared at Rain, almost through her. She remained still and attentive.

"A very short time after, though, it became clear he wasn't, shall we say, together. He would stop talking in mid-sentence, forget something I'd said just moments before, and fall asleep for a good part of the day. He was on drugs, you see. Don't ask me what for. I never inquired. The labels on the bottles weren't clear.

"I thought of him as a simple soul, really. He never troubled me. Although over the six months that I took care of him, it grew increasingly difficult for one person to care for him. His body was giving out."

At this comment, he paused and took a sip of tea.

"Was it in fact Alzheimer's?" Rain asked.

Peter shrugged. "I don't know. I read some on the disease, asked once when a doctor came to the house when Mr. Granger had a bad cold, but never got an answer."

"What happened?" John asked.

"What do you mean 'What happened'?" Peter asked, his eyes on his garden.

"To Granger? Where is he today?"

Malmkoviz remained still, his eyes fixed a distant spot in the garden. "I don't know."

John could tell he was lying. The octave voice had lowered. The man was still, like an animal sensing danger.

"Is he dead?" Rain asked.

Malmkoviz took a few seconds, longer than it would take for a "yes" or a "no."

"He's not dead, not that I know of."

"Did he ever get better?"

Malmkoviz shook his head, then looked down into his tea. Except for the chirp of a bird, not a sound was heard. When he looked up, a glimpse of fear was erased before he smiled. "I simply don't know. He was taken from my care with no word. One day, the chauffeur didn't appear. I waited that day, and the next. I had no phone number to call to find out what was going on. I waited. A check came in the mail, posted from Boston, with the agreed-upon salary and then some. I was paid very generously."

He stood and began clearing the dishes. "I've already said enough." His eyes fell onto Rain again. "I'm sorry. You'll have to go now."

"Did you enjoy that work? Taking care of Mr. Granger?" she asked.

His lips were pursed, and then they loosened and his face cleared of a few worry lines on his forehead. He grinned, stood, ushered them towards the front hall.

"You know, it was like having a child, a helpless child for whom I could care and who was grateful for my attention. I'd never had that in my life. Yes, I suppose it was enjoyable. It wasn't until after his disappearance that I realized my days had filled with the activity of caring for him. It took some time to settle into other activities after he left."

"You worked for Yvette, also?" she asked.

The question caused him to start. "Yes, unfortunately."

"Unfortunately?" John asked.

"Unfortunately for me. She was, is, a very demanding sort. Not like her ex-husband. I only did it for Deborah."

"Oh?" asked Rain.

"Yes." Almost too quickly he opened the door and with his hand made a gesture that pointed them out.

Rain extended her hand to shake. "I noticed your car has New York license plates. Are you from the city by any chance?"

"Uh, yes, actually!" he exclaimed, his eyes dancing for a second.

"Do you get to shows very much anymore?"

He shook her hand but, when John extended his hand, Malmkoviz's hand hung by his side. John withdrew.

"I wish I could get there more. Never got around to changing my license plates." He chuckled. "Was going to say, 'Don't tell the police!'" He nodded to John as he opened the front door.

Rain laughed, thanked Malmkoviz, and they left. In the car on their way back to Winslow, Rain voiced concern about the veracity of what Malmkoviz said. John concurred. Malmkoviz wasn't telling everything. They agreed to try and contact Granger's offices in Boston.

That night, after dropping Rain off, John returned to Harley. By then it was about 11 P.M., very dark and still. A single porch light illuminated Malmkoviz's house. The interior appeared void of activity. John parked a half mile away and returned to the house on foot. In the shadows of trees, he watched and listened. Either Malmkoviz had gone to bed or gone out. There was no car in the driveway as there had been earlier. After lingering with no results, he decided to get his car and go home.

Driving along the road, he wondered about New York. Why would someone after all these years, for Malmkoviz had to have been here for at least ten years now, retain his license in another state unless he also claimed residency in that state? Perhaps Malmkoviz still had an address there. He would check it out in the morning. And where was Granger? New York as well? Perhaps. It seemed Malmkoviz still had much affection for the man. If so, wouldn't he try to keep in touch with him? Or at least inquire about his whereabouts?

The road rose in front of him, no streetlights, and the lonely, country-road darkness that spoke to him about returning to an empty house, being alone, either drinking himself to sleep or watching television. Why hadn't he asked Rain to come out with him? She had been yawning, excusing herself for her fatigue. He'd suggested taking her back to the Turners' and she'd agreed. Best to leave well enough alone.

She didn't seem to be showing him any interest other than friendship anyway. Why bother? But when he thought of why, he realized he was thinking about her body, having her body and her heart and that was why. Why get into that only to be disappointed? It was time to realize that he lived in a dream world when it came to women, placing them out of reach in his mind so that when he was with them he didn't have to reach for them and get into trouble. Only the drink loosened his restraint, and then he had another form of trouble, like the night with Michelle. "Give up, Jordan," he whispered out loud.

Maybe he should visit Jean, his counselor in Manhattan. It might be good for him to get out of Winslow for a break. After tomorrow. Tomorrow was the funeral. Emily would be buried first thing. He'd been avoiding that thought all day, but now he was alone and could no longer push it aside. He would go. He would try to compose himself. He would stand and watch her casket be placed by the grave and listen to the priest. It wasn't her, though. She really hadn't died. Her wide smile and petite childhood form running through the trees captured his mind. Tears formed at his lids.

Yes. New York would be a good idea. He gripped the steering wheel and turned into his drive.

Surprisingly, Rain's Toyota stood in the driveway. She was about to get into the driver's side when he pulled up beside her.

"Hi!" she said. "I left you a note."

"What brings you here?" he asked. She was dressed as she had been earlier in the day. They walked up the front steps and he unlocked the door and let them in.

"I wanted to tell you that Betty knows Peter Malmkoviz," she said.

They stood in the hallway. John flicked on a light. "And?"

"And, she said he lives in New York more than he lives here."

"How does she know him?"

"Flowers," Rain said.

"Flowers?"

"She bought some orchids from him years ago. At a town flower show. His were the only exotic ones on sale. She struck up a conversation, bought some orchid cuttings, and occasionally visited him to see his collection. She said he has since stayed out of the local flower happenings. Something about him disagreeing with the Winslow ladies' commission, the people who organize the annual flower event here."

John chuckled. "Flowers," he said, shaking his head.

"I also wanted to know if you wanted company tomorrow. At the funeral," she said.

He felt his face muscles relax in a way they hadn't for two days. She stared without expectation, her eyes so direct. He couldn't suppress a smile.

"You have the best poker face," he said, noting the softness creeping into his voice.

Her face cocked to one side, questioning.

He took her hand and led her to the couch. "Sure. Thanks, sure I'd like to have company. How did you guess?"

She settled at one end of the couch and crossed her legs. "Well, it's selfish, too. I don't really want to go alone, or with the Turners particularly."

"Let's go together then," he said.

He settled across from her in his chair. He would offer her tea in a minute. That would be nice. Right now, he was going to sit and chat, let her lead the conversation, allow her to stay until she decided to go, leave his own thoughts at bay. Her eyes were on him now, calm and pensive. Poker face. How did she do that?

Chapter Eleven

I t was a gray day when she was buried. He stood, as did twenty or so others, staring, unmoving, as one was taught during these events. Stand, in respect for the dead, pray, do as you're told. If you're a man, try not to cry. If you're a woman, cry. Grip someone near. Hold as if it were life itself, for a life has left us and we need to single it out, otherwise we have no understanding.

Inside a coffin, he had decided, during the experience of his mother's death meant nothing. You could make it what you wanted. Make the person beautiful, make the person bones, but in truth you would never know. Somehow, he found it all very disgusting and had at that same time decided he would be burned. Gone is gone.

Yet, today, it was Emily, and that wasn't someone from whom he'd been detached. This reality was his. He wanted to reach out and open the coffin, kiss her cheeks, jump in with her and beg her to return. If she did, then there was hope that he wasn't going to have to face this awful future without his finally returned companion.

Rain chose not to wear black. A gray and beige suit spoke to her western background, that tinge of defiance against the status quo and that inability to face weather other than long hours of sunshine that simply didn't allow for drab, dark colors. Her hair was shining and straight, as if the wind had blown any hint of curls. She watched the priest, half studying, half in a trance. He felt her reach for his hand and he gripped hard. We need one another.

The priest, Father Dominion, had known Emily as a child. A tall, hearty-looking man whose first burial had been a double suicide. John recalled that detail from one of Father's speeches during religious training when John was seven. Father had told them about his first days as a priest, how frightened he'd been. John, who hadn't been paying attention, had straightened up at the mention of suicide. This was an adult who'd been afraid and not ashamed to tell about it. Double suicide. How many other tragic deaths had occurred since then? How many had been brought on by the deceased themselves?

He studied the casket. Her body was long and thin. Even so, she'd fill half of the box. He felt the bones of her fingers, her cold touch, her hand grazing his skin, her fingers gripping his forearm as she laughed at some silly joke he'd just told. How could you have gone away from me? Just when you'd arrived, Emily?

Rain. Think of Rain. She's real. She's holding you now. She knew Emily.

It didn't help. Rain was not Emily. He noticed his heart now, how her name was special. Would another ever replace her? He would be forty this year and always there had been Emily. And his mother.

He glanced over the knoll. Darcy's grave marker was barely visible over the stone wall that separated the Protestants from the Catholics.

She was surely bones. But Emily. She hadn't begun to rot, or had she?

Grant them eternal rest, O Lord.

His only recourse was to study Betty and Walter. In doing so, his emotions shifted to a safer haven, that of his profession. Study them. They're hiding something. Or are they?

Betty, strangely, was not in her typical hysterical state. All in black with a half veil that covered her eyes and hung over an elaborate black felt hat, she seemed remotely elegant, her sophistication built into her wardrobe and her kid-glove hand laced around her dapper husband's arm. Every time John studied them, however, he was perplexed.

This union, and their offspring, never made sense to him. The parents of Emily, and still he could equate nothing of her to them. Walter's strut, his stolid countenance, for otherwise he'd break. Betty's fragility that so juxtaposed the slender yet indestructible embodiment that was her daughter. In between, this younger creature of nature, this child of laughter and release, constructed of two with hardened edges, undemonstrative actions, closed feelings. A hint of spring in the dead of winter.

What Emily really was, was his mother. She had Darcy all over her, except for the recklessness. Emily and Darcy were cut from the same mold, effervescent, fervently in love with the moment, careening towards life second by second. Darcy fell victim to the weakness that destroyed her. Emily had fallen, too, but not from a drug that could be inhaled or smoked or injected. What had captured her? Who?

Betty raised a handkerchief to her nose, blew. Walter adjusted his arm to allow for her movement. John determined to uncover the mystery. Her death, a death, the dying, that of course would remain a mystery. Strange, he somehow didn't want to know where Emily was now, didn't care about her body. He wanted to know something more, something that went deeper than Emily herself. Some truth that had gnawed at him for how long now?

Rain gripped him and for the first time he sensed her need for him, for his strength, if nothing more than a physical presence to hold her together as she collapsed as were others around them at that gut knowledge that they would never ever see Emily Turner again.

He held her and gripped, too, sensing not so much that he needed the support as that he'd need it later, when he was alone, for John faced the truth when he was alone, not in daylight, and certainly not in front of these mourners.

Where you are Emily, you see us now. There were some things that were as sure as the dawn. As certain as the night.

Holy water sprinkled across the casket. Betty watched the casket as if she wanted it, wanted to possess it, be it. Or was John reading too much into that haphazardly senseless stare that he'd seen not on her but on others, people who had no ability to comprehend. Betty sniffed, then smiled a smile that seemed to ease a tension she'd held by holding Walter. Now she stood on her own and watched the flowers that adorned the casket. Gently, she placed two of her orchids on the casket. Two white with purple strains and tied together with a white ribbon. Two delicate specimens that she delicately placed as if into a vase. Only the air caught their petals and began its work to wilt them, to destroy them as they gave off their beauty.

Orchids. Peter and his orchids. The orchid house. Two orchids on a casket.

Good-bye Emily, he attempted to think, but her eyes blazed again on him and she wasn't gone, not ever, not this time, not ever. He would see her again tonight in his dreams. He would know her for all the days of his life, as he had till now, and he would until he himself wilted away. Why they had never consummated a future he would now never know.

It was over as it began. Deborah made a point of inviting him to the mansion. Yvette had appeared at the service, and was presently getting into a limo some distance from the grave. Her purple suit and wide hat disappeared under the roof of the vehicle. Deborah followed, her wide bottom noticeable underneath the light blue suit she wore. Why a get-together there?

John followed her with his eyes, until the limo drove away. Rain's hand had slipped under his arm.

"Shall we go to Yvette's?" he asked.

"More information," she said. "Let's."

He admired her stamina. "You're not grieving, are you?"

Her eyes returned to the beautifully flowered casket. "What we live is what remains. She was a vital and energetic person. I have her memories. How can I be sad?"

"You're saying it makes no sense to mourn?" he asked.

"I will mourn, John. It will happen. That's normal. But I will stop mourning one day." She gripped his forearm. "Will you?"

He didn't answer her. It was one of those questions a man could get into trouble answering.

✳ ✳ ✳

The mansion was done up as if for one of Yvette's parties. He found Deborah right away, in the kitchen, commandeering the spread of food and wines. She was one sexy broad, he determined. Hidden under her layers of muscle, her rolled-up hair, was a tumble of woman. What did she do in her free time, he wondered? She eyed him suspiciously as he approached.

"I met Peter Malmkoviz," he said.

She nodded. "How's Peter?"

"He knew of Emily's death."

"He reads all the papers."

"Is he from Scandinavia, like you?"

Startled, she stopped what she was doing and gave John a steady stare. "Mr. Jordan, what does that matter?"

"How do you know him?"

She looked down at the tea cups she'd been arranging, her thoughts miles away. For an instant he pitied her.

"He was my husband, Mr. Jordan."

"Was?"

"Yes, he brought me into this country — sponsored me if you will. I owed him, plenty." Her sarcasm did not go unnoticed.

"He's much older than you."

She smiled, her gaze whimsical. "And I suppose he owes me as well." She stood straight, eyed John directly, without qualm. "And you?"

"Me?" he asked, gripped with a familiar tenseness.

118

"Why no marriage for you? Was it Emily all along?"

He wanted to resent this comment, and give it its requisite snub, but she'd hit on the very thought over which he'd mulled for many years. How many others knew him better than he knew himself?

She touched his shoulder and then he figured her.

"Why should you be alone? There are so many women. Me, for instance," she said. As quickly as the words came out, she let the comment pass, as if a reaction to it was his choosing.

She resumed her work. How to throw curves at an investigation, he thought. Luckily, the thought of embracing her did nothing for him. He stood tall, chose to ignore it.

"Then you and Peter go way back," he said.

If she was disappointed, she didn't show it. "Of course. To the fifties. I divorced him only a few years after getting permanent residency. I had no more need for him, nor he for me."

The bitterness in her voice was clear.

"Oh?" John asked.

Her eyes blazed as she gave him a final dismissive stare. "Get it straight, Mr. Jordan. People do what they have to do. Or are you perhaps too young to understand?"

With that, her tea cups neatly arranged on a tray, she excused herself.

Rain sat with Betty and Walter. John joined them as Deborah was placing tea cups on the coffee table in front of the trio. Walter was studying Deborah's breasts, not with the lust John would have imagined, but with a vacuous stare. Betty sniffed and patted a handkerchief to her nose while Rain whispered comforting words.

When Yvette appeared, it was in the company of Paul and Michelle, who had just arrived, Paul having gone to the station after the funeral to address other pressing issues. Michelle walked comfortably towards them, her simple black shift emphasizing her blonde hair. She nodded to John and sat in a chair opposite the others.

Yvette entered, waving to other invited guests at the far side of the room, then rushing to Betty and Walter and settling in a chair near them. She crossed her legs, adjusted her lavender skirt across her knee, and reached for Betty's hand.

"Betty, darling, how are you holding up?" she asked.

Betty coughed into her handkerchief and squeezed Yvette's hand. Walter looked down at the floor.

"So terrible," Yvette whined, "at her age, a heart attack of all things! Betty, cherie, why didn't you tell me? I could have seen to it she. . . ."

"Not an issue any longer," Walter growled, keeping his eyes down.

Yvette blinked and threw him a wide-eyed glare before turning to Rain. "You must be just beside yourself! Coming all the way from California to find . . . this!"

Rain replied, "It's a shock. The last time I saw Emily, we were driving along the Pacific Coast highway, heading for the airport. I gave her a lift so she wouldn't have to drive herself."

"Tell me, did she just love it out there? The weather alone is enough to draw one there, I must say. It's been an awful winter here. I'm thinking myself of moving back."

Walter stood. "Where are you going?" Betty asked him, her eyes watery.

"Out," he said, nodding to Deborah and ignoring Yvette.

Betty fell back against the back of the couch, watching her husband leave and placing a hand across her forehead. "So tired," she mumbled.

"Can I get you anything?" Rain asked.

Betty raised herself slowly from the couch, "No, it's fine. I'll just get myself to the bathroom. I'll be right back."

With that she disappeared towards the main hallway.

Paul pulled John aside. They walked to the hallway where John gave a glance up the staircase. The bathroom door was closed. "I'm heading to the office," Paul said. "There's a list of guests still to be addressed. I'll start that. Rain talked with Michelle. You're going to New York?"

"Peter Malmkoviz may be there. Also, Granger was relocated to a sanitarium somewhere around the city."

"You think you can find out where?" Paul asked.

John nodded. "I'll stop by the precinct. They'll help me."

Paul's eyes roved to his wife. "Going alone?"

"I'll ask Rain."

"Good idea."

"Paul, we should see what we can get on Deborah, her past, her arrival in the country—sometime in the fifties, her marriage to Peter Malmkoviz." He told Paul what Deborah had just told him.

Paul answered, "We'll get right on it. You going to be all right?"

John nodded. Paul was making an effort, a good sign. "I'll find out where Granger is."

"You think he's alive?"

"Maybe. If he is, he's probably not in very good shape. Someone should find Cheever. I've been thinking a lot about him and his relationship to Granger."

"I'll start looking into that, will fill you in on your return. Staying long?"

John shook his head. "The day tomorrow. Any longer I'll let you know."

Paul patted John's shoulder then squeezed. "Sorry about yesterday. You must be having a rough time."

"No excuse," John answered. "I'm sorry, so sorry."

Paul placed his officer's cap on his head. "So am I. It's forgotten now. Have a good trip."

John watched Paul let himself out the front door. Yvette appeared at his side.

"Hello," she murmured. "I was wondering if there was anything more I could do to help."

He didn't bother to look her way, turned his head instead to the closed bathroom door on the upper level.

"John?" Her voice was childlike, helpless. He smirked. What an act.

Her fingers dug into his upper arm and he had no choice but to look into her black eyes, now lined carefully with black makeup. Even in the subdued lighting of her hallway, she seemed to have a youthful appearance, as long as you didn't look too close, which he was doing now. Deep creases in her eyes, across her forehead, lining her mouth. He shivered.

"Stay until we tell you you can go," he said quietly.

She released her grasp on him and whined as she circled him. "But I absolutely have to get to France! They're expecting me!"

"They'll have to wait."

At the sound of a door opening, Yvette also looked up. Betty stood there, outside the bathroom. Her face was streaked with tears and makeup and she was unmoving, staring through John, her hands clenching the banister. He decided not to engage her, and returned her stare equally and unabashed. It made him think of the looks he gave Walter when, as a kid, John had been caught playing with the dog in the flower bed. Yvette, too, was oddly silent. Steps came from behind. Walter had let himself in as Paul exited. He passed John and made his way up the staircase, wordlessly moving towards his wife. Betty seemed not to notice, her eyes trained on John.

He wanted to ask her what she was thinking, but Walter reached her and touched her forearm, led her towards the top of the staircase. She allowed him to lead her but her face remained blank, her eyes open but not looking, her body straight and compliant. Walter was whispering encouraging words about making it down the steps and being careful. He led her out the front door and closed it behind them. John moved to the window and watched as they walked away, in the direction of their property, through the woods where Emily was found dead.

"Nom de Dieu," Yvette whispered, watching them disappear.

John left her in the hallway. He wanted to leave, too, but first he'd return to the sitting room, say good-bye, and arrange a time in the morning to pick up Rain.

※　※　※

The next day was warm and according to the weather reports would be the first good beach day of the season. John enjoyed days like this, a burst of summer before spring had a chance. The beaches weren't open for the summer crowds and you could walk undisturbed for miles along wild coastlines. Today, they weren't going to the beach.

Rain sat pensively beside him as he drove south on the interstate. When they arrived in southern Connecticut and after stopping for drive-through food, they found a shaded and somewhat secluded rest area to eat before hitting the city traffic. By early afternoon, they had traveled across the Hudson River and were maneuvering within the Lincoln Tunnel into Midtown. Rain hadn't been to New York since childhood and reveled in the strange expanse of what was still considered one of the greatest cities in the world. John enjoyed watching her reactions to the sights that he himself had seen enough of but that to her were brand new. He decided he wouldn't see Jean, it was too embarrassing to discuss in front of Rain, and right now he had other things to do and didn't particularly feel in need of "working on himself" as his kindly counselor would have described their sessions.

The Upper West Side was the location of one Peter Malmkoviz, a five-story townhouse building. A buddy of John's from the precinct had verified the address prior to their arrival. Peter's car with the New York plates stood in front. John and Rain parked across the street, watching for any sign of Peter from the building. It took almost two hours before he appeared at the front entrance and made his way to the car, driving in the direction of the West Side Highway and taking himself up the Hudson River valley. They followed him from a safe distance.

John had already researched the names of several high-priced long-term medical facilities around the city, including one just outside of Nyack, a short drive north from Manhattan where Peter was now headed. Not far from the highway but in a secluded stretch of woods a distance from the town center, a discreet sign on one side of a country road with high hedges displayed "Hudson Manor." Peter's car had disappeared behind the bushes well before John and Rain arrived; however, their entrance into the property was not as easily facilitated.

After passing two large stone pillars that marked the entrance, they drove for over a mile before arriving at an iron gate forming a border along with another bank of high shrubs around what appeared to be the property. Due to their lack of appropriate identification, a guard denied them entrance. He expected something specific that he would not describe. The mention of Stuart Granger did nothing to allow their entrance.

Perplexed, they sat for a minute or two at the guard station and then, due to the impatient and perturbed looks the guard sent their way, they slowly drove back in the direction from where they'd come. Before reaching the outer entrance, Rain asked John to drop her at the side of the road.

"Don't ask questions," she said, "just do it. Continue outside the property and wait for me. I'm going for a walk."

John's questions went unanswered and he finally let her descend and moved along himself, watching her slim form from the rear-view mirror. She sauntered as if on a Sunday afternoon walk, reaching to pick at a dandelion, arms swinging back and forth. From a distance, she looked like a young girl, her white sneakers bright in the sunlight, her hair blowing. What was she up to?

Outside the entrance, he waited for over a half hour before she appeared at the gate and moved towards his car, getting into the passenger side and bringing with her the distinct smell of fresh-mowed grass and spring flowers. She shoved a bunch of dandelions under his chin.

"Butter lover?" she giggled.

Taken by surprise, he laughed. It was the first time he'd laughed in several days.

"Thought I'd never hear you do that," she said quietly.

He wanted to reach for her but was afraid. Was that a good sign or not?

She let the dandelions flop over her closed wrist. "I was waiting for someone to drive by."

"What?" he asked.

"I figured someone, maybe someone who worked there, would drive by. It took a while, but someone finally drove out of the gate. I flagged her down. The woman in the car was irritable but when I explained that my car had a flat just outside the gate and could she give me a lift there, she calmed down. It was a nurse who worked the 7–3 shift. I only had a minute or so but she said that Stuart Granger was one of the patients."

John's face lit up. "How did you get her to talk?"

"She had been mumbling about what a lousy job she had, how she was looking for something new. I mentioned that it seemed a very exclusive place and she said only people with net worth of over $1 million were allowed. I told her my uncle Peter Malmkoviz went to see Stuart Granger, that I was waiting for his visit to conclude and had promised him I'd pick him up so we could get back to a display at the Museum of Modern Art. At that point, our nurse friend said that Granger was very ill indeed, but then caught herself and said no more."

"Good work, detective," John said. Her eyes twinkled and she lay back against the seat. "What now?"

"I'd say we found out what we need to know. Shall we wait for Peter to finish his visit?"

They decided there'd be nothing more to gain from waiting, that John could ask his former work associates to keep an eye on Malmkoviz. When Peter returned to Harley, they'd question him again. Going after Granger with no real reason could produce unfavorable results. Doctors' reports and other information could be obtained only with permission and warrants. They'd have to consult with Paul as well.

They'd made headway. The Malmkoviz–Granger connection was still very much alive. Granger himself had not died, but was very ill. Who then would be tending to the business affairs of Granger? Probably Cheever. He would be the next likely person to question, especially about how the transaction to build homes in the woods where Emily was found was going, as well as Granger's overall financial health. Other than that, things were too speculative at the moment. If Granger was unable to make decisions, and the land deal was on hold, there was really no reason to pursue the reasons that Peter still maintained a connection with the man.

They decided the better route to take would be to follow up on the past. Where was the birth certificate for Emily? Why was Emily pursuing her roots so intently during the last months of her life? What had she discovered? Why had she returned to Winslow when she did?

They mulled over all these questions during a deli lunch near Times Square. Rain picked at her food.

"Should we just let it be? Art ruled the death a heart attack," she asked John during a pause in their conversation. "Art himself said heart attacks occur even to young people like Emily."

He thought for a moment. Realistically, they had to conclude the investigation by finishing the work Paul had decided they should start — interviewing the guests, following up on Emily's health record, working with Betty and Walter. But, in that there was no concrete evidence other than the jeans swatch that John had misplaced, it could also be decided to end this work. Still, he shook his head. "Too many questions."

"For you?" she asked. She stopped picking at the bread and stared at him. "John, you might want to think about what good it's doing for you to continue on this case, to continue pursuing something that may in the end prove futile."

"If you're saying I should get out of the picture, forget it," he said. "If for no other reason than to get a better understanding of why she was running through the woods, running to my house, I must keep going."

"You may be asked to stop," Rain said. "I'm simply proposing what may happen. You need to prepare yourself for that, regardless of what Paul may decide."

He watched her as she talked, her voice full of compassion and her face so sparked with care. Was she like this with everyone?

"A woman has died and there's no reason for it!"

"The reason is, she had a heart attack," Rain said gently. "I don't like it any more than you, but it could have happened just as it appears."

His head was shaking. "Don't. Don't do that, don't do what everyone is going to start to do, what I've even done in the past. As soon as the body's buried and the attention veers to something else, the dead are forgotten. It's too easy to write them off, especially if there's so many fine lines and gray issues. I've seen it here, right here in Manhattan. People stop caring if the answers aren't obvious. I can't do that, Rain, I can't. Something was up that night. She was healthy and enjoying herself and several hours later she was dead. If there's no medical reason, no medical history, what happened?"

"Those are all good points. We'll certainly keep on this, and I'm sure Paul will, too. It sometimes helps to look also at the other options. Just don't lose sight of them."

He nodded, and refrained from saying what he thought, that there were no other options. There was a reason for this and he would discover it. Rain or no Rain. Paul or no Paul.

They took in a late afternoon show and then headed back to Winslow, arriving just before midnight. John left Rain at Walter and Betty's and returned home. Sami had stayed with Paul and Michelle, who kept very late hours. John was comfortable calling on them. They invited him in. Paul wore a stern look as he listened to John's update, then offered John a coffee.

"We have some developments here, as well, John," he said quietly.

Michelle had appeared at John's side on the couch. John, worn and unaware of Paul's regard, stroked Sami's fur.

"Peter Malmkoviz is dead," Paul said.

John chuckled. "He's not. We followed him. . . ."

"He died suddenly in a car crash late this afternoon. On the West Side Highway. Caused quite a traffic jam. One of your buddies from NYC called a few hours ago, mentioned you'd been asking for information."

"Car crash?" John whispered.

Paul nodded. "Collapsed lung and punctured artery. No chance of survival. No next of kin. If no one claims him, he'll be burned. You know the routine."

"No will? He was such a perfectionist."

"Not that we can uncover."

"He was married to Deborah."

Again Paul shook his head. "Nope. Never was."

John's brow crinkled. "I don't. . . ."

"Deborah was not married to Peter. Deborah was married to Cheever. The father of that young broker, Scott."

"Wait a minute," John said.

The two men stared at one another. Paul shrugged. "It beats me why she'd have told you otherwise. It's all documented. She married Cheever Sr. a long time ago, almost forty years now. We got a copy of the license from the county office."

"She's trying to keep me off the track, then," John muttered. He imagined her stare, that direct expressionless look that he couldn't decipher. Yet, at the same time, she seemed to be hiding something just beyond that stare. A familiarity. "I'm going back there."

"Why?" Paul asked. "What will you get from them? I suspect, even if they're trying to throw us off, that they'll stay put and stay quiet, especially to you. You might be better off trying to get answers in other ways."

John paused, looked at his friend. "What are you talking about?"

"If Deborah is lying, she'll continue to lie. How about going after Cheever's son? He may know something."

John thought for a moment and then recalled his first conversation with Cheever Jr. The man had been in a hurry to get out of town. Paul had a point. He'd get Rain to go with him to visit Cheever. She had a way with people. He'd also begun to miss her even after such a short time. Her gray eyes had a way of staying with him, forcing a feeling deep within, a feeling that had no name nor any shape he could discern, but a feeling he wasn't encouraging to leave him either.

Chapter Twelve

At the end of one of Cambridge's oldest streets, a winding brick road on which George Washington himself had trod, stood a stately stone mansion. Looking at once forbidding and venerable, its gardens and lawn enhanced its exterior while lace curtains hanging from tall arched windows protected the interior from curious eyes. Ivy wound around a wrought-iron gate that separated the street from a circular drive that otherwise could have nicely serviced some of the city's eternal demand for parking. Save a fountain bubbling a melody and a chirping sparrow flitting amongst bushes, no movement was seen.

John and Rain stood outside the gate of the home of Scott and Magrite Cheever, each holding one of the iron bars, staring like little kids who weren't allowed to venture further.

"Do you think anyone is home?" Rain asked.

"Sure. They're all in the back watching us fools drool over their multimillion-dollar pad bought for a song years ago. It's how many New Englanders made money—even some of the old-money types."

On receiving a quizzical stare from Rain, he continued. "Real estate. The best overnight success story, the prettiest gamble going for the 'establishment' around here. If you bought in the early eighties or before, your property value has easily tripled today, especially in hot places like Cambridge and Boston. If big daddy Cheever owned this years ago, they're sitting on a gold mine."

Rain nodded, satisfied but not impressed. He liked her for that, liked her ability to integrate facts and not allow them to overwhelm her. She wore a velvet sweater top, odd for the hot day, and jeans. The sweater's color matched her eyes.

John moved towards a gold plate near the entrance, at the center of which was a black button. He pressed and it made a distant noise, ringing from within the house.

A woman opened the front door and peered out. On seeing them, she returned to the house and closed the door behind her. After another few minutes, a man dressed in a black silk suit emerged. Of an age difficult to determine, his eyes, with their drooping lids, made him appear over fifty but his body was as fit as that of a football player.

"Yes?" he asked, slowly eyeing Rain then John.

"We'd like to talk with Mr. or Mrs. Cheever," John said.

"Do you have an appointment?" he asked, looking beyond them to the street where he seemed momentarily more interested in a passing Doberman and its owner, a tall, well-dressed matron who glanced nonchalantly his way. Two joggers ripped the reverie in two, so he looked back at John and Rain.

"No," John answered, "but it's in regards to an investigation."

The man stared blankly. Apparently, investigation or not, an invitation was the preferred way to introduce oneself.

Rain stepped forward. "Excuse us, we really didn't know that an invitation was required, but a friend of mine has died and we're looking into her death. Mr. Cheever is aware of this. We're from Winslow. I'm Rain Danforth and this is police officer John Jordan." She placed her hand into John's.

A shiver quickly gave way to a warm sensation that emanated from John's chest. There she stood, inches from him, holding his hand as if it belonged there. He'd never understand women. Ever. She smiled up at him and then at the man, who bowed and excused himself.

They were alone for several moments. She squeezed his hand then released it. The man returned to the house and closed the door behind him. He reappeared and from the front door released the gate so that it opened for the guests.

Inside, he ushered them through a great room and to the back of the house, reached by following a floor made of solid Connemarra marble. Rain kept pointing to its deep olive shade, admiration pouring from her face. They were seated and served tea before Mrs. Cheever appeared. Rain and John stood.

A thin blonde woman wearing a simply cut yet expensive silk dress of a fawn color that enhanced her blue eyes, she held a burning cigarette in one hand, her other hand she extended first to John, the narrow row of diamonds at her neck sparkling as she moved.

"Magrite Cheever," she smiled, giving John an approving nod. To Rain she managed a quick, fragile handshake, gesturing towards the sofa for them to sit down again. "Please."

For the first several moments, her breeding and composure seemed unrehearsed, as she settled into a straightback Louis XVI chair and crossed her legs, glancing out the window to a spray of phlox and geraniums. But, before saying another word, she inhaled deeply on the cigarette, stubbed it out, then lit another, ignorant of her guests and a maid who had appeared to clear away the tea.

Rain broke the silence. "Did you know Emily Turner, Mrs. Cheever?" She looked at John who nodded.

Magrite focused on the flowers outside. It was as if she'd not heard a word. She opened her mouth, then refrained from comment, only to begin again after another puff.

"Scott knew her. I saw her at the party, though."

"Did you talk with her?" John asked.

She shook her head, then her eyes darkened. She waited until a bird that had landed on the windowsill flew away. Then she stood and went to the window that overlooked the gardens. Puffing, she let out a long breath before answering.

"I was too busy watching Scott. I have to watch Scott when pretty women are around."

Her eyes slid downwards, then without moving she eased her glance to the side, towards where John sat, but she remained immobile, her back to them. She struck a magnificent pose. As the daylight was at its height and the sun streamed in, her body seemed to fill with the sunshine and the dress melted into the colors of the walls and the outside, the green bushes outlining her as if she were an apparition. Her thighs could be made out through the sheer material. There was something extremely delicate about her, yet her body was firm and straight. It was almost as if she preferred being on display rather than talking. She turned and sat down again, her cigarette having reached its end.

Lighting up again, she asked, "Why?"

"We're trying to understand what happened to her," Rain said. "Scott told you she died during that night?"

"Scott tells me nothing," she whispered. Now she looked directly at Rain, so suddenly Rain adjusted herself in her seat. Magrite's eyes were the dusty blue one would think of someone who seemed to melt into nature. Yet they were damp, tears rimming the lids. "Scott is a very busy man."

It was hard to know what to think about her. On the one hand, she appeared about ready to break, all cloudy and torn up. On the other, she sat there smoking, a dark tone taking over her voice as she spoke of her husband. There was nothing clear-cut about her.

"Then you haven't discussed the incident with him?" John asked.

"I read it in the paper," she said. "I read to pass the time." It was a statement evoking neither sympathy nor disdain. She returned her gaze, this time to John, expectant. Waiting for questions so that she could somehow reveal herself, then disguise her intentions so as to not let on really where she was coming from.

"Then he hasn't mentioned that he was at the Turner house the day after the death either," John said. "He told me then that you returned home that night around 2 A.M. Is that right?"

She nodded. "Whatever. I don't keep track of time."

Rain gave John a quick look, then said, "Forgive me for prying, Mrs. Cheever, but you said that you had to watch Mr. Cheever because he was interested in the ladies. . . ."

Magrite nodded, a hint of amusement in her eyes. She must have found Rain interesting, someone who wasn't deferring to the Cheever reputation that typically demanded reserve. "He fucks other women regularly, sometimes right in this house."

Her voice was so soft the words belied it. John found himself shifting uncomfortably. Rain however maintained her even voice and composure.

"I'm sorry to hear that," she said.

"No bother. I have what I want," Magrite said, gesturing to the ornate setup about her. "We made a deal years ago." Her eyes were sad.

"Deal?" Rain asked.

"He married me for money. His father had money, of course, but my family was from the South, real, old-fashioned, filthy-rich money. I was a wild, unkempt daughter that Daddy wanted hitched and out of the way. Scott graced the folks with his charm and education, and the deal was handled quickly and between men, if you know what I mean." As she talked, her accent thickened to an unmistakably southern one.

"Oh, I wasn't such a dumb broad, mind you. I wanted him, too. It's so interesting when you think you have your way and you really don't." She puffed. Her body remained motionless, something she did without thought, still and unmoving, like her attitude. Somewhere, years before, she'd hardened and wasn't going backwards now. "The running around was always a part of my life. I was foolish to think he'd stop. It doesn't even hurt anymore. What hurts is being alone."

"Have you thought of getting out?" Rain asked. "You're a lovely woman. I'm sure you could start again."

"There's no more of my money. Daddy gave it to Scott and Scott spent it, making damn sure I knew it. This new money is his alone. If I leave, he'll keep it. He has a right."

"How long have you been married?"

She smiled, slowly at first then more broadly. "Oh, honey, we're not married. He undid that as fast as he could. I just live here now."

John finally spoke up. "You're divorced?"

"No," she chuckled. "Annulled. We're annulled. He never laid a hand on me after the agreement, then a month or so after our wedding, he went to the church—his church—where he knew the pastor and could 'contribute' to the new rectory. He let a week go by before telling me."

"Why stay then?" Rain asked.

If she'd thought of an answer to that once, she'd thought of it a million times, John wanted to say on seeing Magrite's reaction. Her face paled and she puffed deeply, exhaling so as to release a film of smoke that hung in the air between her and her interlocutors.

"It's the way it is. My daddy made a deal with Scott. He'd blow Scott's head off with a shotgun if he knew. As long as Daddy is alive, I stay."

"In this day and age?" Rain whispered.

"Don't matter," she whispered back, sounding like she'd grown up in a barn rather than in riches. "Don't matter none at all."

"Do you long for someone to love you?" Rain asked.

"Daddy loves me," she said. "Ma daddy loves me."

John and Rain exchanged glances.

"Well, if you hear of anything at all, Mrs. Cheever, please let us know," John said, standing and handing her a calling card.

She smiled up at him, lingering her gaze as he waited for Rain to gather her things.

"We'll let ourselves out."

Magrite remained behind, staring at the flowers and snapping her lighter to begin burning another cigarette.

"What kind of a person does this to his wife?" John asked Rain as they walked away.

Rain was deep in thought. She took John's arm and they continued towards the subway stop they'd taken to get here.

The feel of her hand gripping his arm had a soothing effect and he found his thoughts veering away from Magrite Cheever. They passed several triple deckers. In the front yard of one of them, summer flowers bloomed in a small garden patch. A resident emerged from a doorway, then turned to lock the door behind him. John stopped short.

"A townhouse," he said.

Rain, who'd been tugged backwards by his abrupt move, brushed hair from her eyes. "What?"

"A townhouse, that's what Cheever said to me when he was at the Turners'. He said that he and Magrite returned to their townhouse in Cambridge around 2 A.M."

"Where we were just now was hardly a townhouse," Rain said.

He shaded his eyes from the sun and looked out over the river in the distance. "Let's find ourselves a phone book."

By making a few phone calls and asking Paul Allen to research a few unlisted numbers, they discovered that the name Cheever was found on many titles and deeds to property in Cambridge and Boston. Scott Cheever and his wife owned property throughout the two cities, and also in New York and Palm Beach. The townhouse Cheever had referred to could have been one just outside Harvard Yard, or another on the waterfront. Their research had prompted Paul to include a review of the ownership of the land around Winslow. Interestingly enough, over time, what had once been land owned by local farmers and long-time residents had been bought out by Stuart Granger. In fact, he still held the deed to Yvette's property, although she had taken a small mortgage out several years back and that bank note was in her name alone.

John and Rain took a good part of the next day pouring over documents at the county clerk's office. With the help of a paralegal, they managed to plot out the history of how various land tracts had moved into Granger's possession. Several Winslow developments, now over ten years old and covering miles of what was once pristine countryside, were owned by him. The wildlife sanctuary, a standing attraction for visitors from all over New England, had also been owned by Granger before it was donated to the state wildlife commission. These two pieces of real estate comprised over one-third of Winslow.

"How had he managed to get all this land?" Rain asked. "That parcel that was converted into houses was bought over thirty years ago in his name!" She nudged him, something he'd grown comfortable with over the last few days and the frequency of their togetherness. "Cat got your tongue?"

"Sorry," he said. "I was just remembering something." His eyes pierced a point on some place outside the window. "My mother told me once that she paid her last dime to Yvette so that the land on which my house stands could be ours. Yvette had always made a point to my mother that the land was never ours and so my mother took it upon herself to change that. It was not an easy thing to do. I remember her discussing the incident with Art and her continual visits to the bank to try and get financing. In the end, she lost it because she couldn't keep up the payments. Yvette won."

John stared at Rain. She had stopped listening to him and her distracted gaze wandered out over the landscape, viewable from a sooty, small window.

She pushed aside all the paperwork that had cluttered the desk they were at and sat back in the chair. "I can't help but wonder about Granger. How he's stuck in some sanitarium, helpless and alone. How Peter, who cared deeply for him, was for some reason cast out. How apparently so much of what was once owned by regular folks is now part of Granger's possessions."

"Granger owns half a county, plus lots of prime real estate in the Boston area, no contest, with no fights, except for this last go-around for housing," John said.

"The other interesting thing," Rain said, "is that most of these transactions were taking place at the same time, according to Peter Malmkoviz, Granger was growing incapacitated."

"Rain," John said slowly, then he stopped.

She looked at him expectantly, nudged him again. "What?"

"Why are we even worried about this? This has nothing to do with Emily." He was suddenly very tired. The last week had drained him so thoroughly he'd been running on empty and pushing in spite of himself. He sunk back in his chair and felt a huge feeling of doom drop into his stomach.

"Well," Rain began, "it may relate to why Scott also owns so much property, why Scott may be overly interested in the outcome of this investigation. Isn't he involved with the financial well-being of Granger Enterprises?"

Her methodical, measured voice was like the scream of a wild animal to John. He suddenly stood and began to pace, his voice rising as he spoke. "I'm not talking about that! I'm talking about how we're wasting time here on something that doesn't have anything to do with Emily!"

"But this is where our work has taken us. How can you be sure it has nothing to do with Emily?" she asked.

He hadn't eaten much and the craving in his stomach had been replaced by nasty spurts of bile each time his body sent him a hunger message. Refusing to address it through food, he found himself irritated and on edge, moving away from simple creature comforts to withstand some odd form of torture. What was with him? What was he losing, or gaining? It was a crazy time. Rain's direct question bothered him, to the point where she was beginning to annoy him. He wanted out of this room.

Instead he stood at the window, his back to her, settling into a stubborn, familiar silence, one he'd worked out as a child. His silences used to drive Darcy nuts. It was his only way to get back at her at times. Do nothing because she's expecting something from you. Some swipe of the hand, like his father, or some scream or stream of nasty swear words followed by yet another form of violence. It was why, following periods of John's silences, Darcy collapsed in despair. While for John this was his only way to cope, his mother had never been able to move beyond the quiet, never been able to understand its message, but she never hurt him either. His control, with its discreet side, had the appearance of a together situation.

With Rain, however, he wasn't sure. She wasn't his mother. She was a therapist to boot. She perhaps had his number long ago. Maybe she was staying with him because she realized from the start he was troubled. Really sick troubled. Like he was the one who needed the institution along with Granger. He noted the fear creeping under his skin and wanted to scream to her to say something. That mention of Emily had struck him, and all that followed in these seconds resulted from that. Some stupid watershed of feelings he was supposed to have worked out by now. Shit. The same mess all over again. Now he was in a room with a woman who could read him. He was trapped. Thirst seeped into his brain, through his skin, and into his bloodstream. The word breathed into his bones. He could sense the liquid's power without as much as a single drop.

Her hand on his shoulder. A touch that, had he been drinking, would have been the catalyst to action. Grab her, or hit her, or throw her around, or run out. Something like that. Instead, he felt her turn him gently around. His eyes were closed.

"What, John?" she whispered.

He leaned forward onto her shoulder. A weight so heavy he wished he could cut off his head to be free of the burden. Her arms surrounded him and for a moment he allowed himself the luxury of a sense of calm.

There were no answers. No answers at all. This woman was holding him up, keeping him from doing damage. He wanted to do her harm. How odd was that? How sick?

Her continued hold on him did the minimum. He relaxed and allowed her to walk him out of the place, to the car, where she took the keys from him and drove them back to Winslow and the Allens' where Rain insisted he stay for a few days to rest and take it slow.

"You're totally exhausted," Rain said as she and Michelle sat across from him in the Allens' living room.

"I can't stop now," he said, although he knew the words were unconvincing to them.

"You can and you will. Paul and Rain will continue to work the case. Although . . ." Michelle hesitated. "It may come to an end sooner rather than later."

He shared a look with Rain. Her prediction had come true. The authorities were tossing in the towel on this one. It wasn't worth the time and effort. He lowered his head into his hands. Just as things were starting to ramp up, he loses the support of the cops.

The two women in the room with him stared down at their feet. The silence allowed them to be entertained by the chirping of a lone bird as it hopped on the ground outside. He had a thought. A brief, chilling thought. It whispered to let her go, let Emily rest in peace and close the book without further ado. Even as this notion crossed his thinking, though, he laughed. The laugh caught the others off-guard, for he'd not laughed in days. Why should they stare at him that way? He was losing his grip anyway, why not let it all hang out now? For how could he possibly fight the others? He who was so weak?

Emily would disappear, as had so many others, with no answers. No answers because of ignorance, fear, and laziness. How many times had he seen this, and why should her case differ? He felt his shoulder raise in a shrug, an indication he had no opinion of the words that had just been spoken.

He wanted to sleep, close his eyes, and wake up in the morning and none of this would have happened. He was tired like everyone else. Why not follow the pack?

Then he nodded in agreement, slowly but undeniably. He thought he caught Rain's quizzical stare, but then again maybe not. Right now, he was going to lay back, close his eyes, and sleep.

Chapter Thirteen

When he finally woke up, he pushed the pillows into a pile and sat up against the headboard, staring out the window. Morning had cleared his head from the night before, but not so much as to pummel him into action. He would sit for a few minutes and collect his thoughts.

There was no time, however, because he heard Rain talking with Michelle. The phone rang once, then after several minutes a second time.

Michelle noticed him first as he stood in the hallway. "The Turner house just went on the market. Sarah at Realty Stop has the listing."

He looked at Rain. "Did they say anything to you?"

Rain shook her head. "No, they were both very quiet when I went downstairs today. In fact, Walter was outside earlier than usual, in and out of the barn arranging his outdoor tools and furniture as if they were moving tomorrow. Betty sat over a cup of tea in the kitchen and watched him. She told me I'd have to find another place to stay, that the Realtor would be in and out showing the place and Walter didn't want any more guests."

Michelle said, "The market is not very good right now, and that is a large, rather expensive piece of property. Out here in the country, it's not often that you find the right kind of person to buy it. The sale may not happen all that quickly. I wonder why they're so anxious for you to leave."

"What did you tell them?" John asked.

"I told them I'd start looking for another place today, but if they would allow me to stay on until I was able to do that, I'd be grateful. Betty seemed okay with it, but when she went out to tell Walter, he came storming in and said I had to be out by this time tomorrow."

"You can stay with us," Michelle said. "Don't worry about that. What puzzles me is the rush. Where will they go?"

They returned to the kitchen where Michelle prepared coffee and they continued the discussion. Michelle was struck by the fact that the Turners had lived in the town for so long, with no hint of retiring or living elsewhere and now they planned to leave.

"But I remember Walter that first day I arrived," said Rain. "He cursed this place and called it the 'back end of nowhere.' Perhaps he's always wanted to get out."

"No one was chaining them here," John said.

"Are you sure?" Rain asked. "What about Emily? What about her interests here? Was there anything about Emily's attachment to Winslow that kept her parents rooted?"

John shook his head. "I'd say just about the opposite." He looked directly into Rain's gray eyes. They were so wide and beautiful. He decided then he could wake up to them each day and enjoy them as if for the first time. "Rain," his voice was barely a whisper, "during your stay, did you ever overhear them arguing?"

Rain hesitated. "Yes. They argue constantly, almost every night. Behind closed doors, usually in the evening after they retired to their bedroom. My room was next to Emily's room so I wasn't that far away. I couldn't hear exactly everything they said, but it was the gist of things that bothered me.

"The arguing took a certain pattern. First, I'd hear murmuring, then usually it was Walter to raise his voice first, followed by whimpering or whining from Betty. They'd go back and forth for a while and then I could hear Betty crying, crying and talking at the same time. It was then Walter would start yelling, so loud I could hear every word. 'Shut up, you fucking bitch. If you don't shut the fuck up, I'm going to kill you.'

"That never seemed to do the trick, however. She would continue to cry. In time, they'd stop talking. I'd hear their bedroom door open then close and Betty's footsteps—she always wears these scuffs that make a familiar noise—going downstairs. She'd walk outside, no matter how cold or terrible the weather.

"One night I decided to stay up and wait for her to return, which she did after about an hour. She poured herself something from the refrigerator and returned to her room. I stayed in my room for another hour to ensure they were both sleeping. When I heard Walter's snores, I went downstairs and turned on the light in the entryway. The boots in which she usually gardens had wet grass and dirt on them. I broke off a clump of dirt."

She looked at John. "You'd mentioned Art's comments to me about dirt, so I thought I'd pay attention to the soil around the property. Over the last several weeks, I've taken samples and have read up on topsoils. It's very interesting actually. There can be vastly different types of soil within relatively close approximations. The land around here is a perfect example. Just into the woods beyond the gardens, you can find very acidic, crumbly soil due to the heavy concentration of pine trees. But not ten yards from there, closer to the orchid house but not yet surrounding the house, is this clay-like substance. Good drainage but not great for growing. The Turners must have brought soil in to use for their vegetable and flower gardening, because that area closest to the house is the rich, dark brown soil found on farms and in well-cultivated fields.

"The stuff on Betty's boots was more clay-like than anything. I watched her for the next several nights, especially one wet night when I thought I'd be able to find her tracks the next day. Sure enough I did." Rain let out a big sigh then, as if speaking of this was finally unburdening her.

"During her nightly outings Betty goes to the orchid house."

"That shouldn't be a surprise," John said. "We know her favorite flowers are there."

"I thought that at first, too. But I don't think it's just the flowers. I think there's something about that place for her, something she shares with no one."

"A secret?" Michelle asked.

Rain nodded. "A secret from most. But not all. I think Walter knows Betty's secrets, too. He yelled very loud one night and I heard his words. He said, 'Get that fuckin' chant out of your head: "not ours, not ours"!' He mimicked her voice. She cried and I know he hit her then, for she became silent. The whole house became silent."

"What in the hell is 'not ours'? She's said that before," John said.

"Perhaps their daughter," Rain ventured.

All three stared at each other. John stood, paced the room. His stomach turned and he could feel sweat on his palms, on the back of his neck.

"You mean 'not ours' means Emily was not theirs? Who's daughter would she be?" Michelle asked.

Rain gave a quick look John's way, then continued. "I wondered that, too. If we take that assumption as correct, there are some possibilities. I thought of Deborah or Peter Malmkoviz first. Deborah because we know she's lying about her past, or Peter because of his orchid connection to

Betty and his choice to remain in this area even though he clearly preferred living in New York. Plus now he's dead."

"And can't talk," John said.

"This is highly speculative," Michelle said.

"Believe me, I still have no answers," Rain said. "But no one does at this point. Perhaps it's the business I'm in, the business of digging in the past to sort out the present, but I keep going back to all the things that happened over the years. To you, John."

His back was to the women. He was staring out the window, past the rock bench that Paul had installed in the middle of the yard last year, past to the woods that rose to a ridge from where you could see into the area of town where he lived. Echoing through his brain was the voice of truth, and a confirmation to himself that Rain was onto something, something he didn't want to face. He knew enough to shut up, but he also knew he couldn't help them. Though he said nothing, they'd figure in time his silence meant he would not stand in the way of this line of investigation. He wanted to bury himself in the ground with Emily. That was how he felt and he'd have to hold onto that thought or he'd go crazy. Don't ask me to figure this one out. You're on your own, Rain. Good luck.

Rain accepted his silence and addressed him no further, but she did speculate out loud on Darcy's untimely and cruel death, on the sudden death of Peter, on the fact that Deborah was married to Cheever Sr. but pretended otherwise.

"Secrets. They're the keys that need to be used to open other doors." She said the words so softly, as if each one might pierce John too deeply and wound him.

He kept his back to them, now to hide his tears. So many damn tears in the last several weeks. She's right and she's onto something. There were too many secrets in this place. Takes a stranger to sort them out. We who are too close to them can't or don't want to see. He knew, too, that in being open-minded to the telling of secrets, one finally found peace. He knew it in his head, but his body and heart were still. There was no feeling coming from him. It was as if he'd reached a pinnacle and that was it, you didn't hope for more, you didn't make any more decisions, you left your body and faced what was beyond this life.

"The newspapers," Rain continued. "John, after you told me about your trip to the library I went there myself to review the old editions of the *Post*. There were twins at one time and that was reported in many articles. It was big news in this town. The only set of twins ever. So their lives were documented thoroughly the year they returned from

California, just one year old. Then, nothing, no coverage of the death of the first, no word about what had happened, no nothing. As if the first twin never happened."

"But she died in California, was buried there," Michelle said. "Wasn't there coverage of that? I thought Paul told me there had been a published obituary."

"Apparently, according to Joanie at the library, there was an issue, but she couldn't find it. It was the July 1953 edition and that has gone missing. Joanie was very upset because she wasn't even aware that it was missing. Since there are none at the library, there are none anywhere unless someone has kept copies all these years and they're stacked in some dusty pile in an attic."

"The year Emily's twin died," Michelle said. "Do you think there's a reason that of all issues that is the one missing? What clues could that hold, so many years later?"

Rain hunched her shoulders. "Emily was out west for one reason, in the end. To find out about her twin sister. I don't know everything, but I do know she found about the twin from the birth records, not from her parents."

"And the birth records showed Betty and Walter as parents. Why would you think otherwise now, Rain?"

"Because Emily was distressed about her family life. She never could pinpoint her issues. I concluded therefore, just before she moved on to another therapist, that her memories didn't hold the truth of her origins, that she never really knew the facts, but that being the sensitive individual she was, she knew too that something was not right."

Rain pointed to John. "John has also confirmed her unhappy childhood. You see, I've mulled all this over but unfortunately don't have all the answers, but I do know we need to keep focused on the past. I'd like to bring Art into this. He goes back far enough, he may be able to shed some light."

It was Michelle's turn to sigh. "Paul is leaning towards closing the investigation. Whatever is done beyond tomorrow, he told me, would have to be of people's free will and would not have the involvement of the police."

Rain said, "With the exception of Cheever and Deborah, I think I can work with Betty here and there, and Art seems to be the type who would want to cooperate."

John felt both women's eyes on him. He was out. He'd done what he was capable of. He wasn't able to touch this anymore. He knew one thing, though, he wouldn't get in the way of Rain. She was too strong, too powerful in her own subtle way. She would have to take this one forward. 'Cuz it has to do with me, he told himself. I know this has to do with me, too. And I'm afraid.

Rain met with Art the next day and told John that she'd be working with him and Michelle, that Paul would pay attention but assign no one to any further work on the case. At some point, there'd have to be creativity around their approach to Deborah, but until then they'd work with those who would continue to cooperate.

Michelle made all the arrangements for getting Rain settled with them as soon as possible. Rain would spend the night with the Allens and the next day Michelle would help Rain move her things from the Turners. They set up a time with Walter to ensure there'd be no interference with the house showing. Then they settled down to planning their next level of investigation.

At one point, late in the afternoon, John and Rain walked from the center of town the entire two miles to his place. He asked her if he could join them wherever they went, but explained as best he could that he wasn't really motivated to produce much on his own.

"That's fine," Rain said, taking his hand in hers. "Just being there is help enough. Sometimes just being there triggers something."

She stopped and placed her hands on his cheeks. Her eyes were sad, a look that he found vaguely unsettling and vaguely familiar. He wished he could untie the knot that kept him from reaching for her. But he was not able to. Stiff and distant, he stared back, weeping inside over the battle he was losing. One day, when this mystery is unraveled, you will leave this place and I'll never see you again, he thought. It's a damn shame.

"You've done everything you can, John," she said gently. "I'm very proud of you."

No one had ever said that to John Jordan. They were words meant for others. He tried to smile. He tried to raise his hand to hers but he couldn't. She lowered her hands and they continued towards the ridge, now a deep blue with the late afternoon light. Walking side by side but not touching, listening to the cheep-cheep of the bugs in the bushes. Soon, the fireflies would blink and the cool hill air would draw down the evening and Winslow would move into another day.

Deborah was waiting on the front steps. As they approached, she shifted from one foot to the next. In a navy skirt and shirt, her hair hung down her back in a long braid. From a distance, she looked younger than her years and John thought of her as a teen, an image he'd been working on since the day after Emily's death. She pressed her shirt on either side and tried to act under control but in this setting that was not hers, she was unconvincing.

"I'd like a word with you," she said, her voice barely a whisper. She took no heed of Rain, kept her eyes trained on John.

"Why?" he asked. He was tired. Little did she know she would soon be under no pressure to answer questions. The investigation was winding down.

"It's about your father."

She seemed to know this would give rise to a reaction. Before turning his face from her and staring at the ground, he caught the hint of a smile across her lips.

His father. Why would she want to discuss him? And why now? John didn't even want to discuss his father with anyone close to him, let alone this woman. His father was not the topic he'd choose, not in a million years.

Rain's hand slipped over his forearm. She whispered, "See you later."

He wanted her to stay, but didn't resist. As she moved towards the road again, her thin body blended with the trees and the night dew.

Deborah and he stared at one another. "Come in then," he said.

Behind him he heard her steps as she followed him into the living room. He had nothing to offer to drink so he sat down and let her choose her place. After a minute, she cleared her throat.

"I knew your father years ago. As a young girl. He was very kind to me and I fell in love with him. Your mother didn't know at first. I was alone, married to Scott Cheever's father. Our marriage was based solely on his lust for me, and I was one of many. The marriage allowed me passage into this country and him a reason for divorcing his third wife. I was very lonely, especially living out here. When Granger made some large land deals, Cheever Sr. built a house here to oversee the finances and consult with Mr. Granger. He felt it would be easier to be close to the action. Cheever left me alone in that house, the one that used to be on Norton Drive. It burned in a fire years ago. You wouldn't remember it.

"I would wander around this tiny place, stopping in shops during the day and spending his money, taking bike rides on the country roads. One afternoon, your father was sitting by Short's Creek. I came upon him suddenly and startled him. He was a handsome man. I was struck by his gentle demeanor, even as he was drinking. You knew he drank."

John nodded. He could see his father now, in that familiar crouch by a rock or along the banks. The man loved sitting by the river and thinking, and in later years drinking. John's earliest memories were of them walking along the creeks and rivers in the area. Yes, he knew he drank. How had John himself picked up that lovely habit? He smirked at Deborah, noting nevertheless that she was very serene and serious. A different sort of person than the one who played protector to Yvette.

"He and I talked for hours. It was so sweet. I remember the air that first day, so crisp and sharp with summer smells. He didn't want to fall in love, he said, but he had. We met after that almost every day. We'd spend hours walking and talking. Nights when your mother worked we met at the house after you'd gone to bed." Her voice lowered even though there was no one around for miles. "We enjoyed ourselves, we did."

"Why the hell are you telling me this?" he asked, annoyed now that this woman would presume this subject matter would interest him.

"Because your father knew a lot. He kept a lot to himself. He kept a lot from your mother."

"A lot about what?"

"About the goings-on in this town. Come on, John, you know there have been secrets." She stared at him, unflinching.

"Why did you lie about Peter Malmkoviz and what do you know?" he asked suddenly.

Taken aback, her face cleared of expression and she diverted her eyes from him. "I suppose I didn't want to tell you the truth then, which is why I'm here. Peter was a friend, a lover, but never my husband. Cheever was. If you knew that you'd have wanted to find out about him, and I really didn't want to go back in time on that. We divorced two years into our marriage, after the death of your father."

When they locked eyes this time, it was with the mutual certainty that there was something of value in what would follow.

"His death mattered to you?" John asked.

She nodded as a tear made its way down her cheek. "He and I wanted to marry but as soon as Cheever got wind of the affair, he arranged for Darcy to find out. At that point, your mother had begun to drink. Her drinking increased until neither your mother or father could hold down a job. Though your father and I talked about his getting on the wagon, he never managed to do so. Cheever just sat back and watched, then dumped me after your father died."

"Look," said John, "This is hard enough without you getting to the point. I know he drank and I know he ignored us. What's the bottom line here?"

She drew in her breath. "He knew about Emily's sister, the twin. He knew how the twins came into Betty and Walter's lives."

For a moment, John felt as though he'd been dealt a blow to his stomach. His breathing slowed until he had to gasp. "What are you talking about?" he asked.

"The twins were not Betty and Walter's. They were someone else's."

John immediately thought of what Rain had mentioned earlier. "Who?"

She scuffed the ground with the toe of her shoe. "I'd have thought you'd have figured that out by now."

"Why don't you tell me?"

"I can't."

"Why did you come here then?"

"I wanted to set you straight about my marriage. I'm not a liar. I was used by Cheever. The Cheever family is accustomed to using people. The young one, too. It's them you should keep an eye on. Who knows, what if Emily knew she wasn't Betty and Walter's daughter? What might she have been up to these last few months? Who was she talking with, who did she look up? She surely didn't spend her time at Ms. Peters's house. That much I know."

"I still don't get what you're on about."

"Yes, you do." Her eyes glistened. "You're very smart. Put yourself in Emily's place. Then figure it out."

"If you know and you're not telling, and what you know means we'd find out how Emily died, you're withholding evidence."

She shook her head. "No, it's not like that. What I know isn't worth anything unless confirmed by others, others who won't talk. You need to get to Scott Cheever, find out how they made all their money. Have them confess to the past fifty years of corruption. Therein lies your answer, John. I'm just a poor immigrant who was taken advantage of. I'll no longer put myself in that position."

"But you do know something."

"I know Cheever knows the truth. I know Granger, if you can find him, knows the truth, but whether or not you can get it out of them is anyone's guess." She turned and began to walk away, then stopped and looked over her shoulder. The light had faded and he couldn't make out her face. Was she looking at him or behind?

It was in that moment that he felt sorry for her. A prisoner of earlier choices in her life, she was not free to move beyond them.

"Wait," John said. He stepped towards her. "When I was at the Turners the day after Emily was found, Scott Cheever arrived unexpectedly. He said, 'Mr. Granger is concerned.' Why would he say that?"

Did Deborah know that Granger was in a sanitarium? Did she know why? If so, then she also knew that Granger was incapable of "being concerned."

"Sometimes it's a simpler task to attribute your own interests to others. Keeps the suspicions at bay," she said.

While she strode away, her words sunk in. She had a point. But were these words sincere, or were they tools she used to divert his attention? Something wasn't right about her arrival, this prompt and unsettling revelation, and her as-quick parting. Too tired for even thought, he shrugged and went inside.

✳ ✳ ✳

The dream that night lowered him to a place he'd never been before. Everything was dark as he traveled a rocky terrain, meeting his father's eyes only to find they were bleeding yellow and orange sparks, something spewing from the man's mouth, fearful and angry words shouting from noiseless mouths. He woke with a start. Sweat poured from his body.

Rain called and they agreed to meet later in the day, to try and uncover specifics behind Emily's borrowing of money from Yvette. They also had plans to contact Yvette's Spanish friend by phone. Rain spoke a little Spanish and they decided that whatever they might be able to glean from this woman would be of value.

That night, the Allens would help Rain move out of the Turners. Apparently, an offer had been made on the house already, but Rain wasn't sure who the prospective buyers were.

"They seem excited by this, as excited as these two get," Rain explained.

"You mean Walter's mowing the lawn twice a day instead of just once?" John asked.

Rain laughed. "Indeed. He's scurrying around like a chipmunk, moving boxes down from storage and arranging his tools and paraphernalia repeatedly."

"And Betty?"

"Betty," Rain said with a pause, "is quiet. She sits on the stool at the butcher-block table and sips tea. That's about it. She stares out the window, answers only if spoken to. It's worrisome."

"What about their nightly fights?"

"I haven't heard anything the last two nights, although it could be that I'm sleeping sounder. I'm glad to be moving out."

"Were you able to find anything out from Betty about Emily's bank account?" he asked. They'd agree to try and work the money issue through Betty and if that didn't succeed have Paul Allen authorize a review of Emily's bank activity.

"Betty had no clue. She said to ask Walter, which is as good as saying no way. I decided it wasn't worth it. She did produce Emily's checkbook and let me look at it. But, after a few minutes, she became agitated, started looking around like some sort of trapped animal and grabbed it away. Before she did that, I flipped through the register. No extraordinary sums were visible. It went back two years. She didn't seem to write many checks."

"Walter was a stickler about her not spending her own money. He probably provided for her while she was here."

"Based on how she lived out west and the checkbook, I highly doubt she was into a large sum of money."

"Then Yvette was lying," John said. "Not unusual." His dream came to mind.

"Well, shall I dust off my Spanish and give Marguerite a call?" she asked.

Her smile was wide and he thought of taking her picture. Then, once she was gone, he'd have something to remind himself of these days. He'd bring one along the next opportunity.

They went to the Allens and placed the call to Madrid. It took some time to bring Marguerite to the phone but, once she was connected, Rain entered into a lively discussion in Spanish. She spoke better than she let on. When she hung up, her face was flushed.

"You speak very well," John said.

She smiled, "It came back easier than I thought. The woman knew both Yvette and Granger. She said that Yvette did change her plans to return to Europe. The day after what we know was the day Emily died, she received a phone call explaining that Yvette would be arriving that day. Marguerite, who seems to be a very organized person, was flustered with the change in plans. She must be involved in philanthropic activities because she mentioned a charity dinner in Madrid that Yvette wanted to attend with her and she had been worried about getting the okay from the attendees.

"Then, within a twenty-four-hour period, Yvette reverted her plan back to the original one with no explanation."

"How do you know she knew Granger?"

"I explained what had happened. Marguerite was very upset to hear about Emily. She said she knew the child."

John squinted. "How?"

"Well, that's where I'm not sure. Without seeing her facial expressions, it's hard to say. She said, in a rather hesitating voice, that she'd been to Winslow and met the twins years before."

"But the twins—the two of them as babies—were only in Winslow for a short time apparently," John said.

Rain nodded. "I didn't quite follow. Marguerite rambled on about some movie Yvette was in years ago. What I did catch was her suggestion to see it. *Something Winning* she called it. She was also wondering when Yvette was arriving, now that the date has come and gone. Apparently Yvette has not been in touch."

They told what they knew to the Allens, with whom they gathered later in the day to collect Rain's things at the Turners'. Neither Paul nor Michelle, who lived in the town since childhood, recalled a Spanish visitor. Michelle said that would have made just as big of a news headline. Unable to further figure out what Marguerite had said, they busied themselves with the task of moving Rain.

It wasn't long into their stay at the Turners' when the news broke. The house had for sure already sold. Walter proudly pronounced this as they were placing boxes and suitcases at the front entrance, readying to move them to Paul's van.

"Yes, sir," he whistled. "In no time this place went, just as I expected." As he spoke, he made sure to inspect all activity while Rain's things were removed from her room, to ensure no one messed or scuffed his floor.

"Who bought it?" Rain asked.

Walter shrugged. "Some corporation. They want it for retreats. Isn't that the limit! What people do today with their money."

John and Rain exchanged puzzled glances. Rain asked, "Where's Betty?"

As he turned to leave the room, Walter said, "In the orchid house."

Rain and John found Betty sitting amidst her plants, as if she would never move from there, as if the flowers were to stay indefinitely. Still and unresponsive to Rain's greeting, it took Rain's nudging her to move her glance in Rain's direction. When she stared up, her eyes were miles away.

Rain placed a hand on Betty's shoulder. "You'll be moving soon, I heard."

Betty's eyes fell. Then she grabbed Rain and pulled her close. Betty shivered and dug her nails into Rain's skin.

"Are you all right?" Rain asked.

But it wasn't in Betty to respond. Her eyes had glazed over and gradually she loosened her grip on Rain, settling into the stool as if she were alone, staring at nothing, still.

"Betty," John said, but received no answer. "Betty, do you need anything? Can we help?"

Rain and John stared at one another. Again John was touched by the look Rain gave him, the familiar and comforting look of someone you knew well. It was becoming so real to him that he wondered how he would go on without it. They sat with Betty for several moments longer but she didn't change her position. There was nothing to do but return to the house. Whatever was going on with Betty was not something they could rightfully intrude upon.

"It's a shock, I'm sure," Rain said as they walked from the orchid house. She scuffed her feet purposefully, eyeing the varying shades of gray and brown.

"Dirt study?" John asked.

She smiled. "It is unusual, John, really. One would think the land was brought in or something. It's so different from right over here." She pointed not far from them, to the nearest vegetable garden.

"C'mon, this place is giving me the creeps," John said. "We should go see Art about what Deborah said. Perhaps he can shed some light."

Rain shook her head and looked back at the orchid house. "I don't know, John. Art has cooperated from the beginning. Would he really have anything to add?"

"I doubt it. Somehow, though, it's comforting to sit and talk with the guy. We'll see."

They agreed to meet later that afternoon. When John arrived at Art's office, he was surprised to see no patients sitting in what was normally a full waiting room at that time of day. He found Art sitting at his desk, the swivel chair turned to face the window.

"Art," John said.

The man waved him in but didn't turn towards him. "Do you know who bought the house?" he asked.

"No," John said.

"Scott Cheever."

"What? He has no business. . . ." John was too startled to go on. He sat in the chair across from Art. "I don't get it."

"I do," Art said. "It's part of the long-term plan. The plan to take over the town and the surrounding natural beauty. It's always been a goal of Cheever's. He knows Winslow is the gateway to the western half of this state, a place that could serve well to those who want to get away from it all and not be too far from home. If he owns the properties, he owns the choice as to how building moves forward."

"The town voted down the last Granger/Cheever venture," John said.

"Yvette Peters voted down the last Granger/Cheever venture," Art said, turning around. "John, Yvette has intentionally squelched everything Cheever has tried all these years. She never wanted Granger to get near this place again, she wanted control, somehow, over the man who dumped her and embarrassed her way back when. Her only way was to mount a massive campaign to thwart any attempt on Granger's part to further his real estate and financial kingdom in this area. That is why she worked on appealing to the local folk. That is why the extravagant parties. The trips here, the middle of nowhere, when she really belonged in Monaco and New York."

"That was so long ago."

"Vendettas die hard, especially ones begun in the old world," Art said.

"What are you talking about? The fact she came from France?"

Art nodded. "It's bizarre, and not really something I fully understand, but the European way of holding onto things seems to be Yvette's way, her main focus unfortunately. I remember years ago talking with Deborah. She came to see me for a checkup. She explained this notion of old-world control, machismo, the not letting go just because, almost the way the Mafia used to operate. Since Granger dumped Yvette, Yvette had to get back."

"It seems ridiculous after all this time," John said.

"Think of what she has to live for."

"Well, she could build a new life."

"She did. And this is it. She began staying in Winslow for longer and longer intervals of time, until Emily's death. Now she can't get out quick enough."

"Therefore, this time it was easy for Cheever to move in. Do you think Yvette will pull out completely once this investigation is over?"

"Don't know." Art looked into his eyes. "How are you doing anyway?"

"I'm tired, and I don't want Rain to leave." It was the first time he'd said that out loud.

Art smiled. "Why should she leave?" He stood, brushed his suit jacket.

"She's leaving," John said, standing as well and readying to leave.

"Have you asked her to stay?"

As he turned to go, he gave Art a thoughtful nod. "I can't do that."

At home he was restless. Art's words played on him, as did the conversation about Yvette. Why was she so anxious to leave now? Did the death of Emily have something to do with it? It had to. She changed her plans with Marguerite following the death. She was unavailable for comment the morning after. Why did she care so much about Cheever not making any financial gains in Winslow? Was it still such a silly notion, this idea of vendetta? And now this revelation by Deborah about his father. He lay down on the couch.

If he had a drink right now he could work this through. He could use those old faculties that allowed him to rationalize life away. He could numb himself to the reasons people did things and the fact he wasn't involved.

This time, he was involved. This time it was Emily rotting in the ground. Like his mother rotted away. They died young, they died vulnerable. Someone or something killed them. Now, as with his mother before, he was witnessing the closing of the books on this case. He could not let it happen.

His heart raced. She was too beautiful, too full of life. There needs to be a full circle here, not for the police registers that would consider due diligence done once all the reports were typed up and a big fat "unresolved" was stamped on the file, but from deep within him. He could feel his mother's hand on him, caressing his arm as she had so many times in her drunken stupor, imagining her little boy to be a man who she loved, or someone who could hold her and take her away from all the misery that she'd visited on herself and that had been visited on her. A stroke of feeling that John interpreted for love, but was really clinging and dependent ownership. It was an ice touch that he feared more than death itself.

Rain had touched him and said she was proud of him, a touch that was not laced with hatred and past angers, a touch that soothed and comforted and broke him. He was confused and it would be better right now, in this very minute, to slip back to his old ways. Then he'd be in control. Alone, in this house, where her spirit drifted, he was victim to the ghosts. Rain was not with him. If he wanted her to be with him, he'd have to open up and tell her, expose himself. He couldn't do that. He kept feeling the ice touch and thinking Rain's would eventually turn into an ice touch.

His eyelids drooped, heavily. He fought it for only seconds and then succumbed, the last flicker of consciousness telling him this was a good thing, to sleep. Sleep meant he didn't reach for a sip. Sleep meant the evacuation of the noises that swept through his consciousness and made him think.

Darcy had looked so pretty that last night. Her hair was pulled up in some European style she had chattered away about. I look like Audrey Hepburn, don't I? Her voice was sweet and she did indeed look like a fragile movie star, another creature than the one he'd been living with since his father's death. Resignation? Was she resigned to something that night? She kissed him good-bye and told the sitter to sleep in her bed. It was a normal scene. Mother going out leaving son with the sitter. Her kiss was wet and full and he didn't feel a chill at all. Still, it was removed. It was distant. She had her mind elsewhere when she kissed him that night.

He went to bed and fell asleep easily, with Jeepers snoring on the floor and the sound of the television in the living room. Safe. Not alone. Protected.

After, when he woke in the middle of that night, with the phone ringing nonstop, he neglected to wonder why the sitter hadn't woken. He picked up the phone and heard his mother's voice for the last time, drugged with drink and screaming at him to help, begging him to come get her.

"They're after me, John. You have to come here, come get Mummy. I know too much and they're going to kill me, like your dad. They're going to kill me!"

The line went dead.

The next morning, Darcy Jordan was found rotting in the woods, her body devoured by wild animals. John was carried from the house to the horrid scene and then to a waiting car where Art took him in for several days. There was a quiet funeral. John Jordan had no mother or father and he was only nine. Art and Min took John in and treated him like their own son. When he was fifteen, he decided to live on his own in the house he still called home.

Forgetting Darcy's last words was what he'd done all these years. Now, a grown man, an aging man even by some stretches, he almost let it get by him again. But this dream held, this dream was what had been sitting inside him. Darcy had called him and told him someone was trying to kill her because she knew too much.

His father had known too much, Darcy, and Emily. They all found out something.

He thought of calling Rain but before he could reach for the receiver, she called him.

"Rain," he could hear his own breathless voice ringing in his ears. "Rain, I remembered something. It's related to Emily. My mother knew something! My father, too! The night she died, my mother, she called me for help. I'd completely forgotten. She was running from someone who was trying to kill her. It can't have been the animals, Rain, she had to have been killed first. Or left drunk."

His eyes watered. Rain's shallow breathing at the end of the line was enough to keep him going.

"Rain, there's a connection, I just know it. I'm not going to give up now. Even if we have to pull my mother out of her grave. Art will help. Someone wanted to hush my mother up. Hush Emily up. Is this making sense or not? I'm sure there's something to this, and I remembered. It's been on the edge of my mind but I've not been able to bring it out. Tonight, something clicked. Rain, what do you think? Am I making sense? Should we get to Art?"

Her voice was unsteady. "John, I, I really don't know right now."

"What's wrong, Rain?"

The whimpering at the other end of the line gave him a chill. So unlike this woman who had provided him so much strength.

"Rain, are you okay?"

"No . . . John," she said.

"Tell me! What?"

"Betty has committed suicide," she said.

Chapter Fourteen

He was outside his house getting into his car when Paul Allen appeared. "John."

John eyed Paul, then lowered himself into the driver's seat. He leaned out from the window.

"Stop. You can't go there now," Paul's voice cracked.

"I'm going."

Paul reached for him but it was too late. He'd already turned the key and backed up the car before Paul had a chance to restrain him. As he drove out, he noted Paul's police car following him, its lights flashing.

By the time he'd reached the Turners', the siren was blaring. He got out only to have Paul follow him and try to grab him. Michelle came out from inside the house. She reached for him as well. Both Allens struggled for minutes as John tried to get away from them.

"Let go! Who the hell are you? Rain's inside!"

"John, you can't go in there!" Michelle exclaimed.

Wrestling one arm free, he slugged Paul with his free hand and broke loose. Running, he made it to the breezeway. Another officer was bent over some paperwork.

"Where's the body?" he demanded. The officer pointed upstairs.

In spite of John's speed and advantage in years, Paul still managed to nab him on the stairway, swinging a punch into John's stomach that was strong enough to stun him and force him to lean against the banister.

"John, you're not going up there!" Paul yelled, calling for the officer downstairs to come help. The two led John to the couch near the fireplace. "Stay here until I tell you otherwise. Frank," he nodded to the other officer, "don't let him out of your sight."

"Where's Rain?" John mumbled.

Paul didn't answer. Stabs of pain continued to radiate from the spot where Paul had slugged him. From the corner of his eye, he could see Michelle moving towards him. She placed a hand on his shoulder.

"Where is she?" he asked again. "Rain."

"She's been taken to the hospital, John. It's only a precaution."

"What? Why?"

Michelle had tears in her eyes. "Walter tried to rape her."

He looked into the usually cheery eyes to understand the words he'd just heard, but Michelle's ability to compose herself had been shattered. What he saw was her suffering. The incident in all its grotesque detail was written in every line on her face.

"I want to see her," he said.

He looked up to the balcony and staircase, from where two medics were raising a gurney. He stood, ignoring Michelle's arm tugging at him. She released her grip. Taking the stairs slowly, he stepped towards the sounds coming from Emily's room. In the doorway of her room he stopped.

The first thing he noticed was a hand hanging delicately from a body that was strung up to the ceiling by a thick rope. She wore slacks and one of her print shirts; her feet were bare. The hair hung over what John knew was by now a bloating and discolored face. He was grateful to not see her expression. Dead, she was helpless, more helpless than she had been in life. The photographer was taking final shots and an officer had begun to fingerprint the room. Both moved around routinely, stopping only to detour themselves from colliding with the hanging body.

He would not be able to ask her what she knew about Emily. And what she knew had to have been a lot. She must have kept it all inside, struggling each day with whatever agreements she and Walter had made to maintain the life they'd chosen over facing the truth. Tortured in her choice, she grew numb and, in spite of the buttress to her emotions that was her husband, she couldn't help spilling her heart. Tears, rages, silent moments, and periods of incoherence marked her struggle. Others observed and commented but did nothing, watching instead from afar the deterioration of a woman so disintegrated in her own pain that she had to take her own life.

In Emily's room.

The aides detached her from the rope, carefully placed her on the gurney. Her open, bulging eyes were closed by a gentle hand. The zip of the body bag rang hollow in his chest. This ending chapter had no mark of finality. On the contrary, he felt as though the story was just unfolding.

He pitied Betty. He felt sorry for her. But why? She's lied to her own daughter, robbing the child of her true heritage and birthright to maintain some secret that brought both of them down. She had aligned herself with Walter, a man equally tortured and with a streak of violence.

Why couldn't they be caught in time, people who in some instant of insanity or intense serenity choose to take their lives? How could have this been prevented, or would that have helped Betty in the end? She would have gone on living a lie and living with the pain. Perhaps this was the best for her. But her secrets died, too.

The room emptied as the body was taken away. For several moments he was alone in the bedroom, emerging from his reverie to note he was staring out the open window at the orchid house. In the emerging daylight he could barely discern several shocking pink flowers. He would have expected her to kill herself there, that place she escaped to when she had to get away from Walter. Instead, she'd chosen Emily's room. Or had it been a choice? Had she her wits about her enough to make a choice? Maybe it had been an odd form of communicating a message, to Emily, to those left behind. There was a spade and hoe leaning against the building, and a rise of dirt to one side. Otherwise, the little house was as usual, waiting for Betty to come inside and become one with her flowers.

Michelle entered and came to his side. "John, why don't you rest downstairs, or at our house?"

"No," he shook his head. "Which hospital is she at?"

"At Trinity," said Michelle, referencing the nearest hospital.

"Is she all right?"

"She's bruised."

"Where is Walter?"

"No one knows. His car is gone and it appears as though he left without taking much. Paul is looking into it now. They can check the bank, too, to see if he's drawn money from their account."

"I'll be at the hospital," John said.

"Do you want company?"

"No."

He left and hurried to the emergency room of Trinity Hospital, a place he knew as well as his name, a place he'd grown to abhor due to the ends he witnessed, many like the one tonight. He found Rain. She lay with her eyes closed in one of the curtained-off beds. A bandage covered her forehead and one eye was swollen and black and blue. A bandaged hand moved up and down across her stomach as her breathing came slowly. She wore a hospital gown. Her hair was caked with dirt and her lips were cut and bloated.

He wanted to kill Walter. Grab the man and massacre him on the spot. Show no mercy. Who would do such a thing to someone so innocent and with such genuine compassion? Who would even try? A madman.

A nurse entered. "Officer."

John nodded. It was Gina, his old friend, a small, graying woman with years of experience in Emergency. Both were no strangers to assaults like this. "Gina, how bad is it?"

"She'll be okay, John. They're running tests now." She touched his shoulder. "She wasn't violated."

He shook his head. "She was violated. She was. Look at her. He smashed her face. He wrecked her hand. She is violated, Gina."

"She's going to be okay."

Rain's eyes fluttered.

"I wouldn't press her too hard right now," Gina said. "You have five minutes." She left.

John watched Rain's eyes open, blink at the ceiling several times, then widen for an instant in a horrified look he remembered seeing on his mother. Their faces blended for seconds, then he noticed she was staring at him.

"Hi" was all he could manage.

A tear curled down her cheek. The fingers of her bruised hand wiggled slightly, then she closed her eyes again.

He reached for her wrist and held, repeating to himself Gina's words that Rain would be okay. He couldn't ask questions, that was clear. Rain was still in shock.

She surprised him, however. Eyes again opened she cleared her throat. "Hi."

Blinking back his own tears, he watched as she tried to compose herself to talk. Struggling with the pain that must have been masked by drugs, she appeared to be making a mental check of her body, piece by piece, gradually realizing that she was all together and that she could attempt to come to. She stared at him, a look of calm mingled with fear.

"I couldn't struggle with him. He was angry and stronger than me," she said.

"You don't have to talk."

"I want to." She squeezed his hand. "I got to the house and he and Betty were standing in the kitchen. It was clear they'd just had words.

Betty was in a corner and then Walter began pacing. The look he gave me . . ."

She stopped, placed her undamaged hand across her brow, felt the bandage. She closed her eyes.

"Rest, Rain, we can do this later."

She turned her head slowly left then right. "No. You have to find him. He's dangerous. Betty ran upstairs and closed the door. He started to follow her, then stopped, turned to me and came real close, grabbed me before I could do anything. He accused me of upsetting the entire house, of getting in the way. At first, I tried to reason with him, but his voice was charged and his body was trembling. I asked him what was the matter, why he was so agitated. He denied being agitated, then he calmed somewhat, but it was only a ploy. His eyes glazed over and he drew me close, hugged me and started to whimper. His hands reached down my back and his embrace was so tight my breathing was interrupted. I tried to push him away. I asked him about Emily. 'What did you do to your daughter?' I asked. This caused him to relax slightly and I detached myself. By then, though, he had made up his mind to have me. I could see it in the way he studied me, his eyes running down my body. I became frightened.

"He said he did nothing to Emily, that Emily did it to herself. 'What,' I asked, 'what did she do to herself?' He laughed, said she had no ability to handle life, that she was a weakling, like me. He grabbed me again and I tried to get away, but he punched me in the stomach and then tried to kiss me. I couldn't breathe, between the hurt in my stomach and his mouth on me. We struggled. He kept saying 'the bitch, the bitch.' I don't know who he was talking about.

"He tore my T-shirt, threw it on the floor. He began kissing me, my breasts. I tried to scream, but his hand was across my face. He had been drinking. As we struggled, I looked up. Betty was watching us, a queer smile pasted to her face. I'll never forget that look. Then he began smacking me again, trying to get me to the couch. I fought with everything I had, but I could feel myself weakening. Then I don't remember anything. He must have punched me."

She closed her eyes. John rubbed her forearm, so thin and white, so delicate. He wanted to take her in his arms and comfort her. She fell asleep. Gina returned.

"Time's up," she whispered. "We're taking her to a room now." Gina prodded John with her hand. They went to the hall.

Two nurse assistants went to Rain and readied her for the ride to another ward. John followed as they maneuvered the gurney to the elevator where the doors closed on her and the nurse. He made his way to the ward and had been sitting in the waiting room for some time before a nurse allowed him to see her. She was sleeping soundly and all he could do was sit and stare, an activity he drew a peaceful pleasure from in spite of her wounds.

For a long time he mulled over her features, her slender arms, her steady and slow breathing. In spite of her arresting presence, he then began to go over the events leading to her being brought in to the hospital.

She had to have found out something. Was she going to remember it? Walter wouldn't have attacked her without reason, would he? Was he simply a dirty old man who had lusted after her? Impossible. The man was running now, he had to have tried something with Rain, he had to have had a hand in Betty's death, if not the actual deed, the events leading to it.

Betty. She must have known that the investigation was closing in on them. Though there was nothing specific, the two had continued to remain reclusive and uncooperative. In staying at their home, Rain must have scratched a very fragile surface. The presence. Her presence. A woman the same age as Emily.

The pain of memory struck. Emily's face appeared, both in her youth and the night she died. Had the same or similar events transpired the night before as on the night Emily died? Had Rain touched on a truth that Walter didn't want to deal with? Had Emily? Something triggered a response from both of them during this night. Had the same thing happened with Emily? This time, it forced Betty's hand. A weak and frightened woman who took her own life.

Scratch that. Someone doesn't necessarily take their own life because they're weak and frightened. It could be an act of great strength. Since his mother's death, he'd gone over and over the notion of suicide, of how it comes in many forms, of how it was plausible that both his parents had in fact taken their own lives rather than fall victim to accidents. It was what he believed in his heart. Betty had a strength. She had raised Emily, that alone proved she had staying power. The dynamic that was she and Walter must have worn her down, especially once Emily was out of the picture.

Rain's eyes opened. The nurse was in the doorway. He wanted to embrace Rain, hold her tight, and assure her everything was going to be all right.

"It's time to go," the nurse said.

Rain stared unblinking at him, then her eyes fluttered and she seemed to drift. "I love you," she whispered.

He leaned forward to hear again, but she had fallen asleep. A warm feeling emanated from deep within him at the same time he began to shake. What had she said?

"John."

He glanced up, then back to the bed, where her small form seemed to disappear into the white sheets. Slowly, he got up. "Rain," he whispered, but she didn't respond.

Outside the room, his legs were weak and he took his time walking down the hall. The antiseptic smell filled his lungs. Hospital noises distracted him. He pressed a bit too long the big, white elevator button marked "Down." In the lobby, he passed wheelchaired people, happy families with newborns, and harried-looking medical personnel. Inside his head was very quiet, very serene, very frightened.

Chapter Fifteen

T he bold gold sign, Cheever and Associates, stood on the corner of one of downtown Boston's main streets. Impossible to ignore, it basked in the shadows of the hot July Saturday, heralding the modern steel artwork entrance to the high-rise offices. Traffic was reduced to weekend visitors and the usual smatterings of workaholics. Pedestrians paused to snap pictures of the forty-five-story structure as they followed the guided path of the Freedom Trail.

John entered the building and announced himself to the guard at the front lobby, who immediately placed a call. Replacing the phone, he nodded to John, indicating the left bank of elevators, the ones that ran to the top of the building and Scott Cheever's private offices. At the forty-second floor, he alighted and was greeted by a young receptionist dressed in a tailored dark suit.

"I'm here to see Scott Cheever," he said, noting her long nails, platinum-blonde hair cut severely to the chin, and a pouting mouth painted vermilion.

Barely nodding, she pressed the intercom and without asking John's name, announced him. "You can go in." She pointed to glass doors.

Once behind them, John followed a corridor carpeted a plush, dark green. The maroon walls appeared freshly painted. Whiffs of cigar smoke met his nose. He wanted to turn and leave but thought of Rain and walked on. This man Cheever knew something he wasn't telling. He also knew about land deals in Winslow, the Turner property being his latest. A grin crossed his face. Funny, he thought, he and Emily had dreamed of overtaking the town by buying out land from Granger. Now, much of the land was Cheever's and John was as far away from being a land baron as he had been as a teen.

Cheever's office door was ajar. He sat at an oversized mahogany desk and contemplated papers. When John entered Cheever looked up, surprise pasted on his face. The tan had faded and, like the receptionist, he was dressed as if it were a weekday. Suit of dark navy blue with tiny pinstripes, a pale blue shirt and green/blue tie to match. Right then, John decided that little in Scott Cheever would be revealed from his facial expressions or body language. Too smart for that. The man extended a hand and gave a broad smile.

"Glad to see you, John. Have a seat," he said, motioning to a leather chair opposite the desk. "How goes the investigation?"

John sat. "Your father was married to Deborah. Why didn't you mention this when we last talked?"

One brow creased slightly downwards, other than that the smile remained. "Of what value is that information?"

"She was married to your father, now she works with Yvette. She's been around all these years, in Winslow, all the time land was being purchased from Granger by your father."

"So what? Jordan, I don't know where you're going with this, but you're wasting your time."

"I don't think so. I think you know more about Winslow and the goings-on over the years than you're letting on."

Cheever, who had settled back into his chair, swiveled around to look out the bay windows at the harbor. John guessed he was no longer smiling. Minutes passed. Then, he turned and stared at John, tapping his fingertips together in an upside down V.

"You're right. I must commend you. I do know about goings-on in Winslow, but it's not like you think. Of course, I'm up-to-date on real estate transactions."

"How is Mr. Granger involved with you?"

Cheever rolled his eyes, an attempt at exasperation at John's switch in subject. As quickly, however, he must have decided to play along.

"Mr. Granger is a client."

"How so?"

"A financial client. My father was the executor of his will, and now I am."

"So you do have contact with him?"

"I didn't say that. I do know where he is, but that's privileged information."

"He's in a sanitarium outside New York. I've been there. Rain's been there. He's been there for years, wasting away while you manage his money."

Cheever looked down at his fingers, grimaced. "You're very astute, clever. Like your mother."

Where did that come from, John thought? Was it a distraction tactic or something more? Without looking into Cheever's eyes, he wasn't sure. He stored it away but didn't react to it. "If you're the executor, then you know what the will says, how his estate is divided up."

Cheever nodded agreement. Was John winning this erratic banter in some strange way? By his apparent meekness, had Cheever backed down?

"All right, Jordan," Cheever whispered. "I'll tell you. The money is divided across several corporations, in which Mr. Granger has at least fifty-one percent stake. Some of the companies I co-own with him, always as a minority shareholder, mind you. One is owned by his ex-wife Yvette. Through this corporation, she is paid alimony and other agreed-upon fees and obligations from their divorce."

"That was years ago."

"True," Cheever said. "Years ago, however, Mr. Granger was a very rich man, then as now. Yvette was no fool."

"Who gets his money when he dies?"

"Next of kin."

"Does he have children?"

Cheever let this pass an instant, then he seemed to decide against ignoring the question. "You know he doesn't."

"I'm not sure."

"What if he has no children, who would his next of kin be?"

"Well, that part's easy," Cheever said, relaxing. "That is the reason for all these corporations, twelve to be exact. It will be easy to ensure that each one passes its assets into various charities. It's all very well detailed in the will and supporting documentation. Granger really is a very generous soul. Unless, of course, his treatments cost so much that his money is depleted. One never knows about such things."

"What is his problem?" John asked.

"A debilitating heart condition that has left his mind feeble as well. It's hereditary. He's like a vegetable. Unfortunate." Cheever took a sip of water.

"Is he going to die soon?"

"No one is exactly sure of the time he has left. In the meantime, I take care of his investments."

"That includes purchasing the Turner property?" John asked.

"No, that I did with my own money."

"With all the property you own today? A townhouse on Beacon Hill, the properties in Cambridge?"

Muffling a chuckle, Cheever answered, "I enjoy real estate. A fine investment, too. Why your mother even tried her hand at it, tried to buy out Yvette once." Scott laughed out loud. "A commendable move if I do say."

This was the second time Cheever mentioned his mother. The effect was distraction in John's thinking. He saw Darcy's face, the lamentable way she defended her ability to pay for a house she could in no way keep up or afford, the way Yvette humored her through the supposed transaction only to reneg at the last moment. Cheever knew this was a button of John's he could press. The more pressure applied, the more John sank. John looked to the liquor cabinet not three feet from him. A bottle of Jack Daniels. He looked back at Cheever.

"Why my mother?" he managed, repeating to himself that if he removed his gaze from Scott Cheever's blue eyes, he lost. "Why?"

Cheever chuckled again. "Your mother. Darcy. What a lively sprite she was. Now, that was a woman."

John wanted to jump over the desk and grab the man's throat. A force he couldn't name kept him seated.

"What do you know about the land on the Turner property?" John asked.

Cheever lowered his eyes again and grew pensive. "The land?" His voice was gravelly, as if he'd been up all night drinking.

"The land, the way it divides into different types of soil. You are aware of this, I presume, since you're now the owner. It would all be documented in a survey, unless of course you haven't done that or it hasn't been done in the last several years. Of course, you know about all that." John could feel his inner strength return. With each calculated pause of Cheever's, a suspicion was confirmed. Cheever wasn't telling all. That alone was enough for John.

"I would have to review the survey documents," Cheever said. "In due time."

"You're closing next week," John said, taking a guess. Cheever didn't seem to be the type to miss a Saturday on the golf course without good reason.

Cheever snapped to attention and stood. "Precisely why I am here today, Jordan. Unless you have other questions, I must excuse myself and get to preparing for the closing."

"How can you close without Walter?"

This question seemed to genuinely surprise the man. "Where is he?"

"No one knows. After he mauled and attempted raping Rain Danforth, he disappeared."

Cheever sat back down, darted looks around the room then closed his eyes, rubbing them hard. "This is terrible."

"Because it slows down your plans, or because a woman is lying half alive in a hospital bed?"

Cheever began to protest but John stood his ground.

"Cheever, whatever you know you'd better come clean. This is all splitting at the seams and your name is on a lot of deals associated with the players. Plus, you think you're smart talking about my mother. Well, you've just opened that can of worms, too. Whatever did they teach you in those fancy business classes? Certainly not how to be discreet."

"Get out." Cheever's eyes turned the color of steel. His lids lowered in an attempt to mean business.

John laughed inside. He'd made major headway, not only with this weakling disguised as a business tycoon but more importantly with himself. Stand up for what you know, for what you believe, and you've got the rest licked. Who had said that to him once? Some teacher in grade school who'd taken under his wings the pathetic child John had once been. Strange what could be recalled at the oddest times. He left the office, passing the secretary. She had bright green contacts on. Fake color. Unlike Rain's wonderful gray eyes.

Outside, he breathed the fresh air and made for the subway. In fifteen minutes he'd be at his car that was located in a parking garage on the outskirts of the city. An hour later he'd be in Winslow. How fast could Cheever dial the phone to warn one of his cronies that John Jordan was onto them?

Chapter Sixteen

John didn't rush to Winslow. Instead he returned to the hospital and, using his policeman's status, managed to get to Rain's room and sit by her bed while she slept. He contemplated the meeting with Cheever. Had Cheever really been working on the purchase of the Turner property? He wasn't a lawyer, after all. Whoever was representing him would be doing all the legwork and interfacing with the Turners.

There had to have been some communication between Cheever and his lawyers. Winslow was a small place and the news of Betty's suicide was all over town. It wouldn't take long for the local lawyers to get word to whoever was transacting business there. Cheever had to have known. Why then would he feign ignorance?

Because, as Deborah had suggested, he knew more than he let on. Then again, how could John be certain of what Deborah had said? She herself seemed to be in the thick of everything, too. If Cheever was in the know, would he necessarily care that the sale might be prolonged? Of course he would. He was not the type to be patient when it came to making a profit. John wondered what the sale price was, and what the Turners had paid for the house. He could find that out, as well as the names of the former owners. It wouldn't take long since the records were still kept in a section of the library. He'd call Joanie right away. She worked until 5 P.M. on Saturdays. Obviously the Turner case would be an open one until Betty's death was ruled a suicide. This meant he could continue to use Paul and the police force to investigate the Turners.

Rain stirred but continued her deep sleep. John figured she was sedated. If she came to and was well enough to leave the hospital soon, they could work together but for now he had to decide how much he wanted to do on his own. It seemed a trivial decision, given the recent events. He'd see this to the end.

He left the hospital. By the time he'd made it back to Winslow, Paul had put the wheels in motion to alert surrounding states and the national police computer network about Walter's disappearance. An all-points bulletin was in effect. So far, there had been no word of a sighting. After inquiring about Rain's welfare, Paul offered John the lead investigator's position on the case, which he accepted.

He went to the library himself and sat with Joanie for several hours in the records room. From the time the town was founded over three hundred years before until the late 1960s, recordings of land sales and purchases were handwritten. They were not what a modern-day real estate attorney would call thorough. In spite of this inconvenience, Joanie and John delved into the ornate script on long yellowing sheets of paper to follow through the history of the tract of land first called the "Wright" tract, after the name of the family who first settled the land in 1783. Settlers from England, they kept what was once farmland in the family until the early 1900s. Following that, a man and his wife bought the farm but in less than two years the property went ownerless because the couple died of the flu the second winter. The third owner's name caught John by surprise. A Stuart Grange purchased the land in 1912. Over two hundred acres, the land encompassed what was now a combination of Yvette's, John's, and the Turner's property.

"Grange. Is there a misspelling?" John asked.

Joanie shook her head. She pointed to several places in the agreement where the name appeared. "I doubt it. Grange is clearly noted more than once."

"Why did the name go from Grange to Granger?"

Joanie winked at John. "Remember that many immigrants changed their names for a variety of reasons? It was not an unusual thing back then. Perhaps it was some error that never got corrected."

"Grange. What kind of a name is that?" John asked.

Joanie mulled it over. "I don't rightly know. Not Irish that I can tell. Most around here settled from Ireland."

"Plus," John added, feeling the adrenaline pumping, "this was the purchase that, if this is indeed Granger's father, gave Stuart rights to all this land, land that Yvette eventually received."

Joanie looked on sympathetically, as if reading his next thought. His mother had been fighting a losing battle trying to obtain ownership of the house he grew up in. As he gazed at the map of the land, he could easily calculate its location, central to the entire one-hundred-plus acres. No way was that ever going to be subdivided as long as Stuart Granger or his vengeful ex-wife had their say-so.

Still, by giving Yvette her slice of land after the divorce, he had relinquished some of his valued possession. John wondered why Yvette hadn't sold out. She could have taken the money and started fresh somewhere else. What held her to Winslow?

Had Darcy done her homework when she had gone after purchasing the land? Had she researched the title or had a lawyer do it? He didn't recall any mention of a lawyer when his mother was trying to gain ownership. She often mentioned the money, how Yvette was changing her mind daily on the price. At one point, Darcy had thought she could swing it only to have Yvette increase the amount by another twenty thousand dollars, an outrage for his mother who had not handled more than a maximum of one thousand dollars at a time and who could barely balance a checkbook. The entire affair must have given Yvette great pleasure. To watch another human being suffer seemed to be a favorite pastime of the woman. Indeed, wasn't it during that time he was introduced to Yvette?

He remembered her red nails to this day, long and hanging off thin, spindly fingers. Her grasping the back of his head and drawing him near to give him a hug. The strong aroma of her perfume, her grip that crushed him. Was it that far back the woman had decided to have him? He shuddered.

"Okay, John?" Joanie asked.

Her question returned him to the present. "Yeah, Joanie," he patted her hand. "Thanks for the help. I think I have enough to go on for now."

They cleared off the table and Joanie carefully carried the documents to a glassed-in case where she placed them in files and locked a double glazed door.

"Is there an alarm system in this room?" John asked.

"No, unfortunately. It was voted down several town meetings ago. Never brought up since."

"Which town meeting? Before I came back?"

"Yes. The same one the conservation committee blocked Cheever's bid to build condominiums."

"Was Cheever at the meeting?"

"Of course." Her voice was laced with disdain. "The man always shows when there's land to talk about."

At the library entrance, they said good-bye. Joanie shook his hand. "I'm so sorry about Emily, John. I know what she meant to you. I hope things work out."

He hugged Joanie and left, thinking as he walked down Main Street that "working out" really had no meaning for him.

✳ ✳ ✳

The next day, Rain was released from the hospital and John was there early to help her gather her things and leave. On their way to the Allens', they were stopped in the center of town by a mini-traffic jam, a result of one of the floats that would be part of the July Fourth parade in two days. Each year the firehouse managed to concoct the largest, usually most gaudy-looking contraption on wheels, big enough to carry all the volunteer firemen and their children down Main Street for the celebration. This year, it was one of the farm tractors pulling a thirty-foot-long wood hauler. As John explained the tradition to Rain, he regaled in tales of his youth when he would jump aboard the fireman's float and enjoy the ride from the town common to the cemetery less than a mile away.

"You did have some good times, then," she said, wiping her forehead.

"Hot?" he asked.

"Just a little. How goes the investigation?"

He detailed his discovery at the library, glancing periodically to her to ensure she was not growing faint. Her eyes widened as he talked.

"Grange. Grange. That's so close. It must be the same family," she said.

"Sure it is. There's no doubt. Either the paperwork contains a misspelling or, as Joanie mentioned, it's a switch from the original European name. Do you recognize its meaning in Spanish?"

"No," she said. "I wonder if Marguerite knows anything. I should call her."

"You up for it?"

"Not right now. Maybe tomorrow."

They drove to the Allens', where Michelle had prepared the spare bedroom and arranged Rain's things. Rain got right into bed and in no time was fast asleep, the trip having exhausted her. John and Michelle talked in the kitchen for a while. It wasn't an hour later when they heard Rain calling to John.

He rushed upstairs and found her panting and sweating. She grabbed him and drew him to her, crying quietly into his chest.

"What's wrong?"

She struggled to regain her composure but the tears kept flowing. "A dream, that's all. This whole thing is going to be with me for a while."

He stroked the damp wisps of hair that stuck to her forehead. "Take it slow. We're here for you."

She gazed into his eyes. "Are you here for me?"

The words struck him but their meaning sunk to a deeper level than he'd ever allowed before. He could tell by her direct gaze, the look that had captured him the day he first set eyes on her, that she was speaking with an affection that had great meaning for her. What did it mean for him? He lowered his eyes, then raised them and returned her stare.

"I'm here for you. I want you to know that," he said.

It wasn't so hard to say, but he felt his stomach tense, his hands grip harder, his own sweat begin to pour. He'd spoken words he was sure of, but then again wasn't at all. She stared back, smiled. The reassurance of her smile helped, but he was still disturbed. Why should comforting words disturb him? Rain needed to hear that he was here for her, and it was true. He was. But. But what? What was his fear? Where was this going? Why didn't he want to talk anymore?

As if reading his words, she said, "You don't have to commit to me, John. That's not what I'm after. I do feel strongly for you, I don't mind saying, but I'm not fishing for a serious relationship."

"Is that what you think I think?" He knew the words were meager even as he spoke them.

"I think you're not sure. That's okay." She lay back on the bed and closed her eyes. In the few silent moments that ensued, she calmed considerably. Her face cleared and her breathing slowed. He let her drift back into slumber and waited for her to come to again.

When she did, she smiled and grasped his hand even tighter. "I just had a thought. We should go see that movie that Marguerite suggested. The one Yvette was in as a younger woman. *Something Winning.*"

Relieved she didn't return to the former subject, he nevertheless noted his desire to tell her he cared. He really cared. He managed, however, only to stare at her, questioning.

"You don't remember?" she asked.

"I do. We'd have to get to Cambridge, though. Old movies aren't readily available here in the boonies."

The day before the Fourth, they finally made it to Cambridge. Rain had had several doctor's appointments and there was the investigation diverting their attention from the movies. That night, John parked near

Harvard Square and they rummaged in a shop offering old movies. They found *Something Winning* and rented it for three days.

Back at John's, Rain settled into a chair and they watched.

Yvette was truly a beauty with deep-set eyes and thick black hair. Playing a French schoolgirl who journeyed south to the Vichy-governed part of France to join the Resistance, she fell in love with a soldier much older than she who had a wife and child back in Paris. Using her dark eyes and a quick, acerbic tongue, she succeeded in carrying secret information from town to town. At the same time she followed her lover as his troops traveled the countryside. A confrontation with the Germans one night killed her lover and she collapsed on top of him, exposing her identity and the documents in her possession rather than run to save her own life. The Germans captured her and in the final scene she was led to her death by firing squad.

"A tearjerker in those days," Rain commented. "I like the old movies, but I'm afraid they don't particularly make me emotional. Too much drama." She reached to turn the rewind button when John stood and went to her.

"Stop," he said, pulling at her arm. "Look." He had been watching the credits and now pointed to a name rolling up on the screen. Quickly he pushed the reverse button until the name had returned to the middle of the screen.

"Oh my God," Rain whispered. "Odile Grange."

"Grange," John said. "Was she married then?"

"Must have been. This film was made in 1952, the man at the store told me."

John shook his head. "I think so. My mother said she married the year I was born."

"1952?" Rain asked.

"Yes. But I don't understand why her name there is Grange and not Granger."

"Odd. Was that her married name or her stage name?"

"Too much of a coincidence to be her stage name, don't you think?" John asked.

"We should check it out. It's bizarre either way, her maiden name being similar to Granger's or her married name so close but not the same as Granger's. I don't get it."

"It's stretching it to think it's an error," John said.

Rain remained reflective for some time. "Let's watch it again."

"Again? Why?"

"I don't know. Sometimes things are more revealing the second or third time you look at them."

John rewound the tape. They began watching, this time paying more attention to detail and rewinding and reviewing scenes in which Yvette had a lot of exposure. Mid-film, Rain grasped John's arm.

"Play that back again," she said, eyes fixed on the screen.

Yvette and her lover were walking along a dirt road at dusk. Her feet were bare and she held a straw hat in one hand, the other swinging with that of her lover. Their eyes locked and then they embraced. The shot was a full-length one of each and, when they separated, Rain called out.

"See?" she asked, her hand gripping into John.

"What?" he asked. Nothing in particular grabbed him.

"She's pregnant. Her belly. Watch."

The couple meandered some more and then the man lifted Yvette up and placed her gently on a large boulder. Yvette, in full frontal view of the camera, wiggled her toes and laughed, throwing her head back.

"Stop!" Rain called.

The shot froze and they both studied Yvette. John noted some girth in Yvette's middle. "I don't really see where you say she looks pregnant."

"She is. Early stages. I can tell. I've seen enough pregnant women— my friends, my patients. There's a thickness around her middle that is not fat."

"Are you sure? I never heard of Yvette having children. Ever."

Rain bit her lower lip, reflecting on the scene. "We should check it out. Just in case. And tomorrow I'm calling Marguerite."

John took her home after they finished their second viewing. It was late and the Allens had already gone to bed. Rain placed her purse on the side table of the entryway and reached up to John's cheek, stroking.

"Thanks, you've been supportive and helpful," she said.

An urge to embrace her surged. He lingered and held her hand, wanting to move closer but unable to.

"Tough few days, huh?" he asked.

She nodded, her eyes focused on the night sky. "I had so many abuse cases, and never was abused myself. Now I wonder if this didn't happen for that reason alone, that I should know of what my patients speak."

"Don't you think that's pushing it?"

Her eyes flashed to him and she smiled. Nodding, she opened the door and walked inside. "See you tomorrow."

✳ ✳ ✳

The Fourth of July dawned hot and sunny, promising a fair turnout. Near Doc McDougal's, children ran in circles, chasing each other with their tropical-colored Popsicles. It was a tradition for Doc to offer free ice cream before the parade, and today outside his small, single-story shop it looked like a school play yard for all the kids.

John inched his way past them and went to the wood counter behind which Doc had stood for over fifty years. Now in his early eighties with deep-set blue eyes and hovering white bushy brows, the man had the spry look of one twenty years his junior. Seeing John he raised his hand.

"Don't tell me you've come for the ice cream, Johnny. You've had your share over the years! I'm afraid your limit has been surpassed." He grinned a toothless smile and pushed his granny glasses up his nose, eyes on two kids running out with Popsicles.

"Here now! You've had enough! What about the others?"

The children laughed and disappeared.

"Town upside-down over Mrs. Turner?" he asked John.

"Seems like it," John said. "I was at the coffee shop just now and everyone wanted to know the latest."

Doc shook his head. "She was in here just last week looking for her aspirins. I order them from New York for her being that we don't get it regular from our suppliers. She was mighty upset that I was out. Really sad. A dedicated lady, she was."

"Dedicated?" John asked.

Doc's eyes darkened. "That so-and-so she was married to had some blinking nerve to get up and leave like that! What was wrong with him? And what about that young girl? Is she all right?"

"She's going to be fine, but she isn't living there anymore. She's with Paul and Michelle Allen," John said.

He noted Doc's disconcerted look, a look the man wore when annoyed. John knew it well because when he was young, his own behavior running around the shop gave rise to the same expression.

"What's wrong, Doc?"

Doc kept shaking his head. "You know, it was not her fault she up and killed herself. Couldn't have been. She must have been pushed along, angered or given to fear, some great big fear. Otherwise, that woman simply would not have done such a thing! She was too nervous, too delicate in her way."

"You think Walter had something to do with it?"

Again, Doc's eyes grew stormy. "I've held my tongue all these years, John, but that man was trouble for her from the get-go. You know what I'm talking about. You do."

But John didn't know. His stomach, however, seemed to be pumping an odd, sick liquid whereby he felt as though he was going to throw up. A notion had taken hold, an old sense of doom, something familiar but long ago. Whatever Doc referred to had to do with him, even though he couldn't pinpoint the details. An urge to get up and run flowed through him. He remained in the shop, however, allowing the distracting children to occupy Doc as he tried to collect his thoughts.

"Doc," he said slowly. "I don't know. I really don't. But I want to."

Doc handed change to one of the children who in turn took the top newspaper from a pile of papers and ran out of the store. Then Doc lowered the storefront shade and flipped the "Open" sign to "Closed."

"Won't hurt to take a break," he said. "Even if the parade is in a couple of hours." A child banged impatiently on the door from the other side. Doc watched the front latch to see if the child tried to come in, but in no time the sounds of retreating footsteps could be heard.

He wiped a stool and sat on it, gesturing to John to join him in the big swivel chair behind the counter. The two sat for a silent few moments, then Doc began to talk.

"The last night your mama was alive, she and Walter came to the shop. Oh, she wasn't by his side, mind you, but I saw her sweet figure in the distance. Darcy was one lovely woman, I don't mind saying. That slender body and that light walk of hers drew many an eye, young man." Doc wiped his forehead.

"She was in his car. He had come to the door and knocked and knocked. In those days, me and the wife lived in the back room. I jumped out of bed and went to him. He claimed to need some of Betty's aspirins, explained she was having one of her terrific headaches. I scowled and complained about opening just for that but in the end gave in. Walter left as soon as he had the medicine in his hands. Darcy even smiled at me from the car. The next morning she was found dead."

"Did you explain that to the police?" John asked.

"Back then the chief of police was more interested in pleasing old Granger than taking the law into his hands. No matter what I'd have said, John, the powers that be would have chosen to see things their way. There was funny business going on in this town back then. I tried to stay out of it. Had a wife and two kids to manage. Art Johnson and I talked, though. Art said he'd do what he felt proper. I'm not sure what that was."

John gripped the chair rung. "So Walter was with her before she died, before she made it to the woods. He must know what happened to her."

"They say it was the wild animals."

"Do you believe that, Doc?" John asked.

Doc shook his head. "If I believed that I'd be a fool. You need to think about what your mama knew that others didn't want her to know, that's what you need to think about." He sighed. "That medicine was a potent form of aspirin, containing a level of drug used for heart conditions."

John froze. Noting his change in demeanor, Doc stopped, his mouth opened slightly.

"Why heart?" John asked.

Doc shrugged. "Sometimes soothing the heart helps headaches and minor pains, I figured. Not rightly sure. I'd ask Art if I were you. Mind you, that woman Betty used it a lot. Daughter Emily used to fetch some for her mother from time to time, too."

"Did Betty ever get prescriptions?" John asked.

"Never from me, which I thought was strange. Given she had some sort of strange tending towards bad headaches, she should have seen a doctor! Other thing. She was a talkative creature—about her flowers and her cooking and the like. But if I ever asked about her health, she never said a word, hushed up like a clam and no two ways about it sent the message that topic was off-limits. I got the message long time ago. Not only that, there was this look crossed her face any time I even mentioned them aspirins. Odd look, like she was looking at a ghost. Even stopped coming for a while once after I'd inquired, until I reminded her I purchased them special for her. Then she started coming around again. Guilt, I guess."

Doc shuffled over to a cabinet behind the counter and took out a box of cigars. He lit one and settled back on the stool, heaving a sigh and looking at nothing in particular.

"Yep. Mighty strange goings-on."

John watched the puff of smoke rise above Doc's head. The air was heavy as no windows were open. Muffled voices from outside grew loud then diminished. The band was tuning up at the common. A French horn blurted, then was silenced.

"Who was her doctor? Art?" John asked.

Doc shook his head. "Nope. Some out-of-town guy. She told me his name once, don't remember though. Was a fellow from Wrightsville.

Must've been the only guy there at the time, that place being even smaller than Winslow. Art would know."

John left shortly after that and headed to Art's office down the street. The office was closed as was expected. He remembered that Art and Minnie always spent the Fourth at their cottage in New Hampshire. They wouldn't be back for a few days. He drove to Wrightsville and parked near the pharmacy. The town was quieter than Winslow, given they didn't have any formal holiday celebrations. The townspeople cooperated with Winslow in that regard.

Inside the pharmacy a young girl directed him to the back where the head pharmacist, Josh Thompson, was getting ready to leave early to enjoy the rest of the day. Josh informed John that a Dr. Simmons practiced in the town back at the time when Emily was a child. For over twenty years he was the only physician, but the man had passed away years before, leaving his eccentric wife who still lived a reclusive existence deep in the woods on the edge of town. John got directions to the house and in less than thirty minutes found himself riding along a road darkened by forest and leading to a solitary house surrounded by a chain-link fence and high shrubs. In spite of the sunshine, the property seemed gloomy and forbidding.

He rang the bell. Since it made no sound, he knocked several times before a woman with unkempt white hair to her shoulders appeared. Stuck to her chin, the remains of dinner. With a dirty hand she swiped her mouth, then brushed back the hair that hung over one eye. Squinting, she eyed him up and down.

"Is this Dr. Simmons' house?"

She seemed to not understand.

John continued. "My name is John Jordan and I live in Winslow. I was wondering if I might speak with you about a patient of his. Are you his wife?"

Again, the woman wiped her face. Her eyes were pale blue and she seemed to stare right past John. Recognition flashed briefly in her gaze, then her eyes widened and she shut them tight. "He's dead. We were married for twenty-two years."

"May I come in?"

She shook her head. "Nobody comes here anymore. Too much work. I'd rather sit on the porch."

He looked around and noticed a comfortable rocking chair and a swing seat for two. A half-filled coffee mug sat on a wooden bench beside the rocker. Mrs. Simmons shuffled over to the chair and began to rock, her eyes fixed on the hills in the distance. John figured she would have a view to magnificent sunsets from there. He joined her, placing himself precariously on the swing chair until he was assured of its ability to hold him. Then, with a foot on the floorboard, he swung back and forth.

"You want to know what?" she asked. She appeared calmer, less anxious. Still her eyes darted to and from John, each time revealing another level of nervous emotion.

"I understand your husband took care of Betty Turner."

Her hand slapped her thigh hard. "I knew it! They told me she was dead and now I knew this would happen! Folks snooping around. Lady was a sick one, she was. He took care of her, he did. Old fool didn't know a fake from the real McCoy. Said she had heart troubles and got her those pills. I never believed her. Told him if he food shopped in Winslow like I did he'd see her prancing around in that fancy car of theirs, running errands like a schoolgirl. No way she had a weak heart. Bull. She was sick all right. Sick in the head, not in the heart."

John tried to piece together the words. "Did you know Darcy Jordan?" he asked.

By her nonresponse, he assumed not. "Did your husband know their daughter Emily?"

Mrs. Simmons swallowed. Kept her eyes on the west. For several moments, it appeared as though she'd say no more. John contemplated leaving. When he stood, it was with the intention of stretching, to see if she'd react. She's stopped rocking but her eyes remained away from him, so he couldn't tell whether his question disturbed her or not.

"Perhaps this isn't a good time. I'll come back," he said.

She nodded slightly. He stood and slowly walked to the car. Before he got to the bottom step, he heard her whisper. Turning, he saw her staring directly at him, a convinced and utterly cold stare.

"No one ever told you what your mama knew, did they?"

He felt an icy chill reach to his heart from a depth he couldn't place. "You knew her?"

"I loved her dearly. She was the only genuine one of the lot."

"What lot?"

"The crew who wanted Emily dead. Darcy—your mama—and I went to school together. We played together until I moved out of town. We shared all our secrets. The last secret she shared with me was the death of her."

John thought he was hearing things. "What?" His voice was barely a whisper.

She smiled, breaking the coldness that had been between them. "Sit, Sonny."

He moved back to where he'd been and kept his eyes on her. She returned her gaze to the mountains.

"On the other side of those hills is Winslow. You were just a little one and, really, if I'm ever asked by anyone, I know nothing. But seeing as it's you who finally showed and not some money-hungry lawyer or that bitch in the big house or one of her sidekicks, you get the story."

He wondered then whether she had it all together. Something bizarre about her spilling her guts to him kept him suspicious. Something human kept him bound to her every word.

"She was a sick child, Emily was. Her sister, too. Weak heart. Both of them. Sick and weak."

John didn't want to hear this. "Emily was healthy and strong when I knew her."

"You knew her before she got ill. My old man said that for her it was a question of time. You're right. She outsmarted everyone by staying healthy." The woman chuckled. "No one could have planned it better than that little one who hadn't a clue, but by going on her health kick and moving out west, she kept herself alive a lot longer than many would have liked."

"What about a sister?"

"She was a twin."

"What happened to the twin?"

"Died. You know that," she said, grimacing. "Don't pretend. You knew she had a twin. You had to know by now. I'm no fool."

"You're right. What did my mother know? Was it about the twin?"

"Your mama knew the twins belonged to somebody else, Sonny. And your father knew it, too."

He felt as though he'd been stabbed. The movie he'd just seen with Rain came to mind.

"Whose children were they?"

She snuck him a quick, sidelong stare, then raised her chin and looked over the hills. "You know that, too."

He folded the fingers of both hands together and placed his head in them. If he stayed like this, maybe he wouldn't have to ever look up, ever face what it was he was about to face. He wanted to vomit and he wanted to scream. He began to feel irritated at this woman. It would be so easy to snatch her throat and shake it hard, so hard she stopped breathing. The words weren't true. She shouldn't be saying them.

"I'd like a drink," he whispered.

"No," she said. "You're not having a drink. Not like your mama, or daddy. No, Jordan, you're facing it and then you'll leave. And if anyone comes around, I'll deny I ever saw you. Just remember that. You can go now, or you can ask more questions. That's up to you. But don't ever come back. Don't ever try to see me again. You'll never be able to."

"Yvette?" he asked.

"I brought them into the world with my husband. Right in that big, fat mansion of theirs across those hills. Late one night. Two beautiful children. They were cleaned, wrapped, and driven away before I could even wash the blood from my hands. Whisked to California. My old man was given a bundle to keep quiet. They were going to get someone out west to forge birth certificates. They had it all planned. My old man got ill that very night. Sick of lying, I say. Sick of holding back the truth. He never could do that. Started drinking. It went from there. I took the money and gave it to a bank, told them to keep it for a while." She smiled. "That was forty years ago. We never touched the money. Now, it's still sitting there."

"What happened to your husband?"

"Died that fall," she said. "Like your daddy. Drowned in the river from being drunk."

John let this sink in long enough to piece together her suggestion that her husband's death had not been an accident.

"Why didn't they come after you?" he asked.

She smiled. "They didn't know I was there when the twins were born. My husband lied about me being away. Said I was visiting my sister out west. Saved my life he did. Cheever came creeping around after the funeral. Hinting we had a lot of things in common, that we could join forces in Wrightsville, purchase tracts of land together. He kept asking me about my savings, my 'considerable savings.' I never let on. It was the last good deed I did for my old man, for myself."

She wiped her face and licked her fingers. A coughing fit ensued. John watched her hack and bend over, then gurgle on the phlegm. When she raised her head, her face was bluish purple.

"Can I help? Do you need a doctor?"

She shook her head, allowed the coughs to subside. "Leave me be. All I ever wanted I had before those folks you're mixed up with showed up in my life. Now there's nothing left. I wait to die."

Her eyes turned kindly. She stared at him a long time. "It's not your fault. It's not Emily's fault. We can't help what we're born into, Sonny. Remember that."

They sat together for another hour. The silence grew between them and John knew she'd said her peace. It was time for him to get back to Rain. Pulling away from the old woman's house, he noticed she kept her eyes on the hills that formed the border between herself, her lonely existence, and the town of Winslow.

Chapter Seventeen

If there was ever a day for a Fourth of July parade, this was it. As noon neared, the sidewalks sizzled. Sunshine uncovered even the darkest corners and alleys around town. Breezes lingered only long enough to ensure long lines at any stand selling refrigerated items. Townspeople and visitors strolled the downtown area, sucking on cooling ice cream cones or taking long sips from soda cans. John arrived just in time to meet Rain at Doc's and take her to a shaded part of the common, from where they could watch the parade while sitting in the gazebo with the press and other town notables.

The barrage of questions that met John took him by surprise. Not only was Steve Rideout of the *Post* quizzical about Betty Turner and the fabulous goings-on of the last several days, others wanted to be filled in by John himself regarding the latest in the investigation. The fact John stood next to a pretty out-of-towner also did not go unnoticed. Eyes flashed his way with looks of approval, and Joanie from the library even whispered to him that it was good he was putting Emily behind him.

He tried to ignore the attention. It wasn't something he'd ever get used to, plus it reminded him of long ago and his parents' tragic endings. Back then the town had lent him the same level of curious attention. He felt he'd been resisting curious eyes ever since.

He remained noncommittal on both fronts. There was still no news of Walter. Following the autopsy that showed self-inflicted wounds to her throat, Betty's funeral was scheduled for the day after the Fourth. The information as it had appeared in the *Post* was correct. Betty Turner had committed suicide. Her husband had left town following an attempt of rape on Rain, their former boarder.

Rain kept her own responses to a minimum and although she allowed herself to be photographed, provided no new revelations. Given the recent events, they both agreed that there seemed a surreal quality to the festivities. They found a corner where they could both sit and watch the parade.

Following the usual tweaking and tuning of instruments, the band struck up a lively Sousa march. This was the signal to begin the walk that for over fifty years had originated at the far end of Main Street. First, the town elders in their military and formal dress appeared heralded by an array of flags on poles being carried by a representative of each of the armed services. Next, the tricycle competition boasted flapping plastic wraps, multicolored balloons, and children dressed to match the decorations on their bikes. A few area militias and then the Boy Scouts rounded out the first wave.

The floats came next, emerging along the hot tar roadway like mammoths from another eon, slowly rumbling towards the crowd and giving rise to cheers as they arrived at each clump of anxious onlookers. All peered to get the first glimpse of the floats as they paraded by one by one. First was the fire department with the wood hauler, next the police department spiced up the festivities with a Latin theme with even Paul Allen using maracas and jiggling about. Others followed, each displaying some element of local humor or creativity.

The antique cars followed. It was at this point John's attention turned razor-sharp. Any year he'd been in Winslow, this was the time he most cherished. First, when he was a dreaming boy of eight and nine, he'd see himself in one of the '36 Fords, the cap low over his eyes, his hands protected by leather, nodding and waving at the "common" folks on either side of the street. He'd be that wealthy land baron who appeared only on occasions such as these to honor the country's birth and to display his wealth. He'd demonstrate to those folks who thought he'd never amount to much exactly what he was made of. He, the son of that lamentable Darcy Jordan, had surpassed most in the town by leaving it. His return would be only for attention-garnering occasions such as these, to drive home the point that he'd left to become and live the life—elsewhere—of a very rich man.

He watched the first car, Cleeve Mason's forest-green Studebaker with shining white walls, slowly putter forward. Cleeve and his wife of over fifty years, Jeannette, looked as they had twenty-five years prior, regal as they graced the town with their smiles and their generosity. Each Fourth, they donated money to the town to continue the upkeep of many of the public places.

Trick Nelson's two Chevys came next, both from the fifties. Following that were antiques from surrounding towns plus some sporty versions from the sixties: a Mustang convertible and Corvette Stingray. John recognized each and every driver. They regularly convened on pleasant summer Sunday mornings to journey throughout the surrounding hills and ended up at one of the local eateries for lunch. In years gone by, John would drive by their rendezvous points, eyeing their parked cars with envy.

Rain tugged him back to reality. "Look," she pointed to an approaching car.

The sun picked up the glimmer of the chrome and the white brilliance of the vintage '30s car, eclipsing momentarily the other cars. This was none other than the Bentley that John had noticed was missing from Yvette's garage the day Emily was found dead.

"Who's driving?" he asked.

Rain shook her head slowly. "Can't see."

But John could now. Her eyes were shaded but the hair was the same taut chignon. Deborah. He felt himself go cold all over and, in spite of Rain's warm hand in his, his fingers trembled.

"What the hell is she doing, under the circumstances?"

Rain looked innocently at John. He could feel her eyes on him the entire time the car made its way directly for them. Something wasn't right. Wasn't it usually one of Yvette's lesser employees who drove the car? Wasn't it usually the fact that the car, so overwhelmingly outstanding and perfectly groomed, obviated any question as to who the owner was, hence the nonappearance of Yvette each year? He couldn't remember. He tried but he couldn't put himself back to when he was a teen.

Rain jolted his memory. "Did Emily watch these parades?"

He nodded. He could see her. The black hair with blue streaks from the sun. Her glittering eyes as she watched one by one the cars pass. Her tremor as the Granger car passed. Her one and only comment he recalled.

"They make me want to vomit," she'd say.

Her eyes had darkened and her voice had an uncommon coolness. She disliked Yvette for the stories John had relayed, but had no inherent reason to dislike the woman from her own personal experience. Oddly though, John had just remembered her phrase that was as quickly wiped from his conscious because, at that time, Emily had looked up at him and laid a gentle kiss on his cheek. Why was he recalling this now?

"She never liked Yvette," he said. Rain was still looking at him. He'd purposely not told her what Mrs. Simmons had told him. He wanted to wait until the holiday was over and until Rain had fully recuperated. At least that was the excuse he gave himself. It was still difficult to imagine Yvette the mother of Emily. The mother of anyone.

Deborah found him with her eyes. A slight nod and destructive piercing gaze, instantaneous and unnoticed by anyone else, struck him as yet another slight. Yet another attack on who he was, yet another patronizing act that reinforced in the woman her superiority, her owner's superiority, and his lesser status.

He fought only momentarily the interpretation of her look. Usually he'd rationalize it away, but this time he held to the notion she was working on him. Again, he noted Rain's look, a look that was strange for its simplicity and compassion, strange only to him perhaps. People did these kinds of things, it was only people like himself who didn't know how to receive these gestures comfortably. Would he ever be able to do that?

The car passed. He studied the back of Deborah's head. Just then, a kid ran out into the street and slammed his fist on the back of the trunk, as quickly disappearing into the crowd. Deborah stopped the car short and in a flash was out of the car racing, not towards the youngster but to the back. She ran a hand across the hot metal, meticulous in her inspection as if there was something more than the paint, the metal, the car itself to discover. John noticed that the trunk had a dent. They were too far away to see if it was recent or had been there.

"Was there a dent from the kid? Or was it there before?" Rain asked.

"Perfection has its flaws nonetheless," he said, shrugging in a gesture of uncertainty.

Rain giggled. "Tut, tut. Perhaps you should be the one to mention it to the owner." She squeezed his hand.

"Perhaps we should ensure that car makes it to the cemetery like all the other parade participants. Then, we could review this with Deborah. It would give me great pleasure to see the look on her face as she describes the car being in her possession as damage was visited on it. In fact, that's what I'll do. As an officer of the law, I should assist at this accident."

He took Rain's hand and led her off the gazebo, noting but letting pass the curious stares coming from the folks on the gazebo. It felt good to hold her hand in public. Plus, why shouldn't he enjoy his one day off in several weeks? The last time he had a day off was well before Emily.

Rain allowed him to lead the way, easing her gait to match his own languorous stride. This felt right. As it had with Emily. He wondered if he was desperate for an Emily replacement or was it Rain herself who drew him into his inner workings, those pleasant physical images that led once in a great while to satisfaction, albeit impermanent? His mind was a kaleidoscope today. He pressed his fingers against hers and they walked. He knew deep down he was trying to forget that Emily Turner was the child of Yvette and Stuart Granger. In that moment, he noted the sweat pouring from his forehead.

At the cemetery, the crowd gathered around the stone memorial to the town's military who died in the major wars. Speeches extolled the bravery and the mission of the deceased, that their spirits held what was best and true about the country.

John looked to the far side of the cemetery where the antique cars were parked. He couldn't see Deborah or the Bentley anywhere. The closer he and Rain walked towards the parking area, the more he was certain she had already left. Why wouldn't she stay until the competition was final? The greatest pleasure for the car drivers was to stand up and be counted as being owner of a well-cared-for antique.

Trick Nelson was the first car driver John noticed. The man sat on his Chevy, taking care to remove his shoes first so that only the soft material of his socks would graze against the car's surface. He puffed on a cigarette.

"Trick," John said.

Trick nodded and smiled at Rain, a wide, thin grin that displayed a smattering of teeth and many more empty spaces. Trick never ventured far from his ranch the other side of town except to show off his cars. He wasn't used to foreigners, as he referred to anyone who wasn't born and bred in town, especially women. "Pleased to meet you, Ma'am, I'm Trick Nelson." He shook her hand and nodded to John.

"Haven't lost your charm, have you, Trick?" John kidded. "Where's the Granger car?"

No friend of Yvette's, Trick scowled then shrugged. "Took off right fast, it seemed. After that kid smacked the behind of her precious vehicle." He slipped on his shoes, hopped off the car, and stubbed out his cigarette. "You'd think he blowtorched the thing."

"I thought Deborah's reaction was rather exaggerated," John said.

"She screamed during the parade, only you couldn't hear for all the music. Cussing up a storm like a truck driver."

"Doesn't someone from the Granger estate usually stay to accept the award that they receive for the car?" John asked.

Trick nodded. "Usually. You know they always get something in this town. Fact is, they run the place no matter what anyone says. Them and that jackass Cheever. Always trying to buy me out, they are."

"Since when?" John asked.

"Since always. Since my dad chased them away with a loaded shotgun twelve years ago. Told that Scott person to never set his dirty ass on the property again. Funny it was, Cheever was only a sniveling kid just graduated from one of those fancy business schools. Thought he could outsmart my old man. Wrong."

"So you never entertained any offers to buy your land?"

"Never. When my old man died that was one stipulation he made, to never ever sell out to Granger or Cheever. Not that I ever would have, mind you. Those folks aren't real Winslow folks anyway."

"So they never tried again?"

"I wouldn't say that. They did, but I wasn't listening. I know what they'd do to my three hundred acres. Condominium city. No thanks. Even for a couple hundred thousand."

"That's all he's offered you?"

Trick nodded.

"You know that property has to be worth a couple of million anyway. It's prime land for most anything," John said.

Trick tried to muffle his surprise, cleared his throat, and lit another cigarette. "Figures that son of a bitch would try to lowball me. Did that to your mama years ago, didn't he?

"It wasn't Cheever back then. It was big daddy Granger himself. I remember, even though I was a youngster. I remember my mama crying when your mom died. Saying how there'd been a murder." He gazed directly at John. "I was never allowed to say that back then. Sorry."

"Why say it now?" John asked.

Trick kicked the ground. "All the goings-on now. All the untold stories continue. Emily. This new event with Betty Turner. Makes me think things are coming full circle. Based on the speculations and discussions of my parents. But each of them is dead now." He took another long, sympathetic look at John. Had John not known Trick to be a genuine sort, he'd have called that look similar to the many forced sympathies that accosted him from most townspeople over the years. He was reminded of why he left for New York.

It was the straw he required. The comment at just the right time. The sway of words and his associated reaction to them. The need to uncover, once and for all, the truth, if not about Emily then about his mother.

"What do you think Art knows?" John asked Trick suddenly.

Trick paused, looked off in the direction of the ongoing ceremony. "Can't say that I know, except my mama always said the doctor kept his own counsel. She said that he knew secrets husbands didn't know about their wives, or the other way around. She said Art knew everything, but Art kept quiet. That kept him safe."

John looked at Rain, who was yawning and appeared rather drawn. "You okay?"

"Sure."

"Up for a trip to Yvette's?"

"Why?" she asked.

"I want to follow up on this accident. Make sure there weren't any damages."

"You're off-duty, John." She looked at him dubiously.

Ignoring her comment, he asked, "Coming?"

"Sounds like I have no choice," she said, smiling and taking his hand. They said good-bye to Trick and walked to John's car.

While driving he kept silent, in spite of Rain's effort at small talk. Eventually, she grew quiet as well. He wondered how much she sensed his apprehension. How could she? She had no idea what he knew, nor what he was about to face. Even he didn't quite understand why he headed straight for a situation that minimally would cause great stress. He would demand information on the Bentley and its whereabouts, in an effort to glean why Deborah was present at the parade instead of some lesser worker. Something was afoot, but he didn't know what. Yvette could easily send him on his way, having protested his entry in the first place or assured him that all was well. More importantly, he was about to face Emily's birth mother.

He wanted to look into her eyes. Yvette knew what had happened to his mother the night she died. Yvette had been at the root of why his mother's life was taken so early. Yvette orchestrated the replacement of Emily's true parents with surrogates who for many years lied and kept their role up, for money or some morbid sense of duty.

When they got to the mansion, there wasn't a servant in sight. In fact, the door was opened and they walked around freely. Upstairs, too, there was no one. They searched every room. Everything was neat and clean, and there was no sign of work in progress. The entire place looked as though its inhabitants had gone on vacation. They returned to Yvette's bedroom and searched the closets. There appeared to be enough clothes to give the impression she was still in town, but with the extensive wardrobe the woman owned, it wasn't clear.

"Is the dress she wore to the party here?" Rain asked. "Perhaps if that's missing, she's left. Isn't she supposed to stay though, until further notice?"

"She's supposed to," John said, eyeing the bank of closets on one side of her bedroom containing racks filled with splendid designer names. "She may have sent some of those clothes to the cleaners, or forwarded them to wherever she was escaping."

John went out to his car and called Paul, alerting him that Yvette may have again tried to leave town. Paul told him he'd check the airports.

"Marguerite," he said suddenly to Rain. "Let's call her. She may have heard from Yvette by now."

But Marguerite was not aware of any of Yvette's plans; in fact she'd become concerned. She'd not heard at all from her. She'd fully expected Yvette to be with her in Spain by now. Rain hung up the phone, her face taking on the same questioning look as John's.

"Something's up," he said. "Why didn't Deborah return here immediately after the parade if she was worried about the damage to the car? Or go to the police station to file a complaint against the assailant?"

The silence between them was shared by the house, the house that, John believed, held too many secrets. Something told him that Yvette was trying to get away from all this, that she'd left town.

"C'mon," John said. "The Turners'."

Rain didn't move. "Why?"

"Something's up," he said, reaching for the phone. He dialed the station again and, once Paul picked up, requested that a car be sent over to watch the place. He told Paul they'd be at the Turners', to join them there. After hanging up, he turned to Rain.

"You don't have to come," he said gently. "I forgot. You haven't been back there since. . . ."

Rain paused, then made for the door. "Let's go then. No one will be there. There's no reason to be nervous."

The mid-afternoon sun blazed through the trees as they made the short drive to the Turner property. The "For Sale" sign stood at the edge of the property, a smaller "Sold" sticker in red at the bottom. Pulling in, they noticed the mailbox bulging with mail.

"Stop," Rain said, "I'll check the mail. There may be some for me."

John watched her make her way the short distance to the box. She'd lost weight and her walk was slow, unsteady. He wondered if the day hadn't been too much for her. Her back to him, she pulled the pile of letters, flyers, and catalogs from the box, trying to keep anything from falling. She flipped quickly through the correspondence as she made her way back to the car. Suddenly she stopped and pulled a white envelope from the pile, eyeing it carefully.

The pile of mail slipped from her grasp, spilling onto the ground. Newspaper flipped with the breeze and some letters tumbled towards the roadway. John got out of the car.

"What's up?" he asked, eyeing the letters but ignoring them on noting Rain's facial expression.

Her fingers fumbled as she ripped at the letter. "I'm not sure," she whispered. Her eyes passed quickly over the single sheet of white paper, then she looked up and gulped. Turning from John, she began to walk quickly towards the house.

"Rain," he called, going after her, then thinking otherwise. The car was still running. He returned to it, picking up what mail he could from the ground. He found the envelope Rain had just opened and noted it had no stamp, no return address, simply the words "Rain Danforth." Driving through the entrance and down the driveway, he could watch as Rain crossed the grass, her gait intensifying.

At the house, he followed her to the breezeway entrance, watching as she climbed to the top of the woodpile and stuck her hand in the gutter to retrieve a spare key. She was gasping for breath and crying.

"Rain, what is it?"

As if hearing him for the first time, she turned his way. Her face had paled and she seemed to be disoriented. She went inside, allowing him to follow and not paying attention to the open door. He closed it behind him, noting the musty smell that had already settled into the house.

Rain stood by the sink. John went to her and placed a hand on her shoulder. He squeezed. "Rain, talk to me."

She bit her lower lip and looked out over the flowers in the front garden. "It's from Betty. For me." She offered him the letter. John began reading an uneven scrawl that ran the length of the page.

I hope you get this. If someone else does, too bad. I killed her. I killed her that night, just like others killed John's parents. I dressed up like the twin and pretended to be the twin, dressed in the nightgown and went to her room knowing she was ill, knowing she would be afraid. One thing the doctor said was to never get her frightened. This is the worse thing you could do. Fright and what it does to her heart will kill her, he warned. I always watched her, I did. I never let her see scary shows on

TV, or go to overnights and share ghost stories like young girls do. She was my little pride and joy. I would have loved her sister, too. I wanted children so bad. But the other was killed years ago by Walter. Killed and buried under the orchid house. My orchids over her. That was our terrible secret. We had the promise of a daughter if the other was killed. I wanted the daughter, but didn't know. I really didn't know what the real deal was. You have to understand, I loved her like my own. I tried. I had to be a good wife, too, and so I did anything he asked. Most anything. Walter said we had to kill her, it would be easy because of her heart. He said this when she showed us her birth certificate and she knew she had a twin. She wanted to know why, why. Who she really was. We didn't look like her, she said. Who did she look like? Those blue eyes and dark hair. Her mother had dark hair in the movies. The real deal was he had to kill Emily, too. That was all part of this money deal. He received more money if Emily were dead, too. But I couldn't do that. I stood up to him, it was the first thing I ever did just for me. The last. I wouldn't let him take her. I encouraged her to travel, to see the world, to get out of Winslow. She did. It made him very angry with me. He hurt me many times, but I didn't care. I didn't want her taken from me. But she found that birth certificate, and discovered the forgery. Walter said we were through, we would be in jail the rest of our lives. The only way was to do her in. I killed her. I walked into her room wearing her nightgown and frightened her that night. She ran from the room and I fell to the floor. She ran outside and Walter chased her, made her run faster and faster. I could hear them in the woods, hear Emily's cries. She was going towards John's to get him. Her buddy. She was closer to him than anyone. They should have been together. Her only shake at happiness was with him. She ran to his house, then kept on running. I stopped hearing things after that. I fell asleep. When I woke he was pushing me, Cheever. He was in my house pushing me to tell what happened. He wanted her dead. Her dead, and he was worth millions. I could see in his eyes that he wanted to kill me. But I got on the phone and threatened to call the police. He left. Then Walter and I began our journey into hell waiting for the money that never came. They'd promised money but it never came. He's going to kill me if I don't kill myself. I can't do this anymore. I was never a liar. I killed my daughter. She was my daughter. Never Yvette's. Never. I killed her.

He put the letter down gently on the counter. Rain was still staring out at the flower garden. In the far corner, the orchid house. He was reminded of the soil, the different soil. Emily. Her one shake at happiness was with him. Betty had always known that. He should be on the phone, should be calling Paul for help, but this silence was all he could bear. Emily was with him in the room, he felt her all around, her laugh, her free spirit, her joy. He knew why the flood of memories came every now and again. It was because she was whispering to him still. She would always be around him. They were meant to be.

"Betty wasn't all that dumb," Rain said finally. "She sent this to the house knowing no one would check the mail right away. Even if they did, this letter was private property."

John marveled at her ability to reason at the same time she no doubt was going through some of what he was. "She cared for Emily."

"But she killed Emily."

"Who really killed Emily?" he asked. "I wonder. Over the years, Emily died a little bit each year. I watched. She believed in life, oh yes, she did. But she was afraid at all times, a timid fawn in the woods, knowing she had to venture out, had to eat from her own branches, stake her own land at the same time she sensed danger at every turn. She knew that her mother would disappear on her at the first sign of danger. She wasn't mistaken. I saw her strong, I saw her falter. I watched in awe because it was also my very dilemma. I knew I had to venture beyond Winslow. I had to move to other adventures, but the childhood pain kept drawing me back. The familiar moan of my mother returned me to this place. That haunting, drunken moan that held me back every time. It was why I loved Emily. Drawn together in pain, a pain we masked through our games, our giggles, our embrace. We sought one another without being free and would have built a prison had we not been separated. The night she left Winslow so many years ago was the saddest night of my life. I will never feel so sad again. A sadness with other meanings, meanings that I dumped on her. A sadness from which I thought I'd never recover. Yet, she knew. Betty knew. My mother knew. Leave and you're free. Stay and you remain its prisoner. My mother died in the prison, my father too. Had she and I found one another again, that night of Yvette's party, what would have become of us?"

Rain's eyes were watery. She brushed a tear. She placed her fingertips across John's lips. "Don't."

He folded her into him, pressed hard on her back and smelled her hair, a musk mixed with lemon. Her hands pressed against his chest as she allowed their togetherness. He wanted to stay like that without ever moving again. Now Rain knew who Emily belonged to. He leaned back and looked into her eyes. The gray was minimized by large black pupils.

Her eyes were bloodshot. Tears kept her from saying words she was trying to form. Finally, she returned to the embrace, shaking her face into John's shirt and allowing the tears.

He closed his eyes and lowered his face into her hair again, wanting to kiss her. *If you only knew how much I've wanted you, without really knowing myself.* This feel of a woman against him had been a memory for so long it was as if he were experiencing all the juvenile urges of twenty years before. What if he kissed her now?

Still against him, he let her lean into him, hugging her hard and passing his hand gently across her back. Each movement, however, generated a sensual need in him, a force he could tell would overtake him if he allowed it. If she allowed it. She was so beautiful in her vulnerability. He wanted only to protect her.

Who had he protected in the past? His mother? Emily? Neither really. Each had died without him, alone and afraid. Who? Anybody?

He knew the answer. There was no one, because he hadn't even protected himself over the years.

Rain broke the spell. Her face, inches from him and torn with shadows of misery like he'd never seen, inched towards his. Her lips opened. "I could love you, John. But I want you to want me, too."

Sensing his tenseness immediately, she patted his shoulder and then released her embrace, stepping a few steps back so that she could rest on the counter. She placed a hand over her forehead.

He stared at her, at her weariness, the open book that she was, her exhaustion. His defenses whispered she had said something she may regret in a day. Or was he simply placing, again, his own trip onto her? Her strength scared him.

"I think we need to go to the orchid house," she said slowly, gradually straightening and collecting herself.

The orchid house. Emily's murder. The investigation. The flood of responsibility that he'd placed to one side for minutes, for too long. He stepped ahead of her to get first to the door. He could hear her footsteps behind him as he opened the breezeway door.

They crossed the yard and followed the path, past the barn and onto the open field from where they could see the orchid house. A loud thud from the barn diverted their attention.

"What was that?" Rain asked.

They stood still for several minutes but they heard only the breeze in the pines.

"Look!" Rain exclaimed, facing the large sliding door that led to the garage spaces for the Turners' cars. "The door is open."

Unalarmed, John said, "It's always open that much. Walter would leave it that way so Betty could get in. She had a hard time opening the door when it was latched. Didn't they tell you that?"

"But wouldn't it be closed now? Walter always closed the barn door at night. It was one of his many rituals," Rain said.

They listened. . . . When they arrived, they looked at the floor. The cement flooring had been broken away and a hole some three feet wide revealed the earth beneath. Some orchids sagged against their pots.

"What's this?" Rain asked.

John held onto her shoulder, keeping her from getting any closer to the hole. "Remember Betty's letter."

Rain took a deep breath. They studied the hole. "Someone came and took the baby." Her voice was barely a whisper.

They heard footsteps behind them. A gruff voice answered, "Right you are, lady."

Reeling around they faced Walter. Muddied and unkempt, he chewed on something and smiled leeringly at Rain. Rain cried out. He tapped a pitchfork on the floor.

"What are you doing here?" John asked, noting the firm grasp Walter had on the tool. An image of Walter angrily pitching hay onto a tractor one summer when John was a child came to mind.

"I might ask the two of you what you're doing here," he said, the smile fading into a grim stare.

John had to gauge the impact of their next move. If Walter had his wits about him, and the man's unswerving stance gave nothing away to the contrary, he would know John could arrest him on the spot. Walter was a dangerous man capable of any move right now. Rain and John were trapped in a corner of the orchid house.

"Where are the baby's bones, Walter?" Rain asked suddenly and in a soft, seductive voice.

Walter glanced quickly at the floor as if seeing the hole for the first time. Trying to recover he laughed. "I don't have a clue as to what you're talking about, you cow." The deprecating tone in his voice sent a chill through John. It could very well be that Walter hadn't known the bones were gone. He'd maybe just arrived, seeing that the mail was still in the box.

"What are you going to do now?" John asked.

"I'm going to kill you," he said. "But first, I'm going to finish what I started with the lady."

His eyes were dark and brilliant as they ran down Rain's body. John had to think, think fast. In seconds they could be massacred with that pitchfork. He already knew he was no match for this man who'd spent years toiling the land and building his reserves of angry energy, becoming one with nature because he had no recourse, no alternative to a life he grew to detest. They might as well have faced an aggravated bull.

Rain stepped towards him. "Take me, then," she whispered.

He kept his eyes on her crotch. "Not this time, not like the last. I'll have you alright but not until he's dealt with." He nodded at John. "Bastard."

"Walter, you can get off easy if you cooperate. You were framed years ago. You were forced to comply with a situation of which you were not totally aware. You'd been lied to by Yvette, by Granger. This isn't all your fault. Cooperate with the police and it'll go better for you. Do you understand?"

"I know one thing, prick. I know you're dead and she's dead, after I get my way with her. Finally." He laughed. "You think you can talk me into anything? After all these years of being made a fool? The last thing I want is to cooperate, mate. I've been cooperating all my life. Betty's dead and I can do what I want now."

Was he really losing it or was John forcing him over the edge on the man so that he could justify wanting to pulverize him on the spot? His gun was in the car, there was nothing but two small garden tools, a spade and small weeder, lying near them.

"Did you kill my mother?" he asked.

For an instant, he saw in the man's eyes a spark of energy, of light, a deep affection. John knew then that Walter had not killed his mother, but had loved her, truly and for many years. All those nights she abandoned him she'd been spending with Walter. He was at a loss as to why his mother had been attracted to such a man.

"Your mother was killed by alcohol and you know it. The fact she was force-fed, heh, that wasn't me. That was Yvette and her own lover, or one of them. Then again, mate, you know all about her lovers."

If they bantered, they bought time, he told himself. "Who force-fed her? I need to know, Walter." Would Walter really kill him, the son of the woman he once loved?

Struck by memories, Walter let his gaze drop. For a few seconds, John pitied the man. His eyes downcast, his body smelling and mildewed with hatred and days on the run, he was a creature of nature rather than human. Desperation in all its forms had driven him to this place. Why had he returned? Slowly, his eyes returned to John, eyeing him evilly once again.

"You're not going to get out, so don't try," he said.

"Who gave her the booze that killed her, Walter?"

"That ass Cheever did. Along with Yvette. They invited her to the mansion and let her think they were on her side. Darcy had found out about the. . . ." He looked down at the hole.

"How?"

"I was moving the bones, from here to another place. Just for a time, so we could move out of here and get on with our lives. So I could leave Winslow forever with your mother. We'd had a big plan. I didn't tell Betty, but she discovered me digging. She confronted me. I acted dumb, except your mother showed up. I beat her up. I couldn't get Betty going. She'd blabber to the whole town, she would, if she knew I was cheating on her. It wasn't worth it. I let your mother bleed for a while and then called Yvette. Yvette said she'd take care of it. Two days later she did. I wasn't a part of the drinking party, or the folks who led her to a field to get eaten by animals."

It was all John needed to piece together the nightmare that was his final memory of his mother. It would be so easy to beat him to death. Give him a taste of his own medicine.

Walter lunged forward. Rain screamed. John ducked the pitchfork and grabbed Walter by the middle, trying to throw him to the ground. Walter turned the fork against John. A shot rang out, blocking John's hearing. He felt Walter go limp against him. Slipping to the floor, he fell onto his back, eyes closed and moaning in pain. John looked up to see Paul Allen.

"I listened from outside. Had to wait to see what was going to happen," Paul said, replacing his gun in the holster. "He's got one in the knee. He'll live."

John turned. Rain crouched in the corner. He went to her and lifted her towards him. "You okay?"

She shook as he held her, her head nodding repeatedly against his chest.

"I'll take care of this," said Paul. "Call the ambulance from the house, then take Rain back to my place. Tell Michelle I'll be along."

John handed Paul Betty's note. As Walter writhed in pain on the floor, Paul read the page, closing his eyes at the end. When he looked up, there were tears in his eyes.

"I'm sorry, John."

John felt Rain's fingers against his back. She was pressing hard. It reminded him of Darcy and her embrace, except Rain's wasn't a desperate move, it was a move of comfort. Someone giving him help, help and support. Paul giving him sympathy and kindness. The truth uncovered, he was already thinking differently.

"Me, too," he said.

"Go on," Paul said. "Take her home."

"What about the others?"

"Yvette and Cheever have already left the country. We'll find them, though. Deborah is still at large."

"I'll drop Rain off and get back to the station. There may be. . . ."

"No, you won't. The case is under control," Paul said.

"Paul. I need to do this," John said, staring into the man's eyes.

"Suit yourself. It may be a long night. You've just been through a lot."

He led Rain to his car. Driving to the Allens', he debated where Deborah might have fled. It took all of ten minutes for him to understand. Deborah needed to hide, and her cronies had dumped her by leaving the country. She'd be good and angry by now.

From his car phone, he called the station and asked the officer on duty to check Hudson Manor in New York to ensure Stuart Granger still lived. On receiving the confirmation, he hurriedly dropped Rain off, leaving her in Michelle's capable hands and promising to return that night.

He then took the highway north, heading to Art Johnson's New Hampshire retreat. His memory served him well, as this had been his summer vacation place for several years following Darcy's death, and he found the shortcut to the lake in less than two hours. A dirt road led to three small cottages that shared a private corner of lakefront property.

Dusk approached and he drove slowly along the single-lane dirt road, watching for underground tree trunks pushing their way upwards that might damage the bottom of the car. Any oncoming vehicle would be forced to stop, as would he, to determine who had the right of way. It would be impossible for cars to pass each other on the road lined with large trees on either side.

He passed one cottage and noted a light coming from the main living area. He assumed all owners would be at the lake for the weekend of the Fourth. Firecrackers snapped from a distance. John guessed them to be going off on the beach. Another several hundred feet, if his calculations were right, he'd be at Art's driveway.

A car approached from the opposite direction, its engine puttering quietly yet clearly heading his way. He glanced to either side of the road to see if there was a spot he could ease into while it passed. Before he had a chance to make a call, his eyes widened in shock as he noted the car coming towards him, its speed now noticeably increased. It was none other than the white Bentley.

Behind the wheel, Deborah. Before she struck his car and he was stunned to unconsciousness, he noted her maniacal eyes, piercing destruction and danger deep into his own. The woman had made up her mind to kill him.

Chapter Eighteen

When he came to, he was staring at the smashed front fender of the Bentley. It had rammed right into the police car, subsequently sending John forward onto the steering wheel. The beginnings of a terrific headache began to take hold, and he felt warm liquid on his forehead. In the rearview mirror he could see that above his left eye was cut. Other than that, he didn't detect any pain.

Taking care to move slowly, he eased from the vehicle and stood, assessing his body from top to bottom. After several deep breaths, he managed to step around the car comfortably. The woods were quiet, save sporadic cracks from the festivities at the shore. Suddenly he heard a branch crack off to his left. A flash of yellow passed before his eyes some hundred yards in the distance. Deborah had been wearing a yellow dress during the parade. Figuring it must be her, he moved carefully in that direction, watching like a wild animal for any other movement.

He had no idea whether or not anyone was with her or if she was armed. Anything could happen under the circumstances. Just then, her voice echoed through the trees.

"Stop where you are, John!"

He waited for a sound but there was none.

"Come forward now," she said.

Her voice floated from the direction he'd seen the yellow. She was hiding from him. Why? He recalled their last conversation, when Deborah had hinted at sinister goings-on but had said nothing further.

"Why? What now?" he asked. He inched slowly through the brush, unsure if she was watching him or not. He couldn't see anything but trees and low-lying bushes. The leaves on the ground crackled in spite of his soft step. She must have her eyes on him from some hidden place.

"Don't ask. Just move towards my voice."

"It will go easier on you if you cooperate, Deborah."

"I have nothing to hide," she yelled. "I'm not running." Her voice was frightened.

"They've left the country, Deborah," he said. "You're on your own now."

The silence that ensued answered his question. Had she been working on Yvette's behalf during the parade, she would have also the right to expect Yvette to help her escape from being caught as well. Now what?

"You're wrong, John. You're lying."

Simultaneously trying to strengthen her tone, she'd allowed herself to emerge from a clump of brush not twenty feet from him. A gun pointed at him. It was one of Walter's. She'd been to the Turners' house. He looked back at the white Bentley, at the trunk.

"They've left the country, Deborah. Now put the gun down."

"No! They've not! They'd not leave without me. I have the secret!"

"The secret in the trunk?" he asked.

They stood ten feet from one another. She poised the gun, clicked the trigger in place. Her eyes didn't leave him, eyes that at once held demons and destruction. Her chest heaved, her clothes were soiled. A foot was shoeless. Her stockings hung in shreds about her knees.

"You're trying to trick me."

John shook his head, aware only of the gun and its proximity. "You can help us, Deborah. What you know can help this case."

"I'm getting out, too," she hissed. "You're going to help me."

He nodded at the gun. "I can't if I'm dead."

Her death grip on the gun, its dark barrel staring at him like a black Cyclops eye, her body looming and rigid, had all the markings of a sick, out-of-place-and-time movie.

"Walter is in the hands of the police. Betty wrote a letter to Rain that tells everything about Emily. I know who her parents are."

She didn't move. The gun remained trained on him. Whatever his words meant to her she wasn't showing, but she wasn't making a move either. He decided to chance continuing.

"Yvette and Stuart Granger. Yvette had the babies after she and Stuart divorced. Granger himself never knew he was a father. She used the money Stuart gave her from the divorce to bribe the Turners, but she had no intentions of allowing Emily to live. The longer Emily lived, the lesser her chances of getting Granger's money when he passed away. She and Cheever stuck around Winslow, watching and waiting. Either Emily's heart would fail, the weak heart she inherited from her father, or they'd figure a way to kill her. Only Emily left and they couldn't seem to catch her. Still, they made sure everyone who knew the truth was taken care of. That's where you came in, Deborah.

"You were to take care of anyone who had a clue about those twins, about the night they were born. That included my father."

His comment had the desired effect. Her eyes narrowed and she raised the gun.

"You don't want to do that, do you?" he asked. "The son of the man you've always loved?"

She gripped the gun but her hands shook. Her eyes closed, she said, "Don't."

"Deborah, I'm not going to hurt you."

He couldn't tell if she was crying or not, but she refused to open her eyes.

A voice, steps behind him, said, "Put the gun down, Deborah."

John turned. Art looked through his spectacles at him, raising his chin in a move of understanding cooperation.

Deborah lowered the gun and collapsed onto the ground. Art went to her. John watched the two. The terrified realization that Art wasn't on his side swept over him. Why would Deborah have sought shelter here otherwise? Plus, all this meant Art was aware of the truth all along.

John felt his hand go to the gun in his holster. While Art cleared Deborah's face of her hair to feel her forehead and reached to her wrist to take her pulse, John raised his own weapon. It would be the hardest thing he'd ever do in his career as a cop.

"Stand up, you two."

They both looked at John, mixed apprehension and surprise. Deborah let out a nervous giggle.

"Precautions, I'm sure you understand."

"John," Art said, remaining immobile.

"How am I to know the truth, given what I see in front of me, Art?"

Art didn't respond.

"Answer me," John said.

The man lowered his face to his chest. Deborah released her wrist from his grip. The two sat like cloth dolls gone limp after children had left them for other pursuits. John wished he didn't have to do what he was about to do. It had been some time since he even recited the Miranda to anyone.

After he was through speaking, he swept the gun past them, gesturing for them to get up. Deborah stood first, tossing her gun away from her.

Minnie Johnson called out for Art from the cottage. The man looked with tired eyes in the direction of his wife's voice, but didn't answer.

They both moved towards John, quietly passing him and heading towards the road where they began the march to the cottage. It would take at least two hours for help to arrive from Winslow. In the meantime, John left the Johnsons in one room while Deborah and he sat on the porch. Once she'd collected herself, she seemed very much at peace, still in her gritty clothes, comfortably rocking back and forth in the old wood rocking chair that had been there since John could remember. The sun was setting and the increasing sound of firecrackers filled the air. The almost full moon made its appearance across the lake. A few stubborn loons maintained their tunes loud enough to compete with the surrounding fireworks. It would be a good night for fireworks.

"May I speak?" she finally asked him.

"What about?"

"Art was protecting you all these years, John," she said.

He almost protested her words, but some deep-felt desire for justice for a man who'd given John Jordan a second chance on life overruled his policeman's instincts to keep the prisoners quiet.

"He knew all along. Everything. But that night your mother was hurt real bad, that night you overheard the phone conversation, you remember?"

Already he was reliving it, that nightmare come true that had lived inside his soul, ruling his every move, keeping him from letting go what he needed to let go. Always when those memories demanded his attention, he would flip his thinking to something banal, the water the trees the dog the bed the floor the chipped cups in the cabinets. Nothing ever worked. This time, a woman emerged. She was so lovely, he marveled that someone so enchanting could be a creation of a mind like his own. She smiled sweetly and the smell of her almost rose from his brain to waft past him as he sat, incense to his damaged sense of smell, his damaged senses in their entirety, softening him to pulp and comfort like he'd never known. He wanted to touch her so badly, he raised his hand. Eyes closed he imagined her touch, ivory skin so soft he was on clouds, sinking into her folds as he contemplated how he might stay there forever.

It was so many women and one woman. It was a good-bye to a type of woman, it was a greeting to another. If she stayed, he'd be complete, but in that completeness he'd draw comfort only temporarily. She was the image of the two women who'd left him years before, but only the image. Reality had never become either of them. If they were ever real he'd not ever known, for he refused to know. They encapsulated his desires and his fears. Each throwing out her true self, wanting him to catch that piece of her too, but never succeeding. He never could face who they really were. Emily was forever the nymph in the woods beholden only to her obstinate belief in her superhuman will to survive. Darcy was forever the queen of pain masking as a country house mother.

It was a good-bye, that much he knew. Moments like these came infrequently if at all in life. The summer so far he'd drank only once. It would be the last time. The woman faded, melting into the night and losing her form to the moon's quiet shine. He looked up and smiled at Deborah.

"Art saved you, John," she whispered. "Art told them you knew nothing, that you should be spared because you knew nothing. But you did, didn't you? You knew but you didn't know. No one explained to you about the night your mother was beaten. That was the night she knew all about the twins, all about what we were planning. Walter loved her so much he told her everything. But he got caught. Darcy got caught in the middle. Art withheld the truth for you."

"Who killed my father?"

"They did. Cheever. Your father knew from me. I wanted to leave with your father, but Cheever is a smart man. He caught on. He killed him. Filled him with liquor and had him thrown in the river. Art was safe because Art was the one to declare how they all died. He kept quiet, let on that the deaths of your mother and father were accidents. I know how you must feel but he did it for you. To keep you safe. He played a dangerous game. You must give him credit for daring. A quiet man, but a daring man."

"Why didn't you tell me this before?"

"I wanted to escape. I wanted to give myself time to get out. I told Yvette I'd take the baby's bones and get rid of them. That would show her I was still loyal. At the same time I could get out, escape. Turns out they left on me, they didn't even wait for me. It was me who stole those old Post articles about the twins. I did so much for Yvette . . ."

"We'll find them," John said.

"Good luck," she said with irony. She was crying. "My crime was anger. I was angry at Cheever Sr. He dumped me and I was alone, no family, not even in my own country. I found your father but it was too late. We were both irrationally in love. It wasn't good all around. To save myself, I had to remain with Yvette. I hated her for what she did to you over the years. She played a vicious game, knowing I loved your father. I had to watch her play with you like a toy without being able to do anything about it."

"You were protecting me, too, then," he said.

Her tired eyes cleared briefly. "I suppose."

Night had fallen. By the time the Winslow police car pulled into the drive, Art and John had talked. There were no bodily injuries in the accident down the road, John explained to the officers. Deborah and Art would be available the next day to aid in the investigation. There was no need to press charges against anyone. The bones in the trunk of the Bentley should be carefully transported to a morgue. The funeral arrangements would be in due time. For the short term, John requested some time off, which Paul Allen agreed to by phone.

Chapter Nineteen

Rain lowered the hood of the Toyota. Everything fit in the back. "I'll have a lot of leg room. That's good." She let the lid go and it banged appropriately shut.

Her face had taken on a nice glow, thanks to the sunny days and the many walks she and John had made in the surrounding hills. Her strength had returned and she was ready to resume her work in California.

John leaned his hand forward, clamping it on Rain's arm that rested on the hood of her car. "You're going to be okay?"

She nodded. "The drive will do me good. Three thousand miles to think."

"That can be both good and bad."

She let her eyes wander over the distant hills. The day before, they'd buried Emily's sister in the Turner plot next to Betty and Emily. Mrs. Simmons had left the area, claiming her asthma required the dry of the Southwest. Walter was in jail, and Deborah was on a plane for Stockholm.

"John, how did you know that Granger was Emily's father? He and Yvette had been divorced for months."

"Math," John answered. "One thing Betty and Walter did was give Emily her true birth date. Emily and I always talked about our birth dates. I knew hers by heart. The month she was born was exactly five months following the end of the filming of *Something Winning*, nine months after the Granger's separated. Yvette made her mark in spite of Granger. She was determined to have his child, married to him or not. It was her grand plan. It continues to amaze me what people do for money."

"Have they found them yet?" Rain asked.

"No," he said. "When they do, I'll let you know." He smiled into her eyes. It had been three days of saying good-bye. He wanted to follow her. They'd talked into the nights about it. Finally, he made the call. He needed some time. Needed to tie up loose ends. Rain had not insisted. In her way he was fast growing very comfortable with, she allowed him the time. It would be the reason he would eventually join her, but he wanted to leave Winslow with no baggage, no dangling emotions, and the case closed.

She got into the car, and before she was out of sight he turned away from the disappearing red Toyota and faced his house. The Realtor was coming in a week for an open house. There would be some cosmetic work to get underway before it went on the market. In spite of his list of things to do, he whistled to Sami. She came quickly from around the back where she'd been sparring with an overly zealous groundhog.

The two headed up one of the paths that led to the ridge. It would be a clear morning, a good day for a hike. He managed to climb without stopping for over an hour, keeping with Sami's jaunt at a surprising clip. When he mounted the oversized boulder that teetered permanently over one of the larger hills, he sat back and caught his breath.

Winslow tumbled below him. There was a new construction site just taking shape in the northwest corner. Some builder from the next town who had gone to school in Boston purchased land at fair market price and wanted to try his hand at custom homes. The vote for the permits and septic had gone smoothly at the town meeting. It was a local kid after all. John sat all afternoon in that spot, getting up only to stretch his legs and ensure Sami hadn't wandered. It would be the last time he'd venture up this hill. In the town center, he could see his mother's grave stone, noting with the relief of his entire lifetime that he finally felt nothing. The sorrow was gone and so were the false feelings of guilt and lost opportunity.

When the view diminished into the rising night, he allowed Sami to lead the way home, stepping carefully but with a sure foot down the rocky side of the hill, wondering did they have such rocky hillsides in the area around where Rain lived. He'd take her on a hike their first Sunday together out west. At that thought, he noted the warm sensation filling him up, that easy notion that what you were about to do with your life was wonderfully right.

It was another week before the news arrived in Winslow. A twin-engine plane had downed in the Pyrenees just miles from Bayonne, France. The bodies were determined to be those of one Scott Cheever and

Yvette Peters. The French authorities researched the victims' backgrounds, discovering that the woman was the once-famous actress Odile Grange, who had left France years before to pursue acting in the United States. A memorial service was held in the small southern town of her birth. During the ceremony, the one remaining Grange relative, an aging woman of ninety-seven, allowed a Paris newspaper to interview her. She remembered Odile as an impetuous and daring child, almost as aggressive and bold as her cousin Stuart. It was divine intervention, the woman canted, that she meet her end while returning home. "They all want to come home in the end," the woman was quoted as saying. Word had it that an ancient family feud had raged for generations about the fortune left behind by the first Grange to settle that part of France over three hundred years before. The old woman had snorted that it wasn't true. No Grange would ever go to such lengths, she commented.